SAVE
HER
TWICE

BOOKS BY HELEN PHIFER

SAVE HER TWICE

HELEN PHIFER

bookouture

Published by Bookouture in 2024

An imprint of Storyfire Ltd.
Carmelite House
50 Victoria Embankment
London EC4Y 0DZ

www.bookouture.com

ISBN: 978-1-83790-352-8
eBook ISBN: 978-1-83790-351-1

ONE

He had watched all the eighties slasher films more times than he could count. His favourite was *Nightmare on Elm Street*. Who hadn't been scared by that film when it had first been released? The sound of Freddy Krueger's metallic razor nails scraping along old boiler pipes had stayed with him forever, and they had haunted some of his teenage nightmares with such ferocity he'd convinced himself that the only way to not be scared of the bogeyman was to *be* the bogeyman.

He'd spent many a lonely night wondering how it would feel to have fingertips of steel and use them to slice apart Janey Cooper at the end of math class, from the base of her throat to her navel. The only problem with that scenario was the metal replica gloves he'd ordered were not even sharp enough to cut through the bowl of jelly his gran had given him the day they'd arrived. He'd tried to chop the heads off her prized carnations too, but all he'd succeeded in doing was bending them and crushing the heads.

Then he'd watched his grandad shaving himself one day with a straight razor, now that was more like it. As he'd sat on the toilet and watched the man press it against the old, wrinkled skin on his face, his grandad had slipped and taken a slice out of his cheek that had bled as if his throat had been cut and he'd hit a major artery. Old George had cried out like a baby for his wife, who'd come running to see what was wrong, taken one look at the crimson mess that had coated the walls and the sink, and she'd fainted on the spot, just closed her eyes and fallen to the ground in a heap.

He didn't know who to watch, his eyes kept moving from one to the other. George had to grab a towel and press it to the cut to try and stop the bleeding, while nudging his unconscious wife with the tip of his boot. Eventually Arlene had woken up on her own much to his relief, because old George couldn't cook a decent meal to save his life, and he knew the pair of them would have starved to death living off tins of cheap beans and tinned hot dogs.

He knew where she lived; he knew where they all lived. It had taken some doing to get their addresses, but he'd never given up and now he was here. Waiting patiently for her to come back from wherever it was she'd gone this afternoon.

If he had to guess he'd say shopping. She wasn't dressed to go to her part-time job in Subway in Kendal that her mum drove her to and picked her up regardless of the time.

He'd closed his eyes to push away the image of his own mother. She'd been too young to care for him properly and had preferred having a good time with her friends than looking after a kid.

He'd been dropped off at George and Arlene's one rainy December teatime and she'd never come back for him. That hurt, a lot. He used to dream about her reading him a bedtime story and tucking him into bed, but she left him before that ever happened and he often wondered if she could even read; maybe that was why she'd pushed him away, the fear of him asking her to read him a story. George and Arlene had been as surprised as he was when they opened the door and she'd pushed him towards them.

'You're going to have to take him, I can't feed him right and I can't look after him like he needs.'

Arlene had hugged him to her, holding him close, and the three of them had watched as she took his small case out of the taxi with the engine idling and the clock ticking that had brought them to their house. She'd bent down and kissed the top of his head, whispering, 'Be a good boy, I'll come back when I can.' Then she'd run back to the taxi and got inside, slamming the door shut on him and their life.

The three of them had watched as the car sped away from their cottage at the end of the lane, the tyres hitting a pothole and spraying water like a fountain all over the road, and then it was gone.

The lane was quiet, the only sound was the pitter patter of the rain and Arlene saying, 'Well I never.' Over and over. She did that a lot, repeating herself. He'd noticed that the first day he'd been there, but she'd been kind to him, a lot kinder than she had to be. Unlike George who regularly used to hit him with his slipper, but he didn't mind. Living with those two was better than being locked in his bedroom for hours while his mum had her friends around.

He looked around, damn he'd drifted off again. He had a habit of thinking about his past and reliving every little memory when he should be concentrating on the here and now.

He scanned the street – the house was still in darkness. Good, he'd have been furious if she'd walked straight past him while he wasn't paying attention.

He went back to thinking about his favourite horror films. He had chosen to emulate neither good old Michael Myers nor his favourite, Freddy Krueger. No, he'd gone with a different one and, when it had come down to it, being able to breathe and do what he wanted to in a full face mask like either of those two had been impossible. The smell of rubber had been unbearable, and the fact that he couldn't see properly out of the eyeholes was never going to work.

He picked up the piece of hard plastic, which wasn't much better, but wearing it he could breathe and see what he was doing.

Movement caught his eye, and he breathed a sigh of relief.

Finally.

She was hurrying home as if she was late for something. A smile crossed his lips. As he suspected, it was going to be a lot of fun.

TWO

Rydal Falls police station was alive with people. The owners of the busiest café in the town, The Coffee Pot, had turned up earlier with trays of sandwiches, pork pies, sausage rolls and so many vol-au-vents they could have lined the entire set of desks in the report writing room and still had some left over. As soon as duty sergeant, Paul Madden, aka Mads to everyone, had put the call out over the airwaves, everyone had turned around and driven straight back to the station from wherever they were.

Amy and Cain had done CID proud and procured a tray of each of the café's offerings, which they had brought upstairs.

Detective Morgan Brookes had been out to pick up some CCTV footage from the newly opened boutique hotel, The Square, in Ambleside, regarding a suspicious car, and walked into the atrium to an almost party-like atmosphere. There were officers, PCSOs, support staff, custody staff all filling paper plates and chattering among themselves, which was nice, but for Morgan far too many people in one space. She went straight up the stairs to the safety of her office, where Amy and Cain were discussing the merits of the vol-au-vent fillings.

'What's going on, is someone retiring?'

Cain shook his head. 'Nope, the owners of The Coffee Pot did a booking for a hundred people, and it got called off last minute.'

'What do you mean, what kind of booking?'

'Some poor bastard realised he didn't want to marry the love of his life and never turned up at the church.'

'Poor, poor woman,' Morgan said.

'Who said it was a woman?' Amy said through a mouthful of sausage roll.

'Well, whoever it was what an awful way to find out. In front of all your family and friends too.'

Cain put three little triangles of sandwich together and pushed them into his mouth. Amy shook her head at him.

'Why didn't you tip the whole tray in there? It's big enough.'

He clutched his chest. 'Ouch, you're so mean and especially with me still recovering from my life-threatening injury.'

Morgan smiled at him; it was his second day back after being stabbed and needing major surgery.

'You still eat like a pig, wounded or not, and anyway you're only here for two hours. I'm not sure how you managed that or what use you are.'

He turned to Morgan. 'Can you not try and train her to be nicer to people? She's so mean.'

Amy tutted. 'It's all part of my charm, Cain.'

The phone on Ben's desk began to ring.

'Where is he?' asked Morgan.

'No idea, he left just before the food turned up,' Amy said.

Cain looked at the phone. 'Should I answer it?'

Amy shook her head. 'No, they'll ring back.'

It stopped ringing and Morgan picked up a sandwich, and was about to eat it when the phone on her desk began to ring. She reached over for it.

'Brookes.'

Morgan heard Amy whisper to Cain, 'A fiver on a body.'

He nodded.

Morgan replied, clutching the phone more tightly. 'Yes, thanks. I'll let him know.'

'Party's over,' she said to Amy and Cain, 'a woman has returned home to find blood all over her front door in Fenton Street.'

She took out her mobile and rang Ben, but his phone went to voicemail.

'He's not answering.'

They both shrugged. 'He'll ring back. I'll come with you for now; Cain you hold the fort and try to find the boss.'

He saluted them. 'Will do, be careful.'

Amy smiled at him. 'It's probably some sick joke.'

Morgan didn't think it was; she had that all too familiar feeling of dread settling deep inside the pit of her stomach, and she wasn't sure if it was because Ben always answered his phone or because the thought of someone finding their front door covered in blood chilled her to the bone.

The house was a small terraced at the end of a quiet street. It would have been in darkness had it not been for the flashing blue lights from the response vehicle illuminating the night sky. There were no houses opposite, just a row of lock-up garages. Scotty was standing talking to a woman who was clearly distraught at her discovery.

Amy glanced at Morgan. 'She's upset.'

'Yes, she is.'

'I wasn't expecting this to be a genuine call. I thought we'd turn up and there'd be a couple of drops of blood off some drunk who'd cut themselves on the way home from the pub.'

'Come on, let's take a look for ourselves.'

Morgan briskly walked towards the police car. Scotty

turned to her, and she could have sworn he breathed out a sigh of relief.

'Boss, there's a lot of blood.'

Morgan glanced back to see if Ben had arrived. Amy was still further up the street, and she realised Scotty was talking to her.

'Do we know whose blood it is?'

The woman who was weeping into her hands whispered, 'I can't get hold of my daughter Lexie.'

'How old is Lexie?'

'Seventeen.'

'Did you check she isn't in the house?'

Natalie nodded. 'Yes, of course and then I panicked the house is in darkness and I didn't see any blood inside.'

Morgan tugged a pair of the blue gloves she always carried out of her jeans pocket and walked towards the front of the house, keeping on the road. She turned her phone torch on, shining it at the white UPVC front door, and felt her stomach clench at the strong, earthy smell that accompanied heavy blood loss. There were spatters of it all over the door, as if someone had been attacked. There were also big pools of it on the pavement.

The neighbour stuck her head out of the door, and Morgan turned to her. 'I'm going to need you to stay inside for the time being, please.'

She had her towel wrapped around her head and a dressing gown on. 'What's going on, Natalie? Do you want to come inside, and I'll put the kettle on?'

Natalie was still crying softly into her hands.

Morgan smiled at the woman, a faint flicker of recognition: where had she met her before?

'Natalie, I think that's a great idea. You've had a terrible shock, and a cup of hot, sweet tea will do you the world of good.'

Amy smiled at Natalie. 'I'll come in and get some details off you so we can get hold of Lexie.' She turned to the neighbour. 'Is that okay?'

The neighbour nodded. 'Yes, I'm Billie.'

Billie went back inside so that Amy could guide Natalie into the house. Amy closed the door behind her, but not all the way so that Morgan could come in if she needed to.

Scotty put his hands together in a praying position.

'Thank God,' he said to Morgan. 'I didn't know what to say.'

'You're all heart, Scotty, have you requested CSI?'

His head shook from side to side. 'Thought I'd let you guys take a look first in case it's not real blood.'

Morgan stopped herself from saying anything sarcastic; he was well known for his lazy attitude.

'Well, do me a favour and ask for them while I try and get hold of Ben.'

She snapped some photos with her phone and took a quick video, then turned back to him.

'When you've done that, I need you to get this end of the street sealed off and the other, too. Is there a trail of blood?'

'Not that I could see.'

She walked over to the passenger side of the car, opened the door and retrieved the big Maglite torch from the footwell. The powerful beam made the blood look even more sinister; she shone it onto the ground to see if there was a trail in case Lexie had hurt herself and wandered off looking for help. There were a few drops on the kerb, but that was the end of the trail, and she knew that she had either got into a vehicle of her own accord, or someone had forced her to. That's if it was Lexie's blood. There was a chance it was a passing stranger's and Lexie would turn up soon, or that was what she hoped. It would be the best scenario. Her phone began to ring, and she felt a tiny piece of the ball of anxiety that had formed in her stomach slip away.

'Ben, where are you?'

'On my way, sorry. I had to nip out. I'll tell you about it later. What's happening, Morgan, talk me through it.'

His echoey voice meant he was on loudspeaker, which also meant he was driving to get to her, and she felt relieved, although the worry that someone could have hurt the teenage girl was niggling deep inside of her, making her feel queasy.

THREE

The small hall attached to the side of the church was a well-used space for dancing groups, Scouts, Brownies, community meetings, choir practice to name a few. Inside of it was an even smaller room, full of boxes of unused jumble sale donations, broken chairs that really should have been thrown away but never had, and a bookcase full of donated books. This room had its own entrance door. It smelled musty, and it looked anything other than a meeting place, which it was. The group of six women and one almost teenage girl met once a month, arriving at separate times, slipping through the entrance as quietly and unseen as possible. Bronte Potter had read a book about final girls, and even though it gave her palpitations and nightmares they were of a different kind to the ones she had almost every other night. It had occurred to her that she was a final girl when she'd looked up the exact definition: *'A female protagonist who survived against all odds and defeats the movie's monster.'*

She hadn't defeated her particular monster or been in a movie, but she had survived being beaten and left for dead by her now ex friend, who had killed the rest of her family, so it was pretty close.

Then she thought about the other surviving victims of the killers who had stalked the area where she lived. She had collected articles about the murders from the *Cumbrian News* and despite not reading them, she had carefully cut them out and put them all into a scrapbook. Maybe she'd known all along that it might come to this, or maybe it was morbid fascination, she wasn't sure, but one day she'd got out the scrapbook and read every single article, writing down the names of the survivors. It had been tough, it had given her heart palpitations, made her sweat unnaturally despite it being a cool summer's day last June, but she had done it and then she had a list.

She hadn't done anything with the list until a few weeks later, when she woke up after a particularly harrowing nightmare. She'd been in the cellar of their beautiful family home surrounded by her dead family, only this time she had killed them. She held on to the heavy piece of wood that had been used as a weapon. She'd smelled the awful coppery tang of so much blood as it filled the air and could feel the sticky wet blood that coated her hands. She'd woken up screaming so loud and for so long that her aunt had called for an ambulance, and she'd been carted off to a mental health facility for a two week stay.

It was while she was there and taking part in group therapy that she'd first had the idea about forming a support group for them, the women like her, the survivors of killers. Surely, she had reasoned, she couldn't be the only one struggling to cope with being so brutally attacked and losing her family.

One by one she'd tracked down all the survivors she could find who lived in the Lake District, and she also included the woman who'd been attacked in Whinlatter Forest, which was not too far away. What united them was that they had all been a victim of a serial killer.

The door burst open, and Milly Blake rushed through it as if she was being chased. Bronte let out a screech. Picking up the nearest thing to hand, which was a broken electric kettle, she held it in the air ready to smack someone over the head with it.

'Sorry, sorry.' Milly held her hands out in front of her. 'It's all good, it's just started tipping down and I've had my hair done.'

Bronte was clasping her heart, and she began to laugh. 'Jesus, you scared the crap out of me. I thought you were being chased.' She took a breath. 'I love it, you really suit that red colour; it looks great with your pale complexion and green eyes.'

A look of sadness filled Milly's eyes. 'Not this time, thank God. I saw Evelyn yesterday, she's good and sends her love. Oh, and thank you' – she touched her hair – 'I wanted a complete change. I was sick of staring at the same old me in the mirror but only not seeing the old me, if you know what I mean.'

Bronte did, she knew exactly how she felt. 'I know, I feel like that some days. How did you manage that?'

'The hair was done by my fab hairdresser, Jo. I had manual handling training at the home Evelyn's in, and I managed to sneak to the toilet and went to her room. She looks so frail; she hasn't been too well.'

'Bless her, maybe we should send her some flowers from the group.'

Milly smiled at her. 'I think that's a lovely idea. She doesn't have anyone to send them or visit; she must be so lonely. She barely leaves her room, even though she lives in a nursing home and is surrounded by people.'

Bronte made a note to do just that.

The door opened and in walked Sara Fletcher, all the way from Manchester. She had been a little harder to find than the local girls, but when Bronte had found her Sara had loved the idea of the support group so much she'd offered to help set it up. Gone was Sara's long brown hair and in its place was a pixie cut.

Sara looked at Milly and they both said: 'Nice hair,' at the same time and burst into giggles. Bronte thought maybe she should have a haircut or colour, too; a complete change might help her to feel better about herself. She'd been feeling pretty rubbish lately, not wanting to leave the house or go anywhere. Her aunt Michelle, who was her mum's sister, was lovely, but she was always dashing around going places, and Bronte always felt as if she was in the way. Michelle didn't have any children of her own and she'd ended up with Bronte at a time when she was wanting to enjoy her life without being tied down.

'Macy is on holiday, the lucky thing,' Bronte told the group. 'Her mum has taken her to Benidorm for two weeks.'

Sara arched an eyebrow. 'I'm not sure I'd call being in Benidorm for two weeks lucky.'

Milly sighed. 'It might not be paradise but it's sunny, hot and it's not here, so I'd take it if I was offered it.'

The three of them sat down and Bronte began to pick at the lime green gel polish on her nails, a habit she couldn't kick no matter how much she got told off by the nail tech she visited every month. It was a comfort thing; she'd last three weeks and then by the time it got to the fourth she was unable to stop herself from picking and peeling the thick layers of gel from her nails.

'Are Lexie and Ava coming tonight?' asked Milly.

Bronte nodded. 'They said they were.'

Lexie and Ava were the most recent of the survivors: both of them had almost been taken out by a woman who had killed an entire family before trying to kill them.

The door opened and Ava walked in. She was dripping wet; her long blonde hair was stuck flat to her head, and her hoody was soaking.

'Erm, nobody sent a memo out about the weather, did they? I'm soaking running from the car to here.'

Bronte jumped up and went to retrieve a towel from the toilet. She threw it in Ava's direction, and she let out a 'Eww,' when she grabbed hold of it. 'Why is it hard and crusty? Actually, don't answer that, I'd rather not know. Thank you, I'll drip dry in the corner. Has anyone heard from Lexie? She wanted a lift but then when I went for her, she didn't answer, and her house was in darkness.'

'Maybe she's getting dropped off instead.'

Milly smiled. 'Or maybe she blew us off for a more interesting offer. I couldn't blame her if she did. I mean I love you guys, but we kind of talk about the same stuff and it might be exciting to go on a date or something.'

Bronte stared at her. 'You'd consider going on a date?'

Milly rolled her eyes then shook her head. 'Actually, probably not but I like the thought of it.'

'Don't we all,' replied Sara.

'Should we get started? Lexie might not be coming,' Bronte said, taking her seat in the semi-circle. Sara walked across to the door and turned the key to lock them all inside. There was another door which led into the church hall, and Bronte had already slid the bolt over. Ava shuddered as she sat next to Bronte.

'Have you ever thought what would happen if someone decided to burn this place to the ground while we're all locked inside, thinking that we're keeping ourselves safe when really we're sitting ducks?'

Sara sat next to Ava. 'Jesus, what a cheery thought that is. Thanks for sharing, Ava.'

The teenage girl shrugged. 'Isn't that the whole point of this? To share our darkest fears. So you can all tell us that the worst has happened to us already; we fought the bogeyman and lived to tell the tale. Then again, look at Laurie Strode: Michael Myers never let her go and kept on coming for her over and over again.'

Bronte stared at her. 'Laurie Strode is fictional – you fought the bogeywoman.'

'Same thing.'

Milly said, 'Actually, I thought someone was watching me yesterday and it proper freaked me out and I thought I saw the same car outside when I dashed in.'

All heads turned to her. 'What?' said Bronte and Sara together.

'It was probably nothing, but there was a guy in a car parked along the street doing nothing but stare at my house.'

'What did you do?'

'I wanted to confront him, ask him what the fuck he was doing, but as I got nearer my hands started to shake and my palms got all sticky. I turned around and walked away in the other direction as fast as I could go with my head down.'

'Did he see you?' Bronte's voice was filled with fear.

'I don't think so. If he was looking for me, he wouldn't have recognised me, as my hair has changed since you know when. I'd just come back from the hairdressers, and it was red instead of brown. I went to Lexie's house and told her; I stayed there last night. I didn't even go home, and I felt terrible for my mum and dad because then I worried he might go after them. Lexie told me I was being stupid, and it was probably someone waiting for someone else and nothing to do with me.'

'Have you spoken to your parents?' Sara's voice was much higher pitched than usual.

'They're good, they're on holiday.'

Bronte exhaled. 'Phew, that's terrifying. Did you think about calling the police?'

Milly shook her head. 'And say what? There's a guy sitting in his car not doing anything on my street and I'm scared. They'd have laughed me off the phone and told me to stop wasting their time.'

'No, they wouldn't. It's their job to protect us. They would have come to investigate, especially if you mentioned what's happened to you before.'

'I don't want to be defined by what happened to me before.'

'None of us do, Milly, but we don't want to end up dead either. If you see him again you ring the cops, better to be safe than sorry. Should I go out and check if the car is outside, what sort was it?'

'No, don't I'm probably being paranoid, it was a Picasso. Maybe just be aware if you see one parked near your houses.'

Bronte reached out for her hand and squeezed the girl's freezing cold fingers. Was it too much to ask that they get to live out the rest of their lives without fear?

FOUR

Ben stared at the blood. Morgan whispered, 'So, what do you think has happened?'

'Who lives here?'

'Natalie, I don't know actually. Amy is in there with her. Natalie can't get hold of her daughter. Lexie.'

Rain began to fall and sent Ben into a panic. It was going to wash away their evidence. He radioed control. 'I need a tent or something super-fast to preserve the scene, as it's started to rain.' He ran towards the boot of the car, to see if there was anything he could find to put over the blood on the floor, but the rain stopped as he got to it; it was a light shower.

'So, we're assuming that Lexie could be in some kind of trouble, right? That amount of blood is serious. Could she have cut herself making something to eat and left in a panic, got someone to pick her up or rang herself an ambulance?'

'Lexie, I know that name, I know Natalie too.' Morgan's face paled as she thought about the two teenage girls and one of the girls' mums who had almost suffocated a few months ago, realising that was where she knew Natalie from. She dashed into the house next door, where Natalie was sipping tea from a chipped mug in the shape of a pumpkin.

'Natalie.'

The woman looked up at her, eyes red and puffy from crying.

'Morgan, I thought it was you, but it's dark and I'm not thinking straight.'

'I'm so sorry, Natalie, I was a little thrown by the house.'

She nodded. 'I left him; it was too hard to stay there after everything. He didn't care about what we went through, which just showed how much he cared about us. Jasper bought us this house, to pay us off I think and get us out of the way. Have you found Lexie? She's not answering her phone, and that's not like her.' She sniffed. 'Not after what happened to us both, she wouldn't worry me like this.'

So much was going through Morgan's mind. Lexie White was the survivor of an evil monster who'd killed an entire family. And she was now missing, leaving nothing behind but pooling blood. Was it her own? Had it been caused by a major injury?

'Amy, have you got a list of friends for us to start checking? I'll get Cain to ring the hospitals just in case she's hurt herself and gone there. We also can't rule out the possibility that it might not be related to Lexie, and someone else could have hurt themselves somehow near to your house.' Morgan tried to keep her voice light, as if it was a real possibility, but deep down in the very centre of her gut her instinct told her it was Lexie. She felt a little light-headed at the thought of someone trying to hurt the girl after everything she'd been through, and she swayed a little to the left. She had to reach out and clamp hold of the back of the chair Billie was sitting on to stop herself from falling flat on her face.

'Natalie, we're doing everything we can, and as soon as we have an update then so will you.'

The woman nodded. She'd aged since Morgan had last seen her. Her hair was tied up in a messy bun, and she had no make-up on; there were creases on her forehead and fine lines around her eyes. She clearly hadn't been able to keep up with the Botox since she'd left Jasper. There was not a pair of yoga pants in sight, which had been the attire she'd worn when Morgan had first met her.

Her own face had lost much of its youthful innocence since she'd first started this job, she thought. She'd blamed it on the stressful situations of dealing with tragic, senseless deaths, and hadn't thought to blame it on the things she'd been through as a person, but now she thought about it, they were just as bad as what Natalie and Lexie had endured. She walked outside and took a deep breath in through her nose to calm down, quietly exhaling through her mouth.

Ben said, 'I want a photograph of Lexie. I've put her as a high priority missing person. Morgan, can you door knock, starting this end, and see if there are any doorbell cameras or dashcam footage that cover this house?'

She nodded. 'It's Lexie White and her mum Natalie who live here.'

Ben squeezed his eyes shut for a second as he scrubbed a hand across his face. 'Crap.'

'I didn't realise at first because it's not the huge house they used to live in, but I just spoke to Natalie and it's them.'

'This makes it a whole different game.'

'I know. Ben, I think we need to check Jackie Thorpe is still in prison.'

'Let's stop it right there, Morgan, in its tracks, eh? Let's focus on the here and now. We would have been notified if she had escaped, so we will concentrate on what we have to work with. You start the house to house for me while I speak to the DI and get him down here to assess the situation and get the info we need to do a cell site analysis. Smithy, start at the other end, mate.'

She couldn't speak, she was so raw with emotion, but she wouldn't let it stop her doing her job. Turning away she walked to the house next to Billie and began to hammer on the door with a closed fist. They had no idea where Lexie was and had no CCTV. She tried the next and the next, realising that this was probably going to prove a fruitless exercise. All of them had their curtains closed, none of them saw anything suspicious, until she knocked on the fourth door and a teenage boy opened it.

'Are you here about that weird guy?'

Morgan felt her heart miss a beat. 'I might be, what weird guy?'

The boy looked her up and down: she was wearing black jeans, black T-shirt, black hoodie zipped up and her beloved Dr. Martens. 'Are you a copper?'

'Yes, guilty. Are your parents home, and what about the weird guy?'

He leaned out of his door and looked at the activity a few doors down. 'Nah, my dad is at work. What happened?'

'The owner of the house at the end came home to find blood all over her door.'

'Natalie? Is Lexie okay?'

'We don't know, can you tell me?'

He laughed. 'Erm, nope. I've been in here on my Xbox playing *Call of Duty* with my mates.'

She wanted to reach over and grab him by the Nirvana sweatshirt he was wearing, but she refrained.

'And what about the weird guy you mentioned?' she asked again.

'Yeah, some bloke in a car just sitting staring at Lexie's house the last couple of nights. He must be a complete psychopath because he literally just sat there watching it, no phone, nothing, not even a radio on in the car.'

'What did he look like?'

He shrugged. 'Dunno, old, bald, it was dark I only saw him from behind.'

'Car, make, model, colour?'

There was a streetlight directly outside this house, and she noticed that his cheeks had gone from pale to a deep, burning crimson colour.

'I think it was a' – he squeezed his eyes shut; his brow furrowed with concentration – 'it was a weird one, a Citroen, maybe a Picasso; it was light in colour. Sorry, I didn't think about it that much. I thought maybe her dad had hired one of those fancy private investigators to watch the house or something.'

'What's your name?'

'Jordan Archer.'

'Okay, thanks, Jordan. I'm going to have to come back and speak to you, or one of my colleagues will try and get a proper description when your dad is in. Did you see the guy tonight?'

'Not tonight. I got home from school, and he wasn't around. I went straight in the house.'

'Does anyone in the street have CCTV that you know about?'

'Can't really say, the house at the other end might; she's a right busybody always moaning about the kids playing football.'

'Thanks, what time are your parents home?'

'My dad is home after nine.'

He closed the door. She would get an officer to go back and get a full statement from him when the nightshift came on. She turned on her phone torch to study the pavement around the house and the walls, but there wasn't a single drop of blood. It clearly stopped in the road outside of Lexie's house. She headed back towards Ben.

'Lad from number eighteen said he saw a man watching the house the last two nights, possibly bald, in a light-coloured Citroen Picasso.'

Ben passed the information over the radio to the control room to add to the open incident log that was running. 'Wendy is on her way, so is Cassie. It's Cassie's day off, but they called her out. If anyone can get a trail it will be Brock.'

Morgan hoped she brought Caesar the big black Italian mastiff with her. He was excellent at chasing down suspects. He was Morgan's absolute favourite police dog, and they had a thing going on where she scratched his ears and belly in return for him slobbering all over her. He had the biggest, brownest, most human like eyes she'd ever seen on a dog.

'Has Cain got any updates from the hospitals? I'm still holding out for this all to be a huge mix up and we're going to find out Lexie sliced off the tip of her finger or something. I don't think I could bear it, Ben, if something awful has happened to her.'

'Morgan, you just told me some guy has been watching the house.'

She shrugged. 'I know, but I'm trying to keep positive for a change.'

He smiled at her and gently squeezed her arm. 'I like that attitude, and you never know.'

FIVE

The group of teenagers always hung around the park at night. At thirteen and fourteen they were old enough to be out quite late but had nowhere in Rydal Falls to actually go to. The park gates were never locked, and it was the best place to keep out of sight of any adults who would tell them to move away from their houses, be quiet, stop kicking a ball; the complaints were never ending. The five girls and four boys had chipped in to get a couple of pizzas they could eat while watching a film on Denny's iPad. There were a couple of ancient wooden shelters with seats in them that they used to shelter from the rain and the wind on a miserable night, but tonight it wasn't too bad. That was why they had decided to get pizza and eat it outside instead of piling into Denny's house. His mum was the coolest and she worked nights at the hospital, so she'd let them hang around in there as long as they didn't smoke inside, didn't cause too much mess or break anything, and didn't have sex. This she had stipulated to each and every one of them.

'I don't mind what you do as long as it's not of a sexual nature. I don't want someone's parents calling me up telling me their daughter got pregnant while I was out at work, okay?'

She had made every single one of them promise her they'd be good, and they had because they were cool with her, but tonight was her night off and she'd chased them all out, telling them she had a migraine and wanted some quiet time without the constant noise of nine teenagers filling the house.

It was dark by the time the pizza was ready and they'd walked down to the park. Denny had his iPad tucked under one arm, Jon, Oscar and Hayden were all throwing a football to each other. The girls, who were walking behind them carrying the assorted pizza boxes, were chattering amongst themselves. Gracie, Kyra, Katie, Hattie and Phoebe were deep in discussion about whether or not they would get tattoos and if they did what sort would they have and where would they put them. The lads reached the shelter first, Denny put the iPad down on the bench and the four of them began to have a kick about on the grass, while the girls put the pizza boxes out and began to divide them equally between everyone. Gracie picked up a slice of pepperoni pizza and took a bite.

'My mum has this huge tattoo all over her back, it's all in black and it's these great big flowers.'

Katie frowned. 'Ouch, I bet that hurt. Doesn't sound very nice if it's all black ink.'

'Not all black, like her back has been coloured in with black ink, the outlines of the flowers are in black, and you can see the skin.'

'What? What does that even mean?'

Kyra laughed. 'Katie, you have no imagination. Show her a picture, Gracie. Have you got one?'

'Er, no. Why would I have a picture of my mam's back? That's just weird.'

'What about on her Instagram? Has she not put any pictures on that?'

The others picked up slices of pizza and sat down on the bench either side of the boxes. Kyra took out her phone. 'I'll have a look at her Insta and see if she has a picture. I want to see it now you've mentioned it.'

'Yeah, well she has more tattoos than anyone I know so they can't hurt that much. I want one on my arm but not sure what to get.'

Oscar came running over to grab a slice. 'I don't know why you're even talking about tattoos because you can't get them for another what, four years?'

Hattie looked up at him. 'And I don't know why you all pretend you can play football cause you're all crap at it.'

As she said that Denny kicked the ball so hard it bounced off the roof with a loud thud and fell to the floor with a splat. He came wandering over to retrieve it but stopped and bent down to look at it, pointing to the once white leather ball that was now coated in something dark.

Gracie lifted her hand to her mouth to take a bite of her pizza when a thick, wet splotch of something dark dropped from the roof of the shelter onto her hand. She jumped, dropping the pizza on the ground. 'What is that?' She looked at her hand. It wasn't water: it was too dark and too thick. Phoebe leaned closer to her, shining her phone torch onto the red splotch, and then she was lifting it to the roof to see where it had come from when another drip fell onto the lid of the pizza box, something dark red spreading like a flower against the white of the cardboard. Phoebe whispered. 'It looks like blood.'

Gracie had now bent down to pick up the football. Oscar grabbed Phoebe's phone off her and took a few steps back, shining it up at the roof. 'There's something up there. Give me a bunk up.'

Denny bent down and cradled his hands together so Oscar could step into it. Reaching up with both hands, Denny pushed, and Oscar grabbed onto the side of the shelter, pulling himself up level with it. Hanging on by one hand he reached out.

'Phoebe pass me your phone.' She did, and he shone the torch onto the roof and let out a yelp so loud it made the others jump. He threw the phone and then himself to the ground.

Gracie screamed. 'What's wrong?' just as she realised that the red stuff on her hand was blood, and she launched the football to the ground.

'Run, we have to get out of here. There's a dead body on the roof.'

Gracie didn't need telling twice. She took off, closely followed by the others. The only one who hadn't run was Denny. He thought Oscar was being an idiot. He retrieved Phoebe's phone and used a finger to wipe the smear of liquid off the screen. It was only then he realised from the coppery smell that it was blood and that maybe something was very wrong. He turned and followed his friends until they were out of the gates and almost at the Co-op, which was the nearest shop to the park.

They ran inside screaming and crying.

The guy behind the counter jumped out of his skin.

'Get out if you're going to mess around. I'll ring the cops. I've had enough of you lot.'

Gracie held up her hands that were coated in blood. 'Ring the feds now, there's a body in the park. There's blood everywhere.'

He stared at her bloody hands and his face paled. He picked up the phone and dialled 999, then screamed: 'Sue' at the top of his voice.

A red-faced Sue appeared, took one look at the crying kids and said, 'What the hell is going on?'

He shrugged, the phone clamped to his ear as he spoke to the 999 operator. 'I don't know, Sue, but lock the bloody doors, there's a maniac on the loose. They said they found a body in the park.'

Sue ran to the doors and turned the key in the box on the wall, then she looked at the kids.

'You lot better not be messing around; he's calling the cops.'

Gracie shook her head. 'Good, because we're not.' She held out her bloodied hands towards the woman.

SIX

The call for urgent assistance at the Co-op on main street was passed over the radio. Morgan took one look at Ben when she heard the report of a possible body in the park, and they both ran for his car. He called out, 'Scotty, keep this area secure. No one near the scene, okay?'

Scotty grunted a reply as they got into the car, and Ben turned it around, mounting the pavement on the other side, narrowly missing a lamppost.

The Co-op was only a few minutes away, the park a few more. 'We'll head to the park and let patrols deal with the situation at the Co-op.'

Morgan wanted to throw up. She couldn't face the thought that Lexie could be the body in the park: it was too cruel.

Ben approached the gates, and she knew he was figuring if the car would fit through them.

'I don't think it's a good—'

It was too late; he drove through the tight space, taking off the wing mirror on her side with a loud cracking noise and the high-pitched splinter of glass as it broke into a thousand pieces, showering the air behind them.

She jumped. 'Jesus, Ben.'

'You were right, that wasn't my best idea. Where did they say it was?'

They hadn't said. She lifted the radio up and asked, 'Where's the body?'

The control room operator answered: '*On top of a shelter apparently.*'

Morgan knew the shelters, there were two; she'd spent many a teenage year hanging around underneath them. Ben knew them too, and he headed straight towards them, flicking the headlights onto full beam as he rounded the bend and they came into view.

There was a figure on top of the first one. 'Oh shit,' he muttered. 'This better not be a prank.'

Morgan shook her head. 'Sick prank if it is.'

He stopped the car, leaving the engine running, and they sprinted towards the shelter where four boxes of pizzas were laid out on the bench along with an iPad. There was also a pool of blood on the floor from the drips coming through the roof.

'I'll give you a boost up.' Ben was talking to her, and she looked at him, then nodded. Mimicking exactly what Denny and Oscar had done earlier, he cupped his hands, and Morgan stood in one. He pushed her up, and she took out her phone torch, shining it on the body that was propped against the peak of the roof.

Despite the head listing forwards, Morgan cried out, 'Lexie.' She knew it was her; she had failed to recognise Natalie, but she would have known Lexie anywhere.

'Talk to me, Morgan.'

'She's got multiple injuries that are bleeding out. She's dead.' Morgan took a deep breath, closed her eyes and readied herself to continue. 'There is no way she's alive, not with this much blood loss. There's a bag on her head too, a clear plastic bag. Even if she'd been alive, she would have suffocated inside of that.'

Morgan let go of the edge of the roof, and Ben helped her to the ground.

Why the bag? Who knew about that? It hadn't been made public knowledge at the time of the attack. She felt chills begin to wrack her whole body, and her hands were trembling at the thought of the brutal death the girl had endured.

'We need to back up now and get suited up. Are you okay, Morgan?'

She was in no way okay with what she was seeing, but she nodded. 'Are you?'

He didn't answer; instead, he asked for units to attend the park and seal off the gates, and for Cassie to bring the dog here instead of the house. Memories of walking into Natalie's huge house and finding her and Lexie at the table gasping for air with plastic bags over their faces filled her mind. What was this? Had the killer got out of prison and come back to finish what they'd started? Jackie Thorpe had cleverly disguised herself while out on her horrific killing spree, surprising everyone when they finally caught up with her. Could she have escaped?

Morgan repeated the question she'd asked back at the house. 'Ben, do we need to check and see if Jackie Thorpe is still in prison?'

This time he nodded. 'Ring Cain, see if he's still at the office. He can chase that up.'

She turned her back on the heart-wrenching scene and walked away.

Cain answered on the first ring. *'What's going on, Morgan?'*

'It's bad, Cain, we found the missing teenager's body in the park. Can you check on Jackie Thorpe's intel record, to see which prison she's in and then can you phone the prison and make sure she is where she's supposed to be?'

'On it now, isn't that the sick bitch who killed that family?'

'Yes, please hurry, I don't want to risk her being free to roam around Rydal Falls and carry on where she left off.'

She hung up. She had been in this position before; her biological father was a cold-blooded killer who had escaped from prison, evading capture for months, so she knew it was possible. She just hoped that wherever Jackie was they kept her under tight security so she couldn't do the same.

And then she realised that if it wasn't Jackie, it could be someone a whole lot worse.

Morgan didn't think she had ever felt so helpless. She couldn't reach Lexie to even whisper some form of comfort to her like the soothing words Declan, the home office pathologist, and her friend, often spoke to the victims in his care. She wanted to sit with her, hold her hand and tell her how sorry she was, spend a little time with the girl and let her know she was here for her now and wouldn't stop until she'd found whoever had done this.

Ben was pacing up and down, staring up at the body.

'How the hell did someone get her in the park and up onto that roof without anyone seeing?'

As if to answer Ben's question, a van with flashing blue lights drove slowly towards them from the opposite direction. It stopped and Amber got out.

'How did you get that in?'

'Service entrance at the back. They leave it open so we can patrol if the kids are being a pain in the arse.'

Morgan didn't look at Ben; she didn't know this either.

'Oh, man. Could have saved smashing the wing mirror to pieces.'

Amber turned to the plain car he had arrived in, with the black plastic mirror casing dangling from its wires. 'Oh, did you drive through the pedestrian gate? I'm surprised you only took a wing mirror off.'

She must have sensed Ben's mood wasn't one to be joked around with. 'What do you want me to do?'

'Wake me up from this nightmare,' whispered Morgan.

Amber turned to her. 'Sorry, wish that I could.' She looked up at the body on the roof and let out a low gasp. 'Oh, my, that's horrid. Why is she up there, how?'

'That's what we're trying to figure out.'

Ben turned and walked away. Morgan could hear him on his phone to the DI. Marc wasn't on duty, but he would come out for something like this, even though there would be a duty DI on somewhere else in the county who could attend and be the senior investigation officer.

Morgan's mobile began to ring. It was Amy.

'What's going on? I heard all that commotion on the radio, and I've come outside to find Scotty and nobody else.'

'Are you with Natalie?'

'No, I left her with the neighbour. Is it Lexie?'

'I'm pretty certain that it is.'

'Oh no, what should I do?'

'We can't get to her at the moment, she's up on the shelter roof.'

'Sick bastard.'

Morgan nodded, even though Amy couldn't see her.

'Should I break the news to Natalie that we've found a body?'

Ben was shaking his head.

'Not just yet, not until we've recovered her off this bloody roof or at least had a closer look to triple confirm it is her. I don't want her turning up and seeing her daughter this way; we can't even get a tent over her.'

'Did you hear what Ben said?'

'Yeah, should I hang fire here? Because there's only Scotty and he's at the other end and you know what he's like.'

Ben was nodding at Morgan.

'He said, yes please. Can you let us know if Natalie tries to leave the house? I want to be the one to pass this message on. I feel as if I owe it to her.'

'Yeah, I will. Poor woman. I know we're in a position to help stop a killer, but I hate this job at times. She's in there worrying where her daughter is, and we know exactly where she is but can't tell her and can't let her come see her. Do you think it's her for sure?'

Morgan turned away from Ben. She had felt it in her bones that it was Lexie the moment she saw her, but she knew they had to follow procedure, until they were sure it was Lexie. The victim's face was obscured by the bag on her head, so it may not be her.

'Did Natalie give you a description of what Lexie was wearing when she last saw her?'

The sound of Amy rustling the pages of her notebook filled the speaker.

'Black leggings, black Nike trainers, black hoodie with Hollywood Vampires on the front. Apparently, she lives in it since she saw them in concert last month.'

Morgan sighed. 'Then yes, it's definitely her. I'll tell Ben, the clothing description is a match.'

Amy hung up, and Morgan crossed to where Ben was staring up at the body.

'I'm shocked beyond shocked if I'm honest,' he said. 'I honestly thought I'd seen it all, but this is just...'

As if called on cue, the CSI van drove along the path towards them and stopped next to the van. Wendy got out, with a guy that neither of them had seen before.

'Guys, this is Ian, the new crime scene manager. He started yesterday.'

Morgan smiled at the blond-haired man; he looked around the same age as Ben. 'Well, this is definitely a crime scene that's going to take some managing. How lucky we are to have you on board.'

Wendy turned away, but not before Morgan caught the smirk on her face and she wondered if Ian was already proving to be hard work. He nodded at her, not bothering to reply, and headed straight towards Ben, his hand outstretched. Ben, who hated office politics and general rudeness, arched an eyebrow at him but took his hand.

'DS Ben Matthews and this is DC Morgan Brookes.'

He didn't even acknowledge Morgan, which shouldn't have bothered her, but it did. She walked towards Wendy who was at the side of the van getting suited and booted.

'What's his story?'

'Don't get me started, Morgan, you know those people who you want to throttle the life out of when you just look at them?'

Morgan wasn't quite sure she'd ever wanted to instantaneously strangle someone yet.

'I suppose so.'

'Well, he's one of them. He came in the office yesterday and completely ignored what I was telling him and began telling me how he wants things doing now he's in charge. I don't know why they even put *must be a team player* on the job descriptions. I can't imagine Ian playing fairly at anything.'

'Is he here permanently?'

'No, just for this week and then he's back at HQ and covering from there.'

Ian came rushing towards the van, a hand cupped across his mouth. Wendy rolled her eyes at Morgan.

'Everything okay?'

His head shook. 'It's the blood dripping on the pizza boxes. I ate pizza for tea.'

Then he was gone, into the bushes, where the sound of his retching filled the air. Ben wandered over to where they were standing.

'Is he for real? I thought having a stomach made of steel was a part of your job requirement?'

'I don't know where they found him, Ben, but apparently not.'

'Help me out here, Wendy, what are we going to do with her? I want her off that roof as soon as possible.'

'Let me get it filmed and photographed. Is Declan travelling?'

He nodded.

'Good, well in my honest opinion you're going to need fire and rescue too, because it might be difficult to get her down without a fire truck with one of those lift things on.'

'Wendy, whoever put her up there must have struggled. If he did then surely, he left us some nice DNA or forensics behind. I want all the bins in the park searched in case he's discarded any evidence inside of them, clothing, the weapon, and what about footprints? Please, please find me something.'

'I'll do my best.'

'That's all I ever ask.'

Ben and Wendy stood to one side as Ian came back to the van.

Wendy asked him, 'What's your plan?'

'Erm, I haven't got one right now.'

Morgan looked at him, her eyes wide in disbelief, and he glared back at her, but she didn't look away.

'I'll let you do what you usually do so we can get the body moved and then I'll work out a plan for the whole area.'

Wendy was shaking her head. 'Wow, amazing. I could never have managed to think of that without you.'

She walked away, and Morgan followed her, whispering, 'Is he being serious?'

'Unfortunately. Complete waste of my time, and the force's money. I'd rather call Claire in to come and help me; she'd have a plan within seconds of being here.'

'Just like you.'

Wendy smiled at her. 'Yeah, we make a great team. Just like you, Ben, Cain and Amy do. I can't be bothered with jumped-up-I-am-the-big-chief when it's teamwork that makes the dreamwork.'

Morgan nodded. 'You're absolutely right, it certainly does.'

She stood next to Ben while Wendy began documenting the crime scene. The whole situation was obscene. Whoever had thought it was okay to do this to Lexie and then leave her like that was in for a shock, because there was no way Morgan would let them get away with it. She had never felt such anger and a deep sense of injustice in her life.

SEVEN

Home Office Forensic Pathologist Declan Donnelly arrived fifteen minutes after Wendy had begun to work the crime scene. He strolled towards them carrying his heavy case and waved his hand in greeting to Morgan and Ben.

'Blimey, I'm unfit. It's almost killed me walking here from the car.'

'Where are you parked?'

'At the front gates, next to a van. Some idiot must have driven through the pedestrian gate, there's pieces of broken wing mirror everywhere. You might want to get CSI to bag it up in case it's relevant.'

Morgan smiled at him. 'Ben was that idiot.'

Declan turned to Ben. 'You were? Well I suppose I should be impressed then, it's not every day you get someone who thinks they're a stunt driver and can drive through gates that are far too small. You're lucky it's only a wing mirror and not the side of the car.' Declan stopped to look at the damaged side of the car and whistled. 'Wowee, you did that proud is what you did, Ben. Good job it's not your BMW.'

'I'd rather it was my car, far less paperwork.'

'True, so what have we got here?'

Ben pointed to the roof, and Declan, who was standing with his hands on his hips too busy surveying the damage to the car, looked up and let out a low groan.

'Dear God, is it me or are things getting much worse around here? I mean that's brutal. I've seen some awful stuff, but why put her on the roof, and why is the bag wrapped around her head?'

'I'm hoping that's what you're about to tell us.'

Declan shook his head. 'I won't be telling you anything unless we get her down from there and out of harm's way, God rest her soul. I need to get up there, not sure how, but I need to confirm she's deceased.'

As if sent by an angel, a fire and rescue engine slowly came into view, driving towards them, the lights flashing but no sirens. Ian began to run towards it, waving his hands furiously in the air. The driver stopped and leaned out of the window.

'Problem?'

'Yes, this is a crime scene. Who gave you permission to enter it?'

Declan folded his arms and leaned towards Ben. 'Now, who the hell is that because he's stolen your line?'

Ben looked as if he would rather be anywhere than here, and he began striding towards both Ian and the driver, who was now out of the cab.

Morgan whispered to Declan, 'New; a crime scene manager who doesn't do violent crimes and had to go puke in the bushes when he saw the blood dripping through the roof and congealing on the pizza boxes.'

Declan arched an eyebrow at her. 'Sounds like he's not the right man for the job.'

Wendy was slowly walking backwards towards them, snapping photographs of the area. She agreed. 'He isn't, but I'm stuck with him.'

'What do you think, Wendy, can I get up there to take a look?'

'Be my guest, this scene has already been contaminated by a load of teenagers who were here for a late-night picnic. Just let me see if they have a ladder I can use to get some close-ups of the shelter roof and body, then she's all yours.'

She rustled towards Ben in her paper suit, shouting, 'Have you guys got a ladder I can use?'

Declan shook his head. 'I feel as if I'm in some kind of alternative universe.'

Morgan smiled. 'I wish that I was.'

He turned to her. 'You know the deceased?'

'If it's who I think it is then yes.'

'Morgan, I'm sorry. This must be tough for you. Should you be here?'

'I knew her through work, well I saved her life not that long ago when she was attacked by the Lawson family killer, and now...'

'She's here and almost certainly dead. Wow, that was a tough one to deal with, that poor family all killed at the same time. I still have nightmares about them. Some deaths stay with you long after the victims are buried. You must feel the same way. I didn't know about the survivors, I only deal with the ones who aren't so lucky. Do you want to talk about it?'

'I ripped a plastic bag off her head when the killer tried to suffocate both her and her mum. It was a close call, and this is so unfair.' Her voice broke as she stifled the sob trying to break free.

'Is her mum okay? Well, obviously not okay but has anyone checked she's not come to any harm?'

'I spoke to her mum not too long ago; she reported finding a lot of blood on her front door and couldn't get in touch with her daughter. Declan, is there any way she could have done this to herself, driven herself here, climbed up on that roof and put the bag over her head?' Morgan had been considering death by suicide. Lexie had been through so much, perhaps she had been struggling…

He pursed his lips and blew out a long sigh. 'I can't tell you that, Morgan, until I get her to the mortuary, but personally I would think not. It's a lot, don't you think?'

She nodded. 'No, me either. It doesn't make sense, does it? If she wanted to kill herself there are easier ways than this.'

'Unless she wanted to cause a huge fuss. Some people would enjoy that you know.'

'I don't think it was Lexie's style. I don't think she would be the kind of person to self-harm that way.'

Wendy came back with two firefighters carrying a set of ladders. 'Thanks, guys, I'll take it from here.' They put it down and she grabbed hold of it. Declan had already suited and booted at his car, and he went to help her manoeuvre them into place.

'Do you want to check she's deceased first?'

He nodded and leaned the ladders at an angle safe enough for him to climb up to the roof, which wasn't very high, but an awkward angle to get to. As he got to the top he called down.

'Drag marks along the wooden tiles or shingles whatever they're called. There's a lot of blood seeped from the injuries too. I need to move along; if we put them a bit further around, I might be able to reach her.'

He climbed back down and carried the ladders around to the side of the building and tried again.

'Much better angle.'

Reaching out he took hold of her bloody hand, pressing his fingers against her wrist and felt for a pulse. He knew by how stiff her body was that she'd been dead some time.

He whispered, 'Well, Lexie, this is terrible and I'm sorry, I really am that someone has done this to you. I'm Declan and I will take care of you now, sweetheart. We'll get you down from here and cleaned up so your mum can come say goodbye.'

Morgan felt the lump form in her throat on hearing Declan's whispered conversation with the girl she'd felt a connection with because she'd saved her life once. Why hadn't she been able to save her twice? Did you only get one chance to survive? No, that wasn't right because she'd had more than a few run-ins with killers and had lived to tell the tale.

EIGHT

He strolled around the car wash as if he hadn't a care in the world. While tourists and locals filled up their tanks and bought family sized bags of chocolate and confectionery, he was washing away the girl's blood in plain sight. No one paid him the slightest bit of attention, which he found both amusing and annoying. Not that he wanted to be caught so soon in the game, but credit where credit is due; he would accept a little acclamation.

As he hosed down the sheet of plastic, he watched the blood run from it along the tarmacked floor to the drain, where it swirled away in a pinkish foam of soap suds and water before disappearing. This he knew was a problem. Although the blade had dealt with her swiftly and put her completely out of action, this much bodily fluids wasn't good. What if he'd got pulled over by some overeager cop out on traffic duty? The back seat of his car looked and smelled like an abattoir; how would he get out of that? *Sorry, officer, my dog got hit by a car and I've just had to get him put down at the vets.* That was his excuse, if he had been unfortunate enough to get stopped, but he was lucky that he hadn't. He supposed that this area was so busy with tourists that the traffic cops didn't really park up and wait to catch them speeding. The roads were far too busy with snail-like traffic that crawled more than anything. It was rare that anyone got the chance to drive over forty on the windy lanes that the Lake District was well known for.

He fed some coins into the machine and began to hoover the back seat and floor mats just in case she'd left some hair behind; it couldn't hurt to be overly cautious. Once he was satis-fied the car was clean on the inside, he rolled the plastic up and put it into the boot. Closed the doors and began to use the power washer on the outside of the car. He concentrated on the wheels because he was sure that he'd read soil samples could be taken and compared to the crime scene. He supposed tyre tracks could too, but this was a common car, or it used to be, so he wasn't too worried about that. When he'd finished and was soaked to the bone with the spray from the powerful jet, he got back inside the car. He was chilled now. He needed to go home and have a hot shower, change out of these clothes and burn them. Then he was going to pour himself a large glass of vodka on the rocks and relive every single moment from the second he approached her.

As he drove home, he checked his mirrors in case he was being followed. Someone may have noticed him at the garage and phoned the cops. The road behind him was busy, but not with police. No cars were following him marked or unmarked. He could go home and enjoy the rest of his evening. He didn't think he had anything to worry about. His instincts told him that he was fine, the cops weren't that good at finding killers. Except for maybe that one: Detective Brookes. She was his most likely opponent in his game of catch me if you can. How scared would she be when she realised that the victim was one she knew a little too well? That amused him. The thought that she might have a sleepless night tonight, knowing that the girl she had saved had died.

He left the car in the street behind his, in case someone had seen him driving away from the girl's house. He had false plates on – the number plate he'd bought off eBay for a couple of quid, no questions asked. It didn't lead back to him or at least he didn't think it did.

As he stood outside his front door he heard a loud miaow. The cat strolled up behind him and began to rub himself against his legs. He kicked it away, but it didn't go far. It was hungry. It was always hungry. As he opened the front door it darted through his legs almost tripping him up. He reached out a foot to kick it, but it was too fast and sprinted up the stairs. He shook his head; the fact that his wife had left him with nothing except a mangy cat that needed feeding more times a day than him really irked his sense of justice. If it wasn't for the fact that he was lonely and needed some form of company, he'd have caught it and taken it to the cat shelter. Somehow, he thought the bloody thing would escape and find its way back here anyway. He put up with it because it was easier that way, and it helped him to look a little less strange to the neighbours if he still cared for a pet.

NINE

There was a sombre crew standing around waiting for Wendy and Ian, who had recovered sufficiently to advise the best way to handle the body without risking contaminating any possible forensics. Morgan knew they were going to have to use the lift thing on the engine to do it, and she was just waiting for Ben to give the go ahead, even though Ian was standing there trying to tell everyone what to do.

In the end Ben turned to him.

'You're not helping, okay? Just shut up for a moment. The only way this is going to work is if three of us go up in that lift and wrap the body tight in a sheet, have a body bag waiting on the platform and put her straight into it.'

Ian was shaking his head. 'I can't do it.'

Ben glared at him. 'Good because no one asked you to. I can't risk you vomiting all over her, so why don't you stand by the van like a good man and keep quiet so I can think this through.'

Ian was about to argue with him then thought better of it, which Wendy noted and whispered to Morgan, 'Wise move, tell him to get his useless arse out of our way. I knew I liked Ben for a reason.'

Ben turned to them. 'Wendy, do you think you can help if me and Declan go up there as well?'

'Absolutely, boss.' She emphasised the boss part, and Morgan knew she did it to wind Ian up.

The fire crew manager told them he would operate the lift, and he then helped all three of them get into safety harnesses.

He said, 'I'm going to be honest, it might be a bit of a squeeze all three of you and the body on the lift at the same time.'

Ben nodded. 'Well, I'm happy to wait on the roof while the body is lowered to the floor. Will that work?'

'That roof doesn't look too safe, if I'm honest.'

'What's your name?'

'Rob.'

'Rob, I'll take that risk. It's currently holding its own and, if it does collapse, it's on my head; besides, it's not that far to the floor.'

Morgan looked at the ladder. 'Ben, why don't you use the ladder? Let Wendy and Declan see if they can get the victim into the lift.'

Rob looked a little happier at that suggestion. 'I'm happy with that.'

Morgan smiled at Ben and shrugged. 'I'll hold the ladder.'

Between them they managed to get Lexie, who had been tied to a small false chimney with a thick rope around the waist, cut free and wrapped into a sheet, into a body bag ready for the waiting undertakers to transport to the mortuary. The plastic bag slipped off her head, as it hadn't been tied on, and Morgan saw Lexie's blood-spattered face, her eyes frozen in horror at what had happened to her. By the time they had finished, all of them were sweating buckets in the paper suits, but at least Lexie could be given some dignity now.

As she was put into the back of the private ambulance with blacked-out windows, everyone at the scene bowed their heads as a mark of respect. Declan was the first to leave. Another CSI van from Barrow arrived with Claire inside, ready to work the scene. Morgan saw Claire look at Ian then roll her eyes at Wendy, who nodded. That guy had his work cut out for him if he was pissing off every CSI that worked for him.

Finally, the scene was lit up with floodlights and the fire engine could resume now that Lexie had brought down. The techs could get on with working the crime scene. Ben stripped off the protective clothing and shoe covers, and Morgan did the same.

'Now what?' Morgan asked Ben.

'Now we need to go and speak to Natalie and break the news to her.'

'I was afraid you were going to say that.'

'If you want to head back to the station, Morgan, that's fine. Amy is already at the scene, so she will come in with me.'

She shook her head; as much as she'd like to take Ben up on that offer, she knew that she had a sense of responsibility that meant she couldn't walk away because she was upset. She owed it to Lexie to pull up her big girl pants and do what she was so good at: catching the sick bastard who had done this.

She couldn't get the metallic tang of copper out of the back of her nose. It had been so potent she could taste it and it made her feel sick. Even though she had none of Lexie's blood on her skin, she still felt as if she needed a painfully hot shower to wash the smell away.

Marc had arrived as they were getting Lexie off the roof and had stood next to her watching in horror. He was now talking to Ian, and she figured that the pair of them would probably get on like a house on fire, because Marc had marched in to take over their department and totally screwed things up, until he'd realised what he'd done and calmed himself down.

Ben took hold of her elbow and guided her towards the car.

'Let's leave them to it. I need to get away from here and clear my head.'

'Me too.'

They got into the car, and he began to reverse, while Morgan hoped that Marc wouldn't turn around before the car was pointing the other way and he saw the damage to the wing mirror. Ben drove cautiously past the scene, towards the small access road that every other vehicle except his had used to gain entry to the park.

'Why don't you go out the way we came in? The car will fit nicely now.'

'Are you being sarcastic, Brookes?'

She laughed. 'Maybe, a little. Sorry, it is kind of funny though.'

He smiled at her, and she saw the corners of his eyes crinkle which made her happy. She loved those tiny laughter lines and had been worried that lately he didn't seem to have much to be laughing about. It was one job after the other, lots of high-profile cases with lots of meetings and involvement from high above watching his every move, despite not actually doing anything to help lessen the burden that seemed to be getting heavier with every new case that came in.

TEN

Sara, Milly and Ava were all staring at her, but she was lost inside of her own mind in a place far away that gave her waking nightmares.

'Bronte, did you decide what you're going to do?'

She looked at Sara, she was always so calm, so level-headed; she had cried once at their very first meeting and hadn't shed a tear since. Proclaiming that she wasn't letting that bastard rule her entire life with his evil actions. Bronte admired her and wished she could be the same.

'I, erm, not really.'

'Did you speak to your therapist since the last meeting?'

Sara wasn't letting this go, she was persistent.

'Yes.'

'And? He said what?'

'That maybe I should think about speaking to him, that by seeing him in person I'd realise he's not the horned devil I make him out to be inside of my mind, and he's just the same old boy I used to be in love with.'

'Huh, I suppose that makes some kind of sense but it's a

pretty hard thing to do. I'd come with you if you didn't want to go on your own.'

'Oh, no, thank you. I couldn't expect you to do that, you have your own monster to deal with. You don't want to add mine to your list too.'

Ava and Milly were staring at her, and she felt uncomfortable talking about this with them. Even though that was the whole idea of this support group, she still had trouble being open about how she felt.

Milly was nodding.

'I think he might have a point; you didn't get to face him in court because of your age. It was all done by video link, which isn't the same as staring the bastard straight in the eyes.'

'How did you manage to do that, Milly? I don't know if I could even look him in the eyes never mind stare him out.'

She shrugged. 'It's probably much harder for you because you were in a relationship. I didn't know the sicko who attacked me.'

Sara reached out for Bronte's hand. 'I didn't know the guy who took me either. Milly is right, I can't imagine how betrayed you feel. It makes it a lot worse knowing that the person you trusted could do this to you and your family. It might be a good idea to go there and ask him why, then tell him he's a fucking arsehole and you hope he dies a long, painful death in prison.'

Bronte laughed. 'That's the thing though, I don't know if I could say any of those things to him. I would probably burst into tears and look like an idiot.'

'Crying is good, it wouldn't matter. At least you would have had the chance to see him in the flesh.'

'He probably wouldn't agree to it.'

Sara leaned forward. 'He would and do you know why? He would get off on seeing you in the flesh again; he would relish the thought of seeing if you were the same girl he used to date or whether you had changed because of what he did. He'd never pass that chance up. You should write and ask if you can come, get a visitor's order.'

'How are you so sure? He might be ashamed of what he did and not want to face me.'

Sara bent down and plucked a brown envelope out of her bag on the floor next to the chair. She waved it in the air and then passed it to Bronte.

'What is this?'

'A visiting order for Manchester Prison for Friday; visiting time is from two.'

'How did you?' She realised then that the only way Sara could have got a visiting order was if she'd written to him to ask for one.

Sara's cheeks flushed pink. 'I should have asked, I'm sorry, but I'm also not if you know what I mean. I truly think you need to go see that little punk and give him what for, then you might be able to move on a little.'

Bronte had never felt so betrayed since she'd woken up from the coma he'd put her in, when he'd tried to kill her, and found out what he'd done, but she wouldn't say that out loud. She looked down at the envelope that felt as if it was burning her fingers, it felt so hot in her hand. She wanted to throw it back in Sara's face and tell her to keep out of her business, but she didn't. Instead, she tucked it into her pocket and swallowed the lump along with all her fears, which felt stuck in her throat. She would not cry over this, now was not the time, she would cry about it later, tucked into bed in her aunt's spare bedroom, and think this through then.

The meeting came to a close. After Sara's little bombshell, there wasn't much to say. Bronte stood up and hugged each girl as they left, leaving her on her own, making sure the place was how they'd found it.

As she stacked the chairs, she supposed they were women and not girls at all, but she was only just out of her teenage years and despite feeling old and weary way beyond her age she knew that deep down, inside of her heart she was still a girl. One that had been robbed of the best years of her life. Her parents and sister had been brutally murdered when she needed them the most. At the time she hadn't realised just how much she did need them; it wasn't the same having no one to be truly proud of her when she'd passed her driving test, her A levels, when she'd learned to tie her shoelaces again. All the stuff that her mum would happily stand there clapping and shrieking about. Most of all though she missed her mum's hugs – her dad had never been much of a hugger – but her mum would wrap her arms around her, envelop her inside of that love and warmth so much that she'd lose herself inside of it. Hot tears filled the corners of her eyes. He'd taken all of that away from her and for what reason? She still didn't know to this day. The therapist she'd been seeing had told her that maybe she needed to speak to him. She couldn't say his name, refused to say his name after what he'd done to them all. She didn't think she could be in the same room as him, but thanks to Sara whether she had wanted to or not she did have the opportunity to do this and maybe she should.

ELEVEN

Amy greeted them with a sad smile, and Morgan knew she wasn't envious of the horrific task that lay ahead of her and Ben. A CSI van was parked up the street, and a suited-up tech was busy working the scene.

'Who's that?' Morgan asked.

'Joe, they called him out.'

'Good, because Natalie is going to want to go home as soon as she finds out about Lexie. She won't want to stay in her neighbour's house.' She turned to Ben. 'Can we get a clean-up crew here ASAP to clean the door?'

'Morgan, I doubt they will be able to come straight away; they have to be authorised and travel from Carlisle. I'll speak to Marc and see what he thinks.'

'I'll do it.'

'Do what, speak to Marc?'

'No, I'll clean the bloody door. All I need is some buckets of water, wipes, and rubber gloves. We cannot leave her stranded like that for hours.'

'Don't be ridiculous.'

'I'm not. I'm being practical.'

She walked off leaving him standing next to Amy, to go and speak to Joe. He was collecting samples of blood.

'Hey, Joe.'

'Hi, Morgan.'

She smiled at him. 'How long do you think it will take you? No rush or anything.'

He shrugged. 'Not too long, I've filmed, photographed and taken lots of samples. I'm pretty much done. Why?'

'The woman whose house this belongs to will need to go inside it pretty soon, and I want to get it cleaned up.'

'I don't know if they've called the cleaning service out yet.'

'I'm willing to do it, I just want to know if I can.'

'Oh, well I don't think there is anything else, but you'll have to get the okay from the DI. Can she not go in the back way? It's okay; I had a look and there's nothing untoward.'

She felt stupid, of course the woman could get in the back way. Why had she not thought of that?

'I'll see, but I just don't want her to have to stare at this mess, if you get what I mean.'

Ben took her to one side. 'I know you mean well, but seriously we're going to have to search Lexie's room to see if there is anything of evidential value. It might be better if she could go somewhere else for tonight. Better if it's out of this street too, so she doesn't have to watch us coming and going. We can't go inside because we've been to the scene, so maybe we could take her to her ex-husband's house; he's going to want to know about his daughter.'

'What about his daughter?'

Natalie's voice was strained. She was standing on Billie's front doorstep looking at them. Morgan wondered how much she'd heard of the conversation and felt terrible.

'Can we come inside and talk to you?'

She shook her head. 'I'm going home, I can't stay here any longer. Have you found Lexie? Is she okay?'

Morgan knew the woman was grasping at straws, praying that the blood didn't belong to her only child.

'We need to go inside, Natalie.'

'Why do I need to go to see Jasper? What does he need to know about our daughter?'

Neither Morgan nor Ben answered, and she rushed towards them. Morgan caught her in her arms.

'I want to see her; you know where she is.'

Amy stood at the cordon to the street, and she turned away and began to speak into her radio.

'Control we need backup here, is there an FLO travelling to help the victim's mum? And can someone be tasked to go and pass a death message on to Jasper White of Hellsfield Hall.'

Billie appeared in the doorway, her face much paler than the last time Morgan had spoken to her. She reached out for Natalie. 'Come back inside, pet, you can't do anything out here.'

She hooked an arm through Natalie's and walked her back into the living room, gently directing her down onto a leather sofa and sitting right next to her, holding her hand tight.

Ben stood in the doorway, blocking her exit, unsure of what to do if she tried to make a break for it. Morgan perched on the antique pine chest that served as a coffee table, right in front of Natalie; they were so close their knees were touching. Natalie looked shell-shocked; her eyes were staring into Morgan's, and she could feel the trembling of her knees against hers.

'There is no easy way to say this. A body was discovered in the park by some teenagers. It's a female and she is wearing the identical clothing that you described Lexie was wearing. I'm so sorry but we think it's Lexie. Would you be willing to come to identify her at the mortuary?'

Natalie never broke her gaze and gave a single nod. 'All the kids wear the same clothes nowadays; it might not be her.'

'I hope that it isn't, Natalie, I really do, but there is a lot of blood at the scene and there is a lot of blood on your front door.

We have had no other reports of missing or seriously injured teenagers in the area. I'm so sorry to have to tell you this.'

'You know what she looks like, why can't you say it's her? What are you not telling me?'

'This is hard for me, I'm hoping I'm mistaken, but yes, I think that it's her but because of the amount of blood I need you to confirm it. Nobody knows her better than you, you're her mum.'

'If it's hard for you, then how do you think I feel about it?'

'Devastated.'

Natalie sniffed. 'I'll go take a look, but I don't believe it's her. I think you're mistaken and it's a kid who looks like my daughter. Who would be so cruel as to hurt her this way when she almost died once before?'

And that was exactly the feeling Morgan had. Whoever killed Lexie must have known about the previous incident; otherwise, why had they put a plastic bag on her head? She wondered who knew about that detail and then realised that Lexie had probably told lots of people since it happened, and they would have gossiped about it, because that's what people do: they take some piece of gory information, embellish it and pass it on to anyone who might listen, and before you know it the whole town was talking. It was obscene, it was mocking, and it was so bloody unfair.

TWELVE

The FLO arrived just as they were going out of the door to the mortuary. Caroline had transferred from Barrow to work Rydal Falls, and Morgan wondered if she was going to regret ever admitting she was a trained family liaison officer, when she realised how much in demand her services would be needed in this area. She introduced herself to Natalie and gave the woman a hug, which both surprised and melted Morgan's heart a little.

She turned to Morgan. 'If it's okay with you, I'll drive Natalie and we can have a chat on the way.'

Ben nodded and answered, 'Absolutely, we'll meet you there.'

Caroline turned to Billie, she had no idea who she was but asked her, 'Would you like to come too?'

Billie looked from Natalie to Caroline and shook her head. 'I'd better not, I don't think it's my place. I'm just a neighbour, and my husband will be home from work soon. He won't know where I've gone or why.'

Caroline had hold of Natalie's elbow and was guiding her towards the front passenger seat. She smiled at Billie. 'That's okay, thanks for everything you've done.'

Billie smiled at her then went inside and closed the door. Morgan felt bad for the poor woman who had been dropped into this nightmare from a great height. She was probably going to go inside and pour herself a huge glass of wine, which is what Morgan would do if it were her in that situation. Alcohol didn't solve anything, but it sure helped to numb the pain, at least for a little while.

Caroline had followed behind Ben the entire way, even letting him get the car parked and walk to the mortuary first. Morgan rang the bell and whispered, 'She's like a breath of fresh air, isn't she?'

He nodded. 'Yes, she is. I like her, like her whole attitude to what is a terribly difficult job.'

Susie, Declan's right-hand woman and probably the best mortuary assistant there was, spoke through the intercom. *'Can I help you?'*

'Hi, Susie, it's Ben and Morgan.'

Susie let out a little squeal, which made Ben frown and Morgan smile. 'I think she's happy to see us.'

Ben looked around to make sure Natalie and Caroline weren't in hearing distance. 'Then I think she needs to get out a little more, if we're as exciting as it gets.'

The door opened and Susie stood there in a pair of green scrubs, white rubber boots, with hair that was half black and half bottle green.

'I love your hair, that green is gorgeous.'

Ben smiled awkwardly at the woman staring at them both. It amused Morgan how he really struggled to come to terms with the different hair colours and styles she had every time they saw her.

'This is a terrible one, isn't it? She doesn't look very old. Declan said the mum is on her way. I've done the best that I can, but I can't really touch her until the post-mortem, so her face is still quite bloody.'

Morgan grimaced and thought of Lexie again, feeling a wave a grief and regret wash over her.

Voices behind them made them stop talking, as Caroline and Natalie came into view. Caroline's arm was gently holding Natalie's elbow as she led her towards the door. Susie gave them both a sad smile.

'If you follow me, I'll take you to the viewing room.'

All four of them walked behind her, down the long corridor that led to the small, bland room attached to the mortuary. Before they could even go inside there was hammering on the door, someone pounding on it with their fist.

Susie turned to Ben. 'Are you expecting anyone else?'

'Not that I'm aware of.'

She opened the viewing room door and pointed to the sofas. 'Please, excuse me.'

The hammering continued, and both Ben and Morgan followed her to make sure everything was okay. Susie opened the door and a red-faced man with tearstained cheeks stood there facing her.

'Where is she?'

'Where is who?'

Morgan realised it was Lexie's father, Jasper White. He'd lost weight and looked a little haggard from when she'd last seen him.

'My daughter. Some copper turned up at my house and told me she was dead and had been brought here, which is bloody preposterous. Lexie isn't dead, so you better show me the poor girl that is, so I can go tell Natalie it's all some huge mistake.'

There was no officer in sight. 'Where is the officer that came to your house?' asked Ben.

'How the hell should I know? I told them to bugger off.'

Morgan stepped forward. 'Jasper, I don't know if you—'

'Yes, I do. You saved them both from that crazy bitch.'

She nodded. 'Natalie is here, do you want to come and see her?'

'She is? I told that copper not to mention any of this to her until I've sorted this mess out. Jesus why did they do that?'

'They didn't, I did. Please come inside and we can talk.'

He stepped in and must have realised where he was because he went a deathly shade of white and stopped speaking.

'If you come with us we'll take you to the viewing room. Natalie is already there.'

He nodded at Morgan but didn't speak, following her down the long corridor.

Susie caught Ben's eye, and he smiled. For once she wasn't chattering and asking him what books he read. Morgan knew he'd find some relief in this.

Before she opened the door Morgan pulled Jasper aside. 'Are you and Natalie cool with each other?' she asked him. 'I don't want to make this harder than it already is for her.'

His voice was barely audible. 'Yes, we are. She hates me and I don't blame her for what I did to her, seeing that girl behind her back, but we still speak for Lexie's sake.'

'Good, that's good because I want you to be kind to each other.'

She opened the door, and Natalie looked vacantly at Jasper. He walked towards her.

'They're wrong, aren't they? This is all a big mistake.'

She didn't answer him and lowered her eyes, so she didn't have to look at him.

Susie excused herself and whispered to Morgan, 'Knock on the glass when you're ready.' Then she was gone, leaving the five of them crowded into the stuffy room and Morgan wishing she was anywhere but here.

Caroline introduced herself to Jasper, who nodded. He was

busy staring at the window in the wall with curtains drawn across it. Natalie was staring at the vase of dried flowers in the middle of the table, next to a box of hospital issue tissues. Caroline took hold of Natalie's hand.

'I need you both to know that there may be some injuries that will shock you. I believe there is some blood on the face that can't be cleaned off until after the post-mortem, and I'm sorry that you're going to have to see this. Take your time, there's no rush. When you're ready we'll get the curtains opened for you both to take a look.'

Natalie stood up, wiping her hands along the top of her leggings. She walked to the window, standing so close to it that her nose was touching the glass. Jasper took his place next to her, not quite so close.

'Let's get this over with,' he said.

Morgan gently knocked once on the glass. Her stomach was churning, and her legs felt like jelly. She couldn't imagine how the couple next to her were feeling. The curtains opened and Natalie let out a high-pitched scream and slammed her palms against the glass. Jasper was shaking his head, and tears were falling down his cheeks as he stared at the corpse on the viewing table, covered with a grey sheet up to the neck.

'Is that your daughter?' Ben asked.

Jasper turned to him. 'Yes.'

Natalie began to slap her palms against the glass window, over and over. Caroline took hold of her and gently pulled her away.

'Natalie, is that Lexie?' she asked her.

'No, that's not my daughter.'

Ben's eyes opened wide as he stared at the woman. Jasper took hold of her hand, which she shrugged away out of his grasp.

'Don't touch me, you took everything from us when you

found out who I was after everything you did. This is your fault; if we didn't live in that crappy little house this wouldn't have happened.'

The hate and venom in her speech was so intense that he flinched as if she'd slapped him.

Morgan stood in between them and asked, 'Natalie, why don't you think that it's Lexie?'

She let out a huge sob. 'Because I don't want it to be, is that all right with you? I want my daughter to be alive, out with her friends having fun not lying on a slab covered in blood.'

Jasper nodded his head. 'It's Lexie, it is.'

Natalie stared at him. 'I fucking hate you, get out. You want her to be dead. I bet you want me dead too.'

Ben guided Jasper to the door and out into the corridor. When the door closed he said, 'I'm so sorry for your loss. Would you like me to get someone to drive you home? Is there anyone we can contact for you to be with?'

'No, I had a family, and I blew it. She's right, I thought I wanted a different life to the one I had and now that I've got it, I hate it. I'm okay, I'll drive myself home and then I'm going to get blind drunk, so if you need me before the morning, you better hammer hard on my front door because I might not hear you.'

Morgan stepped outside as he finished speaking. She knew exactly how Ben was feeling. He'd had to do the same after his wife's death and occasionally still did on the anniversary of her passing.

Jasper walked away, leaving the pair of them staring after him. He walked out of the door and let it slam shut behind him.

'I feel awful for them both.'

Ben put an arm around her shoulders. 'I know, we think living is hard but it's nothing compared to dealing with the dying.'

Susie appeared; her face sombre. 'Guys, this is just awful.'

They both nodded. Morgan didn't speak. She couldn't find the words because it was well and truly awful. She may not have been able to speak but she felt that tiny spark inside of her ignite. She was going to hunt down whoever had done this, working day and night to make sure they caught them before it happened again.

THIRTEEN

The station was empty by the time Morgan and Ben arrived back. It felt totally different to earlier. Gone was the jovial party atmosphere, along with most of the food. Empty trays were scattered everywhere, and the only thing left were curling pieces of lettuce and dried-up tomatoes along with crumbs and lots of bread crusts. Ben was looking at them in wonder. 'Did I miss something?'

'Only some poor sod's wedding buffet. They were jilted at the altar and The Coffee Pot had already made the food, so they dropped it off here.'

'That's harsh, but I can't believe we missed out.'

She smiled. 'We didn't, Cain and Amy took trays of the stuff up to the office.'

Amy appeared behind them and said, 'I wouldn't get your hopes up that there's any left up there either; we left Cain alone with it.'

Ben grinned. 'He's a growing lad.'

'He's a greedy lad,' replied Amy.

All three of them trudged up the stairs to the office, expecting to find it empty. Cain was only in for a couple of hours a day, to build him back up to full shifts. As they opened the door he looked up from the computer on his desk. There were still trays of sandwiches and vol-au-vents on the desks.

'You thought I'd eat it all, didn't you, Amy?'

She laughed. 'Yeah, I did to be honest.'

Ben, who had spent ten minutes in the toilet at the hospital washing his hands and face, peeled back the cling film and took a sandwich, eating it in two bites. Then he picked up a couple more and polished those off. After three vol-au-vents he turned to Cain. 'Why are you still here?'

'You need a hand. I started checking out Lexie's parents and gathering the intel for the file.'

Amy shook her head. 'Are you trying to steal my job?'

'No, I'm trying to be useful.'

'Let you off then, especially seeing as you left some food for us.'

Morgan still felt sick. She had no appetite and couldn't get the image of Lexie's bloody body tied on the roof of the shelter out of her mind.

'I'll brew up.'

She needed to get out of here, tears were threatening to fall, and she didn't want anyone to see her crying. She left them to it, wiping her eyes with her sleeve once she was out in the corridor.

'Everything okay, Morgan?'

Marc's deep voice made her jump, of all the people to see her when she was at her most vulnerable. She should have just cried in front of the others – at least they'd have ignored her – he was always too busy trying to act like a caring boss and sticking his nose in.

'Fine, well as fine as it can be. That was really difficult at the mortuary.'

He nodded. 'I imagine so, do you need a break, a bit of a breather? It's been intense for you. No one would blame you if you took some time off, had a rest from all of this.'

She laughed. 'Sir, thank you that's very kind, but I wouldn't know what to do with myself if I wasn't here. And I need to be here. I want to help catch whoever did this to Lexie. I have to.'

She purposely didn't say she wanted to be the one to catch the bastard who had done it, because he would read all sorts into it, thinking she was about to go off on a one-woman investigation. Which she probably totally was, but you didn't admit that kind of stuff to bosses like Marc. He'd moved her to Barrow once in the middle of an investigation, and she didn't trust that he wouldn't do it again.

He reached out a hand and patted her shoulder. 'Well, you know my door is always open if you need to talk, Morgan.'

She nodded. 'Thanks, do you want a coffee?'

'Yes, please.'

Then he walked into the office, leaving her breathing out a sigh of relief as she filled the kettle up and turned it on. After over twelve months of him being in charge, she still couldn't figure him out and she was a good judge of character. She found a tray tucked down the side of the fridge and gave it a quick wipe before putting the five mugs of steaming coffee on it.

Taking the tray into the office, she saw Marc sitting at her desk with his feet up as he munched on a plate of food. He didn't remove them when she walked in, and she felt a deep-seated burning begin to rise up her chest. He could be nice one moment and then so irritating it made her want to drop his mug of hot coffee into his lap. She purposely placed his mug on Des's empty desk and cupped her own in her hands as she took a sandwich to nibble on, hoping it might stop the churning inside of her stomach if she ate something. It was like some weird, grown-up afternoon tea, only it was almost ten p.m., and everyone was in an awful mood because there was nothing to celebrate.

Finally, Ben stopped eating and took a sip of his coffee.

'Right, folks, tonight has been hard and we have a long

way to go before we can even think about clocking off. Cain, you're an exception, if you need to go that's fine, I don't expect you to work long hours so soon after returning to work.'

Cain shook his head. 'I'm okay, boss, I'll go if I have to.'

Morgan knew that he wouldn't; he was a team player – unlike the DI – and he would stay as long as the rest of them did.

'Well don't do too much; I appreciate it.'

Cain shrugged. 'Least I can do.'

'Are we having a full briefing, boss?' Ben asked Marc, who was staring into the vol-au-vent he'd been about to put into his mouth.

'Bit hard.' He shoved it in anyway.

'What? the food or the briefing?' asked Morgan.

'Both, the briefing. CSI are working both scenes, although Joe messaged to say he'd finished at the house. Before you ask, Morgan, there is a clean-up crew on the way to sort it out. For now, Natalie will have to use the back door.'

There was a knock on the office door, and they all turned towards it.

Ben shouted, 'Come in.'

They all watched expectantly, wondering who was about to come in, and the door opened, and Caroline smiled at them. 'Sorry to interrupt, is it okay to have a word?'

'Of course. You haven't got Natalie with you, have you?' Ben's voice sounded a little nervous at the thought of having to deal with her all over again.

'No, she went back to Jasper's house. He phoned her in the car and told her to go home, that she shouldn't be alone if the house was a crime scene, and she agreed. I delivered her to his door, and he led her inside and passed her a glass of whisky on the rocks.'

Morgan felt relieved that the pair of them were together,

even if they despised each other. Natalie was somewhere far from that blood-covered front door.

'I asked if they wanted me to stay with them and they said not tonight, they want some privacy to come to terms with what's happened. I'll go back first thing and sort their breakfast out, answer any questions. Well, you know the score.'

'Thank you, Caroline.' Ben smiled at her.

'No problem, can I help you guys with anything?'

'I don't think so. Are you hungry?'

She smiled. 'Not really, but thanks. I'll speak to you tomorrow; if you need me before then let me know.' She waved and left, and when the door shut Morgan said, 'I really like her, she's lovely.'

Amy laughed. 'She must be nice if she gets your seal of approval, you dislike most people.'

Morgan rolled her eyes and looked in Marc's direction; he wasn't paying the slightest bit of attention to any of them. He was staring down at his phone.

Ben stood up, took a sip of his coffee and stretched. 'Right, where were we? Oh right, we're a bit thin on the ground but let's look at what we've got. It's clear that Lexie was attacked outside of her home address; we know by the amount of blood that she was mortally wounded. It stops at the kerbside so whoever did this must have bundled her into a car or van then driven her to the park, where they then drove inside and managed to get her onto the roof of that shelter and leave her posed there for as much shock value as possible.'

Morgan nodded. 'There was the plastic bag around her head, too, which suggests to me this was someone who knew about the previous attempt on her life, when she was almost suffocated.'

Ben continued. 'Dear God, this is going to be impossible. I want the entire street spoken to, checked for CCTV, dashcams, video doorbells, then the surrounding streets. We need to figure out the route he drove; both streets at each end of Fenton Street are going to be canvassed as well, to check for CCTV so we can see if anything is picked up en route to the park. Someone is going to have to work out how many ways there are to drive to the park from Fenton Street. I want to know what vehicle they were in; it must have had ladders because how else did they get her onto the roof? So, any cars or vans with a set of ladders on the roof rack should help to narrow it down, and also the streets aren't that busy. We need to narrow down a time that she was attacked too, see if we can retrace her route from wherever she'd been.'

Morgan reminded Ben that they'd logged a suspicious light-coloured car on the street. 'The neighbour's teenage son, a couple of doors down, said he saw a guy parked up outside the house for the last couple of nights, in what he thinks was a Picasso. His parents weren't home when I spoke to him. Would you like me to go back now and get a statement, see if he can give us anything more?'

'Yes, that's brilliant. Obviously, it would be great if he had a number plate.'

'It would, but he didn't know the VRM.'

Marc was finally paying attention. 'What about hypnosis? We could see if he remembers anything under that.'

Ben turned to him. 'Do you know anyone who could do that for us?'

'Well, no, but it's an idea, something to bear in mind.'

Morgan rolled her eyes out of view.

'It is, but let's go with old-fashioned police work and see if we can find this car on CCTV. There has to be somewhere in the area we can pick it up. Morgan, if you're happy to go speak to him do you want to go now before it gets too late? He might be our only witness; we don't want to waste a minute. Amy, do you want to go with her?'

Morgan stood up. 'I'm okay, I can do this on my own. He

was a little nervy, so if two of us turn up he might not want to talk. I'll arrange for him to come here tomorrow, to see if he can do a photofit.'

'Okay, be careful.'

She nodded, pulled her coat on and left before he could order her to go with Amy. It wasn't that she didn't like her, because she did, but she wanted a little time to think about who could have killed Lexie. She wanted to check if Lexie had a boyfriend or ex who she would have shared the intimate details of her attack with, someone she might have once felt comfortable with. Usually in a case like this, she knew the closest people to the victim were taken into consideration, but she also knew that Natalie could not have done this, though she couldn't rule Jasper out. Then again, his reaction to seeing his daughter's body had been too visceral and raw; it wasn't put on – it was genuine distress. Her mind was spinning. Plus, she had already spoken to Jordan, and she didn't want to freak him out too much by turning up with someone else. She knew how difficult it was to get teenage boys to talk at the best of times, and she was relying on him being able to give her something to work with.

FOURTEEN

Milly could not shake the feeling of being watched as she drove home. Though there were no other cars behind her, she still felt weird. She had learned to drive after being attacked walking home. Her dad had insisted that she pass her test and had even bought her the little blue Fiat 500 to practice in. She tried her best not to act like she was scared of her own shadow, but the truth of the matter, plain and simple, was she was scared. Scared of being on her own, scared of walking anywhere, scared if someone looked at her for more than a few seconds, scared of going out with her friends and getting drunk in case she acted reckless. She had taken up self-defence classes since the attack. Too scared to join a class with other people, her dad paid for her to have private lessons, which were great and helped her feel a little better.

As she stared in the rear-view mirror a car shot across the road in front of her, blaring the horn at her, and she slammed on the brakes, screaming at the top of her voice. The car continued but she was stranded in the middle of the junction, her car had stalled, and she had narrowly missed crashing straight into it, because with a sense of horror and shame she realised that she'd driven straight through a red light. Her hands were shaking so much, and she thought she was going to throw up all over herself. She started the engine and drove across the junction, stopping on the other side once it was safe. What was wrong with her?

She always felt this way after meeting with the others; listening to their terrifying ordeals was supposed to make her feel better, but it didn't: it made her feel even more anxious. It proved to her that her ordeal hadn't been a one-off incident that would never happen again to anyone she knew. In fact, it was the opposite: it proved to her that the world was full of sick people, and they were everywhere. Nowhere was safe.

Why had Lexie not turned up tonight? She always messaged Ava if she wasn't coming. Milly had slept at Lexie's house the night before, and they'd talked about the group, but she hadn't intimated that she wasn't coming. Milly's mum and dad weren't due back off holiday for another five nights, and she wondered if she should go and check on Lexie, maybe see if she could stay there another night. Her mum Natalie was cool; she didn't mind her turning up late. She headed in the direction of Fenton Street, and as she drove past the park, she saw it was blocked by police vans with flashing lights and she wondered what had gone on now. All the local teenagers hung around in there and always had since it had been opened.

As she carried on to Lexie's street, the unsettled feeling in her stomach got worse. As she approached she saw that the entrance to the street was sealed off with a line of blue and white police tape. There was a copper standing behind it. She slowed down and looked past Lexie's house, which was in darkness, and saw another police officer at that end of the street. She decided to park up on Rawlinson Street and walk to Lexie's. As she got out of her car and crossed the road, she glanced at Lexie's house and then she saw the blood on her front door. She noticed the policewoman standing near to the front door with a clipboard in her hand and felt the world begin to swim as her legs gave way and she lurched forwards. She heard a voice call out, 'Hey, are you okay?' And she felt someone take hold of her arms to try and keep her upright.

Milly had never felt so weird in her life, she had tunnel vision and was going to pass out. The voice was soft, and she thought she recognised it.

'Come on, let's get you sat down while you take some deep breaths.' She felt herself being lowered onto someone's front doorstep, but she couldn't do anything about it. 'Put your head between your knees; it helps a lot, it helps me when I get like this.'

She did as she was told, bending forwards and putting her head as far between her knees as possible.

'Should I call an ambulance?' This was a different voice; it wasn't as kind as the other one.

'Would you like us to call an ambulance?'

Milly shook her head. 'No, I'll be okay. I just need a minute.'

'Take your time, deep breaths.'

She did that, breathing deeply and slowly until she finally felt as if she could raise her head.

'I'm so sorry, Morgan, I thought I knew that voice.'

Morgan smiled at her. 'Milly, what are you doing here?'

'I came to see Lexie; I stayed here last night and was supposed to meet her earlier, but she didn't turn up.'

Milly knew by the expression on Morgan's face that something terrible had happened to her friend.

'Oh.'

'Where is she? I saw the blood and that's why I felt a bit woozy. Whose blood is that?'

'I'll tell you everything very soon. Are you okay to sit in the van for a little bit while I go and talk to someone a couple of doors up?'

Milly looked around, she had nothing better to do, and she was scared for Lexie, and she was also scared to go home alone. 'Yes, that's fine. Thank you.'

Morgan helped her up and took her to the van, and sliding the door open she helped her inside.

'I won't be too long; please wait here for me, Milly, I need to talk to you.'

She nodded. She had nowhere else to go, and she had to know what had happened, and as stupid as she felt sitting in the back of a police van, she did feel safe.

FIFTEEN

Morgan lowered her voice. 'I need that girl to stay there in the back of the van. Please don't let her leave; if she tries to, come get me okay. It's very important that I speak to her.'

The officer nodded. It was an officer Morgan didn't know. 'Sure, no problem.'

'Thanks, I'm going to speak to a potential witness but shouldn't be too long.'

She signed herself into the cordon and ducked under the tape, walking to Jordan Archer's house. There were a couple of women further up the street standing on the doorstep talking to each other, but she needed to speak to Jordan first. She knocked on the door and a man opened it. Holding up her warrant card she smiled at him.

'Detective Morgan Brookes, are you Jordan's dad? Is it okay to come in and speak to you and Jordan?'

He nodded and waved her in. Jordan was sitting on the sofa.

'I told Dad you'd be coming back.' He smiled at her, and she couldn't help but smile back.

'Thank you, Jordan, did you tell your dad why?'

'Yes, it's because of that weirdo who was watching Lexie's house.'

'It is. Mr Archer, I'm sure you're aware there has been a serious incident.'

He nodded. 'How serious? I saw the blood on the door and the police blocking the street.'

She swallowed, not wanting to lie to the man but also not wanting to upset Jordan too much.

'Very.'

'It's okay, you can talk about it; Jordan isn't as soft as he looks. He spends all day on his Xbox blowing people to smithereens.'

'Lexie was attacked outside her home, and we need to find the person who did it.'

'Is she okay? Because that amount of blood tells me she might not be.'

Morgan frowned at him. 'Like I said it's very serious. Jordan, can you tell me when you first noticed the car outside Lexie's house?'

'Two nights ago.'

'What made you think the person inside was watching Lexie?'

He shrugged. 'I don't know, just a feeling really. It was only there when she was in the house.'

'How do you know she was in the house and not her mum?'

He pointed to the games console controller on the coffee table. 'Well, I don't know for certain, but she sometimes plays games, and I can see when she's online. Every time I've noticed her gaming, he was out there.'

Morgan wondered if he could be involved and if this was some kind of cover up.

'Oh, okay. That's good, thanks. Do you ever play with Lexie?'

He shook his head. 'Nah, she's not very good and I have my own friends.'

'So, the guy in the car, was he on his own?'

'Yeah.'

'Did you get a look at his face? Would you recognise him if we showed you some pictures, or maybe describe him so we can get the officer who does facial recognition to come up with an image of him?'

'I only really saw the back of his head; it was shaved.'

'Did you see the colour of the Picasso? You told me earlier it was light. Any of the number plate at all?'

'I think it was white, and it had like a sixty-eight or maybe sixty-nine number in it.'

'That's good, thank you, Jordan. Did he do anything?'

'Like what?'

'Get out of the car, go take a closer look at Lexie's house, take pictures, write anything down?'

'I didn't look at him for very long. I just noticed it was there two nights on the row last night and the night before. When I came home, I've seen it before I think further up the street or one similar. I can't be sure.'

'What time was that?'

'About eight.'

She turned to his dad. 'Did you see the car at all?'

He shook his head. 'I work until nine, so don't get home until around nine fifteen. I can't say I noticed a white Picasso, but then again, I wasn't looking.'

'Can I ask where you work, and do you drive, Mr Archer?'

He let out a loud laugh. 'I do drive, but I can't afford to run a car at the moment. Things are a bit tight since his mum left. I work at the printers in Ambleside.'

She nodded. She needed to check if anyone on the road owned a car matching Jordan's description. She gave him her most sympathetic smile. 'The cost of living is a nightmare at the moment, isn't it?'

'Certainly is, why are you quizzing me? I had nothing to do with this, and you can speak to my colleagues. They will confirm I was at work.'

'It's procedure, we have to rule everyone out. Jordan, is there anything you can think of that I should know about this guy? Did you only see the car twice? You didn't notice it last week or has it been there through the day?'

He shook his head.

'What about tonight, did you see it tonight?'

'No, but I did hear a scream.' He lowered his eyes to the floor.

'What time was that?'

'I'd just got home; it was about quarter to seven.'

'Was the car there when you got home?'

'No.'

'What about Lexie, did you see her at all?'

He let out a loud sniff. 'I passed her at the top of the street. I was on my bike. I came in through the back gate, then went into the house and heard a scream outside. I should have opened the front door, but I ignored it and went to get changed. I'm sorry. Is this my fault?'

Morgan shook her head. 'Absolutely not, Jordan, this isn't anyone's fault except for the person who attacked her.'

He lifted his head to look at her. His eyes shone with tears. 'I feel so bad, that blood.'

'I know, it's awful but you weren't to know.'

She didn't tell him that he should have called 999. She also didn't tell him he was probably the last person to see Lexie alive. There was no point in making him feel worse than he did. He was too young to shoulder guilt that would stick with him for the rest of his life, when none of it was his fault.

'Jordan, which direction was she walking home? Did she pass the newsagents on the corner?'

He nodded, and she felt a sigh of relief. Although it wasn't open now, she knew that they had CCTV cameras, good cameras, from the times she'd been there when she was in training on response. They had a lot of bother with teenagers hanging around. She would go and speak to the owner in the morning. At least they had a direction of travel for Lexie, because that meant she had walked along Buccleuch Street where there were a couple of premises also with cameras. If she'd been followed by the guy in the white car, hopefully he would be picked up too. She closed her notebook and stood up.

'Thank you, Jordan, you've been very helpful.'

He looked miserable; his dad stood up with her. 'Will he have to go to court? To give evidence about this?'

'He might do. When he comes to the station tomorrow, we'll get a full statement from him. Is that okay, what time do you start work?'

'One; I'd need to be out of there by twelve thirty at the latest.'

'I'll be in touch in the morning to let you know when to come down. What's your phone number?'

She wrote down the number he recited. 'Thank you both.'

He walked her to the front door, closing the living room door behind him. This time he lowered his voice and asked, 'How badly injured is Lexie?' He looked at Morgan, imploring her. 'Tell me the truth.'

'Unfortunately, she died, Mr Archer.'

His eyes widened in horror. 'Oh my God.'

'I didn't want to say that in front of Jordan, but you'll have to tell him because it will be all over social media and the press soon. Better to hear it from you than read about it online.'

'I will, would it have made a difference if he'd rung 999?'

Morgan shook her head. 'Probably not, she had already been badly injured.'

She thanked him and left him to break the horrible news to Jordan. His face was significantly paler than when she'd arrived. That poor lad was probably going to blame himself for the rest of his life, for not phoning the police, but how many teenagers would think to call the cops out for a single scream? Not many, they'd rather poke their own eyes out with a sharp stick than have to phone the plod; she knew that herself from her teenage years.

Morgan left the house and walked towards the van. She needed to get Milly home and talk to her. Then an awful thought filled her head. If Lexie's killer had been watching the house for the last two nights, had he seen Milly there too? Was she in danger?

SIXTEEN

Morgan phoned Ben, and as she waited for him to answer she walked away from the van towards the top end of the street, where the newsagents was. She didn't want Milly to hear her conversation. When he answered, she relayed everything word for word that Jordan had told her.

'That's helpful, not as brilliant as it could be but it's a bloody good start. Well done, Morgan.'

'I have a bit of a plot twist.'

'A what, what's that mean?'

'As I arrived here, I met Milly Blake who had also turned up to check on Lexie.'

'Milly Blake.' He paused for a few seconds. *'Milly who got abducted? That Milly Blake?'*

'The very same.'

'What's she doing at Lexie White's house?'

'They're friends, such good friends that she slept there last night. Ben, I'm concerned about her. This guy was clearly stalking Lexie, but what if he saw Milly and she's next on his list?'

'*Oh God, you didn't just dump that on me.*'

'We have to take it into account. I'm being serious, he might be watching her too.'

'*Where is she now?*'

'In the back of the van. She almost passed out, and I made her sit in there until I could speak to her properly and drive her home.'

'*Should she even go home, Morgan? I don't want you going anywhere near her house on your own. Wait for me, actually let me send a patrol there first, to check it out and see if there's a car matching the description in the area before the pair of you go there. I don't think she should be at home. Let's sort her out a safe place to stay for the next couple of nights. I'll ask the boss to get that organised. I'd rather make sure she's safe, even if this has nothing to do with her. Bring her back to the station and we'll take it from there.*'

Morgan had this feeling of overwhelming dread that was sitting in the pit of her stomach. A chill ran down the back of her neck, making her shudder as she looked around the deserted street. She turned back to go and speak to Milly; she had to find out if she'd seen the same guy.

Morgan opened the sliding door of the van, and Milly turned to her.

'How are you feeling now?'

'Crap, can I get out of here and go speak to Lexie? Is she at the hospital?'

Morgan wished that she didn't have to be the one to keep on delivering this life-changing, devastating news over and over. She let out a sigh and shook her head. 'Yes, she's at the hospital, but I need to talk to you, Milly, but not here. Would you come back to the station with me while we sort out a few things?'

'Like what? I didn't hurt her, if you think that I did. I was at group; you can ask them.'

'God, no. I don't mean that, I mean about you and Lexie, your safety. There are things we need to talk about, but I'd rather do it somewhere safe.'

'Can you not follow me home and we can talk there? I feel rubbish.'

Morgan tried to push the feelings of guilt to one side. She wasn't completely lying because Lexie *was* at the hospital. 'I can't, look please, for my sake, could you let me take you to the station where we can talk more comfortably.'

Milly sighed. 'Suppose so, it's not as if I have anything else to be doing apart from putting my pyjamas on and reading.'

Morgan smiled at her. 'That sounds like the most perfect evening. What do you read?' She held out her hand for Milly to take as she got out of the van, in case another wave of dizziness overcame her.

'What about my car?'

'We'll get it brought to you after, if that's okay. I'd rather you came in mine to the station until we know you're feeling better.' Morgan grimaced; she knew the girl would not be feeling better once she'd been told about Lexie.

'I love women's fiction. I'm reading *The Cornish Midwives* series by Jo Bartlett; it makes me want to pack my stuff and move to Port Agnes.'

'That sounds amazing. I've never been to Cornwall, I'll have to check them out. I usually read true crime or horror stories.'

Milly looked at her. 'You do this job and read true crime books? Why?'

She laughed. 'It's just my thing, I've always been fascinated by how evil some people can be, and I love scaring myself with a creepy horror story on my days off. It drives Ben, my partner, mad when I have to wake him up when I need the loo in the middle of the night.'

Milly laughed. 'You're too funny and normal for a policewoman.'

She frowned at her. 'I'm not sure if that's a compliment or an insult, but thank you. I try my best.'

Morgan opened the car and guided Milly into the front passenger seat. As she closed the door, she looked around the area, scanning to make sure there was nobody watching them. Not sure if it was the thought of someone stalking Milly so openly or the thought that they might still be out there that had put her on edge, but she felt like a sitting duck and quickly scooted around to the driver's side. Once she was inside, she turned the engine on and locked the doors.

Milly was watching her. 'I'm not psychic or anything, but I get the distinct impression something is freaking you out.'

'You do?'

Milly nodded. 'I know you don't want to tell me about Lexie, but how bad is it? Is her mum okay?'

'Her mum is staying with a friend tonight and, to be honest with you, she's not okay.'

'She's dead, isn't she? It's okay, you don't have to tell me now, but there is no way you lot would be making all this fuss if she wasn't.'

Morgan glanced at her, scared to say yes in case she took it really bad and tried to jump out of the moving car or something. 'It's not good.'

Milly was staring blankly out of the windscreen and nodding. 'Can I tell the others? They need to know something terrible has happened. They have to know to make sure they take extra precautions.'

'What others?'

'The group I was at tonight. It's a support group for the biggest, saddest group of women you ever did see.'

'I doubt that, but who else attends the group?'

'Well, Bronte Potter set it up along with Sara Fletcher.'

Morgan, who already felt chilled to the bone, felt as if her blood had stopped circulating and had frozen inside of her.

Milly continued. 'There's Lexie White and Ava, I can never remember her surname, and we try to check in on Evelyn as much as we can, but it's hard with her being in the nursing home.'

'I know all of those women, they're survivors of killers that I've caught or helped to catch.'

'Yes, we are. Although we jokingly call ourselves The Final Girls, you know after all those horror movies where there's a girl who beats the odds and lives despite being faced with a scary as hell killer.'

It was Morgan's turn to feel a little faint; she had to really concentrate on the road. Her head was swimming and she felt as if her brain had turned to mush. The station came into view, and she tugged the lanyard out from inside of her jacket, unable to speak to Lexie. She put the window down and pressed it against the intercom. The gates slid open, and Milly whispered, 'Open sesame.' Then she looked at Morgan and said, 'Hey, are you okay. We sent you emails to see if you wanted to join, but I guess you never got them; they're probably in your spam folder or junk mail. You should have a look and see if they came through. It would have been nice to have you there. You've been a final girl far more times than the rest of us. It's not too late; you can come to the next meeting. We have them once a month but never on the same day, in case any of those freaks out there are watching us. We like to mix it up to keep us safe.'

She nodded at her and got out of the car, sucking in a mouthful of the chilly evening air to try and shock her system into functioning again. Milly got out of the car and looked around the car park.

'I've always wondered how you guys got into the station, because the front doors lock really early, don't they?'

'Yes, they do.'

Morgan led the way to the side door, which she used the

most. It opened near to the entrance to the custody suite. Neither woman spoke. Milly had suddenly lost her voice, and Morgan felt as if she was living in an alternative universe. They had formed a support group, invited her to be a part of it and she hadn't a clue it existed.

SEVENTEEN

By the time Morgan had led Milly up to the canteen on the first floor, she had recovered from her fainting bout and was non-stop chattering and asking questions about the station. Morgan was regretting bringing her here because she couldn't concentrate. She sat her down.

'Do you want a hot chocolate out of the vending machine? They're about the only drinks that taste okay.'

Milly nodded. 'Yes, please.'

Morgan fed the change into it and got two hot chocolates; she needed something hot and sugary to help thaw herself out. She placed them on the table. The TV on the wall was on a news channel, and she picked up the remote and put UK Gold on, no news, just comedy.

'I need to go find my boss; can you wait there for me?'

'Sure, I'll drink my hot chocolate.' Milly smiled at Morgan, but it was such a sad smile it made her feel bad for the woman. She had to speak to Ben though and not in front of Milly.

She went to the stairs and ran up them, rushing into the office. Amy and Cain were both staring at their computer screens, and Ben was in his office. She opened the door.

'Need you in the canteen, now. Milly is there and she knows something is up. I haven't been able to tell her.'

He stood up, picked up a clipboard and followed her out into the corridor, where she whispered, 'They have a support group; it meets once a month.'

'Who?'

'She calls them the final girls, the survivors of killers we've caught.'

He arched an eyebrow at her. 'Morgan, what's with you tonight? You keep acting all strange. What are you talking about?'

They were almost at the canteen where Milly was sipping her drink.

'Ask her about it.'

Ben smiled at Milly. 'Hi, do you remember me?'

She nodded. 'I do, you're Ben.'

'I am, how are you feeling, Milly? Morgan told me you felt ill earlier?'

'Like crap. I'm scared of what you're about to tell me, but that's nothing new. I've been scared since that afternoon he attacked me when I was almost home.'

'That's perfectly understandable, you went through a terrible ordeal. It's always going to be there at the back of your mind, but you have to be the one to keep it at the back and not let it dominate your every day.'

Milly smiled at him. 'You're good, are you not in the wrong job? You could be a therapist.'

He laughed. 'I'm not that good.' Pulling out a chair he sat down opposite her, placing the clipboard on the table. Morgan sat next to her.

'So, is this the part where you tell me my friend is dead, has been horribly murdered and that I might be next on the killer's list?' Her voice was strained, even though she was trying to make light of what they all knew was a terrible situation.

Morgan choked on the sip of hot chocolate she'd just swallowed, almost spitting it everywhere.

Ben nodded. 'You're very astute, Milly, and yes, we have some tragic news for you about Lexie. She was murdered, attacked outside her own house. Most likely the injuries she received were mortal and she died as a result of them.'

Milly choked back a sob, tears were falling down her cheeks, and she lifted a sleeve to blot them away. Ben went and grabbed a handful of napkins off the counter and passed them to her.

'We're very sorry, Milly. I can't believe it either, it's so cruel.' Morgan was patting her arm, and she gave her a sad smile.

'We knew this or something like this would happen; we talked about it at the group. Do you know who did this? Did you catch him?'

'No, at this point we have a description of a car he may have been using, and a brief description of the guy who we believe may have been watching Lexie's house the last couple of nights, possibly longer.'

Milly gasped. 'You are going to tell me I'm next, aren't you? You don't have to, I had a feeling I was being watched and followed a couple of times the last few days. There was this guy in a silver car outside my house a couple of times when I came home. It really creeped me out, but then I kept telling myself I was being stupid and letting my imagination run wild. I thought I saw it outside of the church where we meet too, but I couldn't be sure; it was lashing down and I was running to get out of the rain.'

Ben nodded. 'It was? You weren't being silly; it's called your gut instinct. You picked up on something that wasn't right, and you knew deep down that this person could be a danger. Did you see the person you thought was following you?'

She shook her head. 'I didn't like staring, but he had a dark coloured coat and a beanie hat. That's about it. I kept my head down trying to make myself look invisible. I do that a lot, make myself a lot smaller, so I think people won't notice me.'

Morgan leaned forward. 'Are you sure it was silver? Another witness thought it was white; and did you get the registration?'

'I'm pretty sure it was silver and no, I'm sorry, I was panicking too much and didn't think to look at it; I was too scared to drive past him last night. I wanted to get away before he noticed me. I thought I was being an idiot because he probably wasn't even interested in me, but I turned around anyway and drove straight to Lexie's house, because I knew she'd let me in and probably stay there. My parents are on holiday, and I didn't want to be on my own.'

She cupped a hand to her mouth. 'Oh God, I led him to Lexie, didn't I? This is all my fault; he probably spotted my car turning around, and he followed me there and instead of me being killed he went for her.' Milly's voice cracked and she sobbed loudly.

Morgan was about to give her a hug when Ben beat her to it, he wrapped his arms around her and held her while she sobbed into his shoulder. After a few minutes he let go and Morgan passed her some of the serviettes. Ben sat back down.

'Could you tell me about the group, Milly?'

She nodded. 'What do you want to know?'

He looked to Morgan and shrugged; she took over.

'Everything, how it started, where you meet? I know you told me who goes, but I was driving and if it's okay with you I'd like to write it all down. We're going to have to speak with everyone.'

Milly was still crying, but they were silent tears that pooled in the corners of her eyes and were gently rolling down her cheeks, and she kept swiping them away with her hand.

'I got a letter through my door off Bronte; she invited me to come to a meeting at the church hall, and at the time I was doing nothing except go to work, come home, and hibernate in my bedroom. I told my mum, who thought it was a great idea, that it would help to have other women to talk to who had been in a similar situation, so I went along.'

'Did it help, does it help?'

She nodded. 'It did until I saw that car a couple of days ago.'

'Which church hall?'

'St Martha's, well it's not in the actual church hall. There's like a tiny storeroom attached to it with its own entrance that we slip in and out of. The vicar is so lovely, he's really friendly and gave Bronte her own key so we could use it whenever. We don't even have to tell him. He said it's ours.'

Morgan glanced at Ben. 'Theo?' Her stomach was churning; Theo had gone from being her number one suspect in a previous case – by managing to somehow be in the wrong place at the wrong time, and in close proximity to the victims in a couple of other cases – to being their friend. The thought that he may be involved made her want to throw up. Not that he was. It was just the association of him and St Martha's that made her uncomfortable. For a house of worship so many bad things had happened at the church, it was hard to describe how it made her feel.

Milly shrugged. 'Yeah, he's nice.'

'Does he ever attend the meetings?'

'God, no. He's never been anywhere near.'

Morgan felt slightly better at hearing this. 'Why did Bronte pick St Martha's, especially after a girl's body was found in the grounds last year? I would have thought it would have been too stressful?' She didn't mention that Des's body had been found inside either.

'You'd have to ask her; I think it's where her family are buried. Maybe she liked the thought of having them close by.'

Ben interrupted. 'I think we should speak to Bronte, don't you, Morgan?'

She nodded. 'Milly, we don't want you to go home. One of my colleagues is currently sorting you out some emergency accommodation for a few days. Is that okay?'

Milly held Morgan's gaze. 'I guess so, I haven't got anything to change into though.'

'You write me a list and, if it's okay with you, I'm happy to go and grab the things you need, that's if you don't mind me going through your stuff to get it.'

'There's nothing exciting in my drawers, knock yourself out.'

Morgan smiled at her. 'Thanks, I'm so sorry about Lexie. It's so sad.'

Milly looked away. 'I know. How's Natalie? I feel so bad for her.'

'Terrible. Why didn't Natalie go to the support group? She was attacked at the same time Lexie was.'

'Lexie said her mum thought it would do her good to go, and she didn't want her to feel as if she couldn't talk freely about her feelings if she was sitting there. Natalie said she had all the comfort she needed in a bottle of wine.'

'She drinks? I thought she was teetotal?'

'I don't know about that; I've never actually seen her with a drink, but I kind of think she said it to make Lexie not worry about her so she'd come to group without her mum.'

Morgan couldn't blame her if she did drink. She'd been through a terrible time, and if it had been her, she probably would drink too. 'What should I get from your house, Milly? Do you want to write me a list?' She passed her notepad to her and the pen, watching as she scribbled down the things she needed. 'My colleague, Amy, will drive you to the safe house and take you in. We'll have a plain-clothes officer parked outside at all times. I'll go get your stuff and then I'll give it to another officer to drop off for you.'

'Can't you drop it off?'

She shook her head. 'I better not, it will be better if it's someone else.'

Milly sighed. 'Are you worried he might be following you too? You're the final girl of all final girls, you're like the Laurie Strode of Cumbria. You better be careful, Morgan, because he could be watching you too.'

'Not at this moment, Milly. I didn't even know about the support group, and I don't think I should be worried at this point. I'm more concerned about everyone who attends the meetings.'

Ben's eyes looked as if they were about to explode from their sockets, they had widened so much. She wished Milly would stop talking about final girls, because she was creeping her out and had just caused her a whole world of grief; she knew that Ben wouldn't let her out of his sight until the killer had been arrested and put in the cells.

EIGHTEEN

Amy had come down to take over with Milly, and show her pictures of silver and white cars to see if she could identify the one that had been parked outside Lexie's house. Morgan had the key for Milly's house, and she and Ben left them to it as they went into the office.

Ben said, 'I don't know what's going on yet, but I do know that you are not, *I repeat not*, to go anywhere unaccompanied. I'm being serious, Morgan, please don't, I'm beyond worried.'

Cain was watching them, but he never said a word.

'Ben, I haven't been followed by anyone in a Picasso, and this has nothing to do with me. I think you're worrying unnecessarily, but I will take extra precautions, okay?'

'Good, that's good. We need to speak to Bronte and find out more about the group. Has anyone taken statements from those teenagers who found the body? I also want the owners of every single silver and white Picasso spoken to and checked out, to see if they have any intel or criminal records.'

Cain shook his head. 'The teenagers haven't been spoken to that I'm aware of. I'm reading the log: there is a list of names and addresses for them though. Do you want me to go make a start? I've asked the PNC Bureau to get a list of car owners to go and speak to. He already told me none of them live close to the scene.'

'Thanks, Cain, that's great. Did you tell PNC it's urgent? And no, you should be going home now, you've done more than enough.'

'Boss, I'm not going yet, not when there's too much to do and yes, they know it's urgent. I spoke to them on the phone and Brendan is on it as we speak. He's going to email it to you and the boss, boss, as soon as he's done it. I can go speak to some teenagers too. Apart from their attitude I don't think it will be too taxing.'

Morgan smiled at him. 'I'll go with you, then we could go to Milly's house and grab her stuff. Come on, Ben, what else am I supposed to do, sit in the office and do nothing?'

'I suppose not, any hint of something not right and you get the hell out of there, okay? Call for backup if you see anyone acting weird.'

Cain grinned. 'I'm not being funny, boss, but have you seen most of the people who live around here? There are a lot of weirdos.'

'Cain.'

He shrugged. 'True though, it's not a full moon, is it? Because then the weirdos will be out in force.'

Morgan began to laugh and realised she didn't know why because she was probably one of the weirdos. She loved nothing more than to sit outside on a clear night, wrapped in a blanket with a mug of coffee, and stare at the full moon. Placing the crystals her aunt Ettie had given her on the patio table and charging them under the moonlight to renew their energy for the next month. She decided not to give that information to Cain because he'd never let her live it down; as much as she loved him, he loved to make fun of her whenever he could. They left Ben sitting by his computer, refreshing his emails waiting for the list from PNC. As they walked out he called after them.

'I'll let you know when we have a list of Picasso owners, and we can work out how many there are locally to be spoken to.'

Morgan waved at him and pushed Cain out of the door before Ben decided it wasn't a good idea letting the pair of them out of his sight.

Once they were in the car, she felt a little better. It was much easier to be out doing enquiries and keeping busy than sitting around, and she knew by the sigh of relief Cain let out he felt the same.

'Ahh, the taste of freedom. Even if it does smell like stale McDonald's and Chanel.'

She laughed. 'The McDonald's is nothing to do with me, the Chanel I'll admit to.'

'This is bad, though, isn't it, Brookes? Do you think Lexie was targeted because she never died the first time around? I mean it's like some kind of *Final Destination* film, which by the way I hated. I've watched them all because I have this fear of not knowing the weirdest ways in which you can die, and I'm telling you I've never been on a sunbed since. Those girls frying to death gave me nightmares for months.'

She glanced at him to see if he was being sarcastic, but his mouth was set in a straight line, and she realised he was being serious. 'Why watch them if you don't like them?'

He shrugged. 'Because I'm sick in the head that way. If something scares me, I make myself do it even more. Like Black-pool Tower, have you ever been to the top of it?'

'On a school trip a long time ago. Are you scared of heights?'

'Yeah, of course I am. But it's the glass floor that gets me. I took my wife up there for a romantic day, and I ended up almost fainting on the spot, and do you know why?'

'No idea but tell me because the suspense is killing me.'

He nudged her in the side. 'Cheeky. That floor could crack at any moment, and you'd fall to your death, landing on God knows who down below, and then you'd kill them too. Some poor bugger just walking along eating their hot donuts, and it could be their last bite before they're splattered to death along with you.'

'Jesus, Cain, that's what watching those movies does to you, it makes you paranoid and see the bad in every situation. My advice to you is to stop watching those kinds of films and watch romcoms instead.'

'You think so?'

'I know so, the chance of that glass floor cracking is like what, one in a million? It's supposed to be able to hold the weight of two elephants.'

'Have you ever seen my ex-wife?'

Morgan smiled, but shook her head. 'Cain, that's awful.'

'I know, she's not that bad, sorry, that was disrespectful. What I'm saying is maybe Lexie was killed tonight because she didn't die when she was supposed to, like she wasn't supposed to survive the first attempt, so now this sick bastard has killed her to make sure.'

'You think he thinks he's the grim reaper, taking the lives of people who shouldn't have survived against the odds but did?'

He nodded.

'Then where does that leave me? Should I have died the night Harrison Williams hung me from the banister? Or the time Taylor tried to kill me? Should I not be here, alive and have lived to tell the tale?'

'No, of course you should. Don't say that, Morgan, I'm just thinking out loud and saying stupid stuff trying to make sense of it.'

'Because if that's true then maybe you're not supposed to be here either. You survived being stabbed in the kidneys, when by all odds you should be dead. Does that mean you're on his hit list?'

'All right, I didn't think of that.'

'No, you didn't. I get what you're saying, though, Cain, and I think what you mean is that whoever killed Lexie could have a list of victims who by all rights should have died when they were attacked but didn't. He's thinking that he's the one to put things right and finish the job, so maybe he does see himself as some kind of mission killer. Where is the first address?'

'At 81 Harrison Avenue.'

She headed in that direction, neither of them speaking while Morgan contemplated if she was in real danger. Maybe he was focusing on the support group, which she didn't belong to, or maybe he would stop now that he'd killed Lexie; but if that was the case why had he been watching Milly too? She didn't like it, not one little bit. It made her feel as if everything was out of her control, which it was but still she liked to think she could read the killers she was hunting, and she couldn't figure this one out nor his motives. She needed to find him and fast before he could kill again.

NINETEEN

By the time Morgan and Cain had spoken to Gracie Crowe about what she'd seen, they realised that they had nothing of any evidential value. Gracie and her friends had literally arrived at the park oblivious to the fact there was a dead girl on the roof of the shelter above them. The first they knew about it was when the blood began to drip through the wooden shingles of the roof onto their pizza, and they'd all run away screaming. Gracie had been adamant there was nobody around when they first went into the park, or when they left. It was getting too late to keep knocking on thirteen-year-olds' doors. As they got back into the car, she sighed.

'I wish for once someone could say oh, yes. I saw a guy who looked like Vin Diesel, sitting in a silver car the registration is...'

Cain was holding his side where he'd had surgery, and he nodded. Morgan thought his skin looked a little clammy.

'Right, I'll drop you off at home; that's enough for one day.'

'I'm okay, just need a couple of painkillers.'

'No, you don't. You need to go home and rest. If you overdo it, you won't be in a fit state to come back in tomorrow. There is no point calling on the rest of Gracie's friends; it would take a couple of hours. We'll let the PCSOs go speak to them on our behalf tomorrow, and if one of them has anything that is important, we can go back for a full statement.'

'My car is at the station, and I can't let you drive back on your own.'

'I'll pick you up tomorrow, and yes, you can. I'll literally drop you off and drive straight back there. Nothing's going to happen on the way back.'

He let out a short bark of a laugh. 'Famous last words, what about that time you got ran off the road?'

She stared at him. 'Do you keep a log of all the incidents concerning me, Cain?'

'Nope, they're so traumatic I have every single one of them stored in here.' He tapped on the side of his head.

'Oh.'

'Yes, oh. I don't know how Ben sleeps at night, the guy must be a nervous wreck living with you.'

'Cheers, I'm not always in a mess.'

He reached over and rubbed the top of her head affectionately, the same way she imagined he would greet a dog he liked.

'Of course, you're not, you just seem to attract trouble like flies are attracted to horse shit.'

'You are definitely going home; I've had enough of you for one shift.'

He winced, and for once he didn't argue with her. She drove him to his house and parked outside with the engine running. He got out of the car and leaned inside.

'Are you not going to come and tuck me into bed? I won't tell Benno if you don't.'

'Sod off, Cain, you're old enough and ugly enough to tuck yourself in.'

He clutched his heart. 'The pain, I can't take it.'

'Yes, you can. Goodnight, thanks for tonight.'

'Straight to the station, Brookes, I do not want to be knocked up by an angry Benno in thirty minutes because you decided you fancied a double cheeseburger and a chocolate milkshake.'

'I promise, even though I do fancy just that.'

He slammed the door shut, and she locked the doors after him. He gave an appreciative nod of his head then waved in her direction as she drove away. He was sarcastic, but she cared about him and wished that he could find someone to take care of him like he deserved. It made her sad to think about him on his own; he said that he didn't mind it and he probably didn't, but he was such a great guy and had a lot of love to give to the right person.

When she walked into the office on her own, Ben arched an eyebrow at her. She smiled.

'Took Cain home and came straight here; he was in pain, his brow had gone all sweaty and his face a funny colour.'

'Is he okay, do you think? I knew he had done too much.'

She nodded. 'He said he needed painkillers. I'm pretty sure he'll have crashed out straight away.'

'How did you get on with the kids?'

'Not so much kids; more like thirteen going on thirty. We only spoke to Gracie Crowe, who according to patrols was the most vocal and loudest about the incident when they reached the Co-op. They saw nothing, they literally arrived at the park to mess around and eat their pizza; no one was hanging around, no suspicious vehicles. He must have been long gone by the time they arrived. If he'd been hanging around when a group of teenagers turned up it would have looked suspicious. I thought we could get Tina and Sam to go speak to the others tomorrow and report back if there's anything more we need to know.'

Ben let out a yawn. 'Good plan, I don't know that we can do much more. We're waiting on the newsagents opening in the

morning, to retrieve the CCTV. It's been confirmed that Jackie
Thorpe is safely behind bars, where she should be.'

'Oh, crap.'

'What?'

'We never went to collect Milly's stuff for her. Cain really
looked awful, and it slipped my mind.'

'Come on then, let's go find a patrol officer to give her list to.
They can go get it.'

'No, I want to.'

'Why?'

She shrugged. 'I don't know, I feel as if I need to. I want to
take a look around her house and gardens while we're there.'

'Come on then, but we can't take it to the safe house, as it
might compromise it. In case someone is watching us. We'll
have to bring it back here to give to an officer.'

'Fine.'

All the way to Milly's house both of them kept glancing at
passing cars, parked cars, any kind of car, hoping to spot a
Picasso, whether silver or white, or light in colour, but with no
luck. Milly's house was in darkness – there wasn't even a lamp
burning in the hallway as they parked outside. Morgan reached
for the door handle, and Ben put his hand on her arm.

'Just wait a minute, let me have a look around first.'

She didn't argue, there was no point. He got out of the car
and stretched then walked around, looking up and down the
street.

Opposite was the riverbank; with its grassy overgrown paths
there were lots of trees and bushes. If their suspect wanted to
watch Milly, he had plenty of places he could do it and be
discreet. It bothered Morgan that he so openly had watched
both Milly's and Lexie's houses in plain view, sitting in a car
that could easily be identified. What did that say about him that

he would be so brazen? That he was purposefully trying to scare them before he attacked? Her door was opened, and she jumped.

'Right, looks as if we're good to go.'

She smiled at him, glad he hadn't noticed her body leave the car seat and levitate momentarily in fright. She had Milly's key in her pocket, and they walked up the path which was lit by some solar spotlights along the edge of the lawn. When they got nearer to the door a halogen security light flashed on, almost blinding them.

'Christ, that's bright, but thank God they have that. Did you ask her if she had a burglar alarm?' He was pointing to the alarm casing above the door.

'Oh, crap she never mentioned it.'

'Maybe it's not armed.'

'We'll soon find out.' Morgan inserted the key and opened the door, but there was no furious beeps like when they went into their own house and had to reset their alarm. 'Looks like she forgot to turn it on.'

He shook his head. 'I bet her parents would go mad if they knew. She's home alone, thinks someone is watching her or the house and she doesn't bother to turn it on.'

Morgan got that, she hated messing around with Ben's, but unfortunately, he was a stickler for using it, and his only real bug bear was her arming it every single time. She supposed he had an excellent reason for it and didn't blame him. After his heart scare last year, the least she could do was to use it. She lived in his house, that he insisted on paying for, so she supposed it wasn't much to ask and it did make her feel better when she was home alone with her thoughts that sometimes got a little too much for even her to cope with. She liked to pretend that she was fine, that she didn't harbour any anxieties about her near brushes with death at the hands of killers, but it was a front and the biggest lie she ever told him. Partly because she hated to worry him even more than he did about her and partly because she was in denial. When it all got a little too much for her, she would lose herself in a book, and live someone else's misery and pain for a while until her own subsided to a dull ache that she could ignore.

Ben had found several lamps which he'd turned on, giving the dark house a warm glow. 'That's better.' He pointed to the stairs. 'Lead the way, have you been in her bedroom before?'

She nodded. She had been in far too many victims' bedrooms, searching for clues as to their whereabouts. He followed her up the stairs, and she turned on the light in Milly's room, closing the blinds in case anyone was looking in; she didn't want to give them a prime view and give away what was happening. She saw a cabin-sized suitcase on top of the wardrobe and pulled it down. Placing it on the bed and opening it, she began to search through the drawers for everything Milly could need for the next couple of days. When she'd packed sufficient clothes, she grabbed the make-up bag off the dresser, a bottle of perfume, hairbrush and straighteners. There was also an iPad that she shoved in too. Not sure if Milly was going to be in the mood for anything, but it was something to keep her occupied; there was also a book on the bedside table that she picked up. *The Cornish Midwife*, its pages were well thumbed, and the cover was bent on one corner. She tucked it into the case: this must be Milly's go-to comfort book. If she had to choose one hers would most likely be *It*, by Stephen King; how opposite they were in their literary choices, yet connected still the same because they'd survived terrible things most people wouldn't.

'Are you done?'

Ben's voice broke her out of the trance she was in. 'Yes, sorry I was thinking.'

'I wouldn't do that, it's dangerous at this time of night.'

She smiled. 'I was thinking I could eat something really stodgy and covered in cheese.'

'Pizza?'

'Bork, no thanks. Not after seeing those pizza boxes earlier covered in big splats of blood.'

'Oh, yes. Sorry, I wasn't thinking. Come on, let's get this dropped off at the station and go home for a couple of hours to recharge. Kevin will probably think we've deserted him. He'll be starving, and we have so much to do tomorrow, I'm not sure where to even begin.'

She smiled. 'Kevin is always starving. We'll start at the beginning like we always do and take it from there.'

There was a creak on the stairs, so loud that it made them freeze. Ben lifted his finger to his lips. Neither of them had CS with them, nothing to protect themselves. Morgan's heart was racing so hard it began to thud against her ribcage. She looked around, then picked up a tin of hairspray off the dresser. It was better than nothing. Whoever had stepped onto the second stair hadn't moved. There clearly had to be someone there because it had creaked when they had walked up, but who the hell was it? Ben turned and stepped out into the hallway that was cloaked in shadows, and she followed close behind. The stairs were enclosed and not open, and they couldn't see who was down below from here because of the turn at the top.

'Who's there?' Ben shouted, then he waved at Morgan and ran towards the stairs. She followed him. There was the sound of footsteps running down the hallway. Ben was on the radio.

'Control urgent assistance, break-in in progress.'

He gave the address and ran towards the open front door. She was right behind him. The gate was wide open – they had closed it – and they ran into the street. There was no sign of anyone. They couldn't hear footsteps, and they had been so close behind that if a car had driven away, they would have heard the engine start.

She whispered, 'Whoever it is, they're hiding.'

Ben was standing with his hands on his hips, scanning

neighbours' gardens for places to hide. Morgan was staring at the riverbank; it was too easy to get lost over there. She pointed across the road to it, and he nodded.

'Is Cassie still on duty control?' Before they could answer her voice came over the airwaves.

'I am, on my way.'

Morgan felt as if someone had walked across her grave the chill that had settled over her was so cold. 'Should we go and take a look along the riverbank?'

'Absolutely not, they could be waiting to ambush us like what happened to Milly when she was attacked.'

'But they'll get away.'

'Maybe, but your safety is important, and they might have left us some nice prints on the door handle. We closed it behind us on the way in. They had to have touched it to open the door.'

The front door of the house next to them opened, and a guy in a pair of Captain America pyjamas came out.

'What's going on?'

'Police?'

He looked them up and down, neither of them looked like police officers. Morgan pulled out her warrant card. 'CID, did you see anyone running out of this house? Do you have CCTV?'

He pointed to his front door. 'Got one of those doorbells, but it's anybody's guess if it's working or not. My wife is on nights; she has the app on her phone, I'll ask her.'

'Thank you, could you maybe ask her to check it ASAP and let us know?'

He nodded. 'I'll message her. Where's Milly? Is she okay? We're supposed to be keeping an eye on her.'

'She's fine, we just came by to check the house for her.'

He nodded. 'Good, tell her if she needs anything to give me a ring.'

'I will, what's your name?'

'Jack Andrews.'

'Thanks, Jack, have you noticed anyone in a silver or white Picasso hanging around the last few days? Do you know anyone who drives one?'

'Well, I have a Picasso. It's white. I park on the drive and my wife uses it for work. She's been on nights the last three nights. I can't say that I've noticed anyone, but I work days, go to the gym and come home, then my wife goes out to work, so we're kind of like passing ships. I'll ask her about that too.'

'Okay, thanks, that would be great.'

He went back inside, closing the door behind him.

'Think it was him?'

Ben shook his head. 'He didn't look sweaty enough and too calm.'

'Yeah, that's the impression I got.'

'Still, we should take a closer look at Jack Andrews and his white Picasso, to see if he's got anything on his record we need to be aware of.'

Sirens filled the night air, and she felt better. There was a lot to be said for wearing body armour and carrying a taser that was far more effective than a can of extra-strong hold hairspray.

TWENTY

He wouldn't say that he hated his job because it paid okay and that meant that he could pay his bills, but he did dislike the people he worked with. They were as miserable on the outside as he felt on the inside, only he did a better job of hiding his feelings. In fact, he did too good a job of hiding his feelings, which was why Miranda was sipping her coffee from the cheesy mug he'd got her in the Secret Santa, with a quote about being the best work colleague in the world, while she was blowing billowy clouds of peach-flavoured vape in his direction. At the same time boring him to death with her son's karate grading. I mean who gave a shit about her snot-nosed, mamma's boy managing to remember some weird dance that you do with your fists and your feet to get a different coloured belt?

'So, I told him I'd take him to the cinema on Friday, if he passed, and he can even have one of those bloody extortionate slushy drinks they sell and some popcorn, because I'm so proud of him. Do you want to come along with us? Do you good to get out of the house you're always stuck in moping.'

He looked her way as he sipped the coffee she'd made for him, which was revolting because Miranda couldn't make a decent brew to save her life, but the caffeine kept his mind sharp which was the only reason he tolerated it.

'What?'

'Jesus, it's like talking to a brick wall. Do you ever actually listen to anything I tell you?'

He nodded. 'Of course, I do, I was listening. I have a lot on my mind.'

She looked him up and down. 'Of course, you do, but don't we all? If you don't want to talk about it, I can't exactly help you, can I? What colour belt did Dominic get then, if you were listening?'

He felt his hands begin to get clammy and his cheeks flush a little at being put on the spot like this, a trait which betrayed him greatly much to his annoyance.

'Blue.'

'Pft, that was a lucky guess, because you definitely weren't listening to me.'

He wanted to tell her to go and jump off the nearest cliff edge, but smiled instead. What kind of person called their kid Dominic anyway? 'You have so little faith in me. What are you going to watch at the flicks?'

She laughed. '*The flicks*, I haven't heard it called that since I was a kid; my nan always called it that. The new *Haunted Mansion*, it's supposed to be funny and not too babyish. I was thinking of taking him to the Royalty because they do the best popcorn.'

'They don't do those frozen drinks though.'

'Do they not? I thought all cinemas did them.'

He shrugged. 'I don't know, maybe they do. I'll think about it, I might be busy this Friday.'

She let out a loud cackle that irritated every last nerve ending in his body. 'Busy my arse, doing what? Are you washing your hair?'

He stared at her. She was a nasty cow as well as being

boring as fuck, because he had no hair and hadn't for years. 'Yeah, how do I keep the shine on this handsome head, if I don't spit and polish it now and again?'

The bell sounded and that also grated on his last nerve; it was like being back in school. He tipped the last of the disgusting lukewarm liquid onto the floor, relieved he didn't have to finish it, and turned around to go back inside.

'Hey, you should think about it. You can't sit in and feel sorry for yourself every weekend. It's not healthy.'

Glancing back, he was greeted with another vaporous cloud of vile, peach-smelling fog. 'I'll let you know.' What he really wanted to do was to pluck that Elf Bar out of Miranda's hand and shove it so far down her throat until she choked on it, coughing up synthetic, peach-flavoured blood and mucus while simultaneously gagging on it.

'Yeah, make sure you do. I might get a better offer myself.'

He glanced at the sky and thought to himself *if there is a god up there send someone her way to get her out of mine. Preferably someone mean as hell who will beat the shit out of her every time she opens her mouth.* Then he went back to work. It was hot and noisy in here, which to him was a relief. As he pulled the ear defenders on, he was thankful that they would drown out any further noise Miranda made in his direction.

He much preferred to be alone with his thoughts than going through the motions of being a person who cared. He found it more exhausting being nice to idiots than he did killing. He smiled to himself, now killing that girl had been everything he had hoped for, and the chase leading up to that moment had been even more fulfilling. He hadn't expected it to leave him feeling so satisfied. The only downside was he wanted to do it again and again, but he knew that he needed to be cautious if he wanted to make this work like he'd dreamed about for so long.

TWENTY-ONE

Morgan disliked briefings, not because of the purpose of them – they were an important part of the investigative process – but because of the number of people who would crowd into the blue room at the same time. Too many people made her uncomfortable, unless it was at a concert and, even then, she only put up with it because wanting to see the singer or band made her endure it for a couple of hours. She'd dragged Ben to see Hollywood Vampires in Manchester, and luckily for them they'd ended up on a row that hadn't sold out, so she didn't have to sit too close to anyone.

Cain hadn't appeared yet, and she sent him a quick message.

Morning. Are you okay?

Three dots appeared instantly on her phone.

I'm good, wouldn't recommend this taxi service though they're way too late!

Ben was talking, and she let out a loud, 'Oh shit.'

Everyone turned to look at her, making her feel even more uncomfortable. 'Sorry, forgot to pick Cain up.'

Amy grinned at her, but she didn't smile back as she felt terrible. Ben carried on talking. He had a map of the park up and one of the surrounding area to Lexie's house. He pointed to the riverbank across from Milly's house.

'I want a couple of search officers to go here ASAP and search the riverbank for anything suspicious.'

'Like what?' asked Daisy, who had done nothing but smile at Morgan since she'd walked in.

'Like something that may be of evidential value. We entered the property across the street last night, to gather some things for a potential witness, and someone came into the house while we were inside. They left before we could catch up with them, but they exited that way and may have left fingerprints or footprints or lost belongings in their haste. At this point in the investigation, I'm praying for anything.'

Daisy nodded. 'Yes, boss.'

'There's a lot to be getting on with. I've asked Mads to spare me Tina and Sam to go and speak to the teenagers who called it in, to see if they have anything. Once they've finished that they'll join the rest who are currently canvassing the whole of Fenton Street, then the surrounding streets. The newsagents at the top of the street opens at seven a.m., so Amy, can you go and speak to the owner and get them to download everything from their CCTV in the last couple of days? We're looking for a silver-coloured Picasso.'

Morgan held up her hand. 'White, too; remember Milly's neighbour has a white Picasso. Jordan said it was light coloured, when I first spoke to him, and then he thought it could be white. It's hard to tell in the dark.' It would be so nice and easy for a change if they could trace everything back to Jack Andrews. He'd seemed cool and pretty calm when they'd spoken to him, but he might be the kind of person who wouldn't break a sweat under duress.

'Okay, we have a witness who gave us a partial reg, only it didn't come back as a silver Picasso: it came back to a Ford Focus, so I'm thinking either the witness may have got a little mixed up or it's got a false plate on, which is highly likely.'

A groan went around the room.

Ben held up his hand. 'I know, it would have been nice, right? But it isn't, so now we're looking for any Picasso that is in the area. We can get the registration numbers and go speak to the owners, surely they're not a hugely popular car?'

Nobody answered him. 'Right, well PNC Bureau sent over a list of all the local Picasso owners, and I'm pleased to tell you the good news is they stopped making them a few years ago, but the bad news is there are several models out there. The list has twenty-seven cars on for the local area, covering from Bowness down to Barrow, which is not a huge number but it's big enough, so I'm going to have to assign someone to work their way through it and tick them off, which is what Cain can do when he arrives. Obviously this doesn't include unregistered vehicles. We'll start with the silver models then he can work his way through the rest of them, to be sure and get them checked off. Wendy, did you find anything at the crime scene last night?'

Both Ian and Joe were sitting next to her; Ian was frowning but Ben didn't look his way. He was focused on Wendy.

'Not much, boss, there was a lot of blood. No hair, there were a couple of partial prints on the edge of the wooden roof tiles.'

'Shingles,' corrected Ian.

She glared at him and carried on. 'I wouldn't hold out too much hope though, boss, they could belong to the kids who were there last night and discovered the body.'

'We may get lucky.'

She smiled at him. 'I hope we do, that was horrific, poor lass.'

Everyone nodded in agreement with her. They were focused but they had hearts and Morgan could tell by the sad expressions on their faces this had touched them more than others had.

Wendy held up a hand. 'Just to add there were no prints recovered from Milly Blake's house either.'

This time it was a collective sigh that whispered around the room.

It was the blatant disrespect and mockery he'd shown towards his victim that bothered Morgan. He had wanted to shock them, shock whoever found her, and he'd certainly done that.

Ben continued allocating tasks to everyone else, and when he'd finished, she excused herself and slipped out to go and get Cain.

He was waiting on the front doorstep for her with his arms folded. When he was inside the car, he said, 'Don't expect a good review for this service and, whatever you do, don't leave this job and become an Uber driver. You wouldn't last a day; to be fair I don't think you'd manage the morning.'

'I'm sorry, I was so busy thinking about last night you completely slipped my mind.' She told him about going to Milly's house and someone following them inside.

He looked horrified. 'Who do you think it was? The killer?'

'It had to have been, anyone else would have identified themselves, but we didn't see a Picasso in the area, so if it was, he was on foot or lived close by. Guess what car the neighbour drives?'

'A Picasso.'

She nodded. 'Too much of a coincidence, if you ask me. I think we need to look at him closely.'

'Totally agree, did you speak to him? What did he say?'

'His wife had the car at work, she's on nights. He was really calm though, he didn't look shifty at all, but he could have killed Lexie, cleaned the car then took it back in time for his wife to use to get to work.'

'Shifty or what?'

'Definitely, he didn't even look bothered though. If he had followed us inside to see what we were doing, then had to run out, he would've been out of breath and sweaty. He wasn't in the slightest. He was as cool as a cucumber, standing there being genuinely concerned about Milly.'

'Not if he's a complete psychopath, he wouldn't. Anyway, you can buy me coffee to make up for being late.'

She laughed. 'It's any excuse to get out of paying with you.'

'I'm not the one who screwed up. I could have walked in and got myself a coffee waiting for you to remember me. Do you know how much that hurts, Morgan? You didn't remember to come get your friend in his time of need. I thought you loved me.'

'I'll buy the coffee, stop with the emotional blackmail. And for the record, I do love you, most of the time, except for when you're being dramatic.'

'You're forgiven, if you get me cake.'

'What happened to your strict training regime and the half marathon?'

'Screw it, I was only doing it for the fitness test, and I managed to get stabbed instead, so it got me out of this year's quite nicely. I'll start again next year, so for now I'm basking in the glow of all the drama and eating as much cake as I want.'

'Hallelujah, then the bet is off; we can call it a draw and I don't have to pretend to enjoy trying to wobble down the street and pass it off as jogging.'

'It's definitely off.'

They both managed a laugh as she parked outside of The Coffee Pot and dashed inside. Morgan ordered the coffee and cakes, but she was too busy thinking about Lexie and Natalie White to engage in any kind of conversation. She thanked the barista, and as she was walking out of the door, she saw a silver car drive past. She could just make out a male driver who turned to stare at her for a second, then he was gone.

She almost dropped the coffees as she ran to the car and thrust them at Cain.

'What the hell?'

'Where did that silver car go? I need you to keep an eye out for it.'

The road was busy, it was the main road through Rydal Falls, and she indicated and began to nudge the car out into the oncoming traffic to a cacophony of blaring horns. A bus stopped to let her out because it couldn't pass her anyway, and she drove off, but it was nowhere in sight.

'Where did it go? It can't be far.'

But deep down she knew that it could. It had taken a couple of minutes for her to get out, and the driver could be on the way to Ambleside or Windermere, not to mention the little side roads that led off to different villages.

'Fuck.'

'Morgan, calm down, it might not have been him.'

'What are the chances of another silver Picasso driving past me? You didn't see him. He turned to look at me, it was only for a split second, but he stared at me before turning away. Why would he do that if he wasn't looking for me or following me?'

'Is there any CCTV at the café?'

'No, I've been before on enquiries, and they don't have any.'

'Did you get followed to my house?'

'I don't think so, I don't know. I wasn't even looking for it. I was too busy thinking about everything that's happening.'

'You better be a lot more vigilant than that, Morgan. If he was following you, that's pretty scary. Can you describe him?'

She tried to picture his face. 'White, black baseball cap, no beard, black coat.'

'Eyes, distinguishing features?'

'I saw him for like a second, Cain. I don't have a photographic memory. It was a guy.'

'It could have been any guy, was it even a Picasso?'

She didn't know, it was a silver car that was for sure. 'I couldn't say for definite.' She knew she was doubting herself now, even though she had initially thought it was. Her imagination could be playing tricks on her and making her paranoid when there was no cause to be, but – and there it was, hanging in the air: *but* – the thought of someone watching her made her skin crawl.

TWENTY-TWO

Morgan drove in the direction of Milly's house, to see if the neighbour's Picasso was parked on the drive. If it wasn't that was another possible cause for concern. There was a search van parked up by the riverside, and she immediately spotted the white Picasso parked on the drive of Jack Andrews's house. Cain took a sip of his coffee and pointed to the van.

'Let's go ask Daisy if she's noticed anything strange.'

Morgan parked up and they walked towards the riverbank, where Daisy and Al were searching.

'Hey, did you guys notice if the car over there has been out this morning?'

They both looked up and shrugged. Daisy smiled at her again.

'Sorry, Morgan, we've been a bit preoccupied.'

'That's okay, no worries. Have you found anything?'

Al frowned. 'We've found lots, but nothing useful, if you get what I mean.'

'Ah, never mind. Keep up the good work.'

She turned to cross the road, and Cain followed. 'Now what?'

'I think we should go and ask Jack's wife where he was last night.'

She was opening the gate before he could talk her out of it. As she passed by the car, she pressed the palm of her hand against the bonnet: it was warm, but not hot. She knocked on the door and wasn't surprised no one answered. He was probably at work, and he said his wife worked nights, but then wouldn't he have needed the car to get to work? She curled her fist and hammered on the glass with her knuckles. The bedroom window above them opened and a woman peered down at them.

'Can I help?'

'Police, have you got a minute?'

She shut the window and a few moments later the door opened. The woman glaring at her had purple smudges under eyes which were squinting against the daylight, and her brown hair was coming loose from the messy bun; she looked tired, and Morgan felt bad.

'Sorry to wake you. Detectives Brookes and Robson, we have a few questions that can't wait.' She held her warrant card for her to see, but the woman waved it away, disinterested.

'You better come in then.'

They followed her inside; she didn't take them anywhere just made them stand in the messy hallway, with shoes scattered along one wall and a stack of coats hooked on the balustrade at the end of the stairs; there were piles of unopened letters on the hall table. It was chaotic and the complete opposite of Milly's house. Cain closed the front door behind them.

'What's going on? I got some garbled message off Jack about Milly and then she's not here. Is she okay?'

'She's fine, there has been a murder though, and I'm very sorry to say it's one of Milly's friends.'

'Oh dear, that's awful.'

'Did Jack not tell you this morning when you got home?'

'Jack left for work on his cycle before I got home. He's on an early today.'

'Oh, where does he work?'

'Blacks Printers.'

'In Backbarrow?'

'That's the one.'

'That's quite some bike ride.'

She laughed. 'He's fitter than he looks, been cycling to work a long time. He enjoys it, unless it's tipping it down, and then he takes the car.'

'Was he out in the car yesterday afternoon, do you know?'

'I don't know, probably, it was his day off. Why are you so interested in what Jack is doing?'

Morgan paused. 'It's just standard questions we need to follow up on.'

'Oh, right. Well, you'd be far better asking him. I didn't see much of him yesterday; I was in bed then rolled out of it to go to work. Probably said hi, goodbye to him.'

'Thanks, we'll do that. What time is he home today?'

'Maybe around six, if the roads aren't too bad.'

'What's your name, if you don't mind me asking? It's just to say we've spoken with you and can tick it off the list.'

'Shauna Andrews.'

'What's your date of birth, Shauna, and can you give me Jack's too?'

Shauna rhymed off hers and Jack's then crossed her arms. 'Anything else?'

'No, thank you for your time; we'll let you get back to bed.'

Shauna rolled her eyes at Morgan; they left her to it.

Once they were in the car Cain glanced back at the house. 'She was happy to see us.'

'You think so?'

'I know so, you could tell by the look in her eyes.'

Morgan couldn't help it, she laughed so loud it made Cain spill his coffee.

'Jesus, Morgan, you scared me.'

'Do you think we should go to the printers?'

'And do what? You better ask Ben about that. Is this guy a suspect?'

She shrugged. 'Not officially.'

'Right, well if he's at work on his bike, he didn't drive past you thirty minutes ago.'

'Actually, you're right on every level, because it was definitely a silver car that drove past me. I don't know what I was thinking.'

She didn't know why she hadn't realised this sooner and turned the car around to go back to the station. She needed to speak to Bronte and the others in the support group. For now she was making that her priority, and she was certain Ben would agree with her.

TWENTY-THREE

It turned out Morgan didn't have to go very far to find Bronte Potter. When she arrived back at the station, Brenda, who had just made herself a mug of coffee and was coming out of the small kitchen area, yelled at her. 'Morgan.' She shouted at the top of her voice, making everyone stop what they were doing and turn around to stare at her.

Cain whispered, 'You've been summoned.'

Morgan waved at Brenda. 'What's up?'

'There's a young lass waiting at the front counter to speak with you. Poor thing has been here at least an hour. I told her you were busy out on enquiries, but she said she was happy to wait.'

'What's her name?'

'Bronte—'

Morgan finished for her. 'Potter? Amazing, I was going to go and find her.'

'I tried to ring you, but it went to voicemail.'

Morgan frowned, and taking her phone out she saw that she had two missed calls off an unknown number. 'That's weird, it didn't even ring, sorry.'

'Signal's not been too good around here the last couple of days, anyway you're here now.'

Morgan walked into the office to take a look at Bronte on the CCTV monitor, unsure why she felt a little nervous to speak to her. The girl, well she was a young woman now, was sitting staring at the wall in front of her, not on her phone like most people are when they have nothing better to do. Her hands were neatly folded on her lap, and she was dressed from head to toe in black, not too dissimilar to Morgan, except for the Dr. Martens boots that Morgan rarely left home without. Bronte was wearing a pair of Nikes.

Morgan let herself into the small side room and opened the door, calling Bronte's name.

She turned around, took one look at Morgan, and burst into tears.

'Do you want to come in here so we can chat in private, Bronte?'

She nodded and walked into the room, looking around before taking a seat.

'Is it safe?'

'We're in a police station, yes, it is.'

Bronte sniffed. 'You can't be too sure. Is it true about Lexie? Milly phoned me last night to warn me and to let the others know. Is she okay? Because she wouldn't tell me where she was or what was happening.'

'It's all very complicated, but Milly is safe.' She didn't add that by using her phone she had put herself at risk; Bronte didn't need to be scared more than she already was. She could see the tremors in her hands as she lifted a tissue to wipe her eyes.

'Then what the hell is happening, Morgan? Who would want to hurt her? The rest of the girls are all terrified now, we don't know what to do.'

'I need to speak to you all. Is there any chance you could call an emergency meeting at some point today?'

'I suppose so, though I'm not sure about Sara, as she has to travel from Manchester, but I'll ask her.'

'Thank you, it's vital that we talk about the safety of everyone and what we can do. Bronte, Milly said she thought she'd been followed, which is the reason she'd gone to Lexie's house. Has anyone else mentioned a guy in a silver car hanging around?'

Her head shook. 'Milly mentioned it, and Sara was shocked that she hadn't reported it to the police. Nobody else has had any problems.'

'What about Lexie, when did you last speak to her?'

'Probably at the last meeting; we meet once a month. Lexie is, was.' She paused. 'This is so hard to try and get my head around, but she's very close to Ava. Has anyone spoken to her because I haven't been able to get hold of her.'

'How do you usually contact everyone?'

'We have a WhatsApp group.'

'Could you message now and ask them if everyone is okay to meet today, and if they have anything they think I should know?'

She nodded. 'Of course.' A few taps of her screen and the message was sent. Bronte looked at her. 'We invited you along when we first got together. I guess you never got the message. I've added you to the group now.'

'I didn't see it. Where did you message me?'

'I emailed your work address.'

'Ahh, it no doubt got pushed into the junk folder; if we get emails from outside of the organisation it has a tendency to throw them in there. Thank you for the invite though, it's very kind of you. Who else knows that you meet once a month?'

'No one, it's one of the group rules: we don't discuss the group outside of the group.'

'You meet in the hall at St Martha's. What about the vicar, Theo? Does he know what the group is about?'

'Yes, but he doesn't ever attend, and he never knows what nights we are meeting, because we change it every month so we're not sitting ducks. He even gave me my own key to the hall so I could come and go as I please. You don't think he has anything to do with this, do you?'

Morgan felt her cheeks begin to flush, betraying her a little, as she shook her head.

'No, he's a good guy. I'm just trying to work out who would know about the group.'

'Good, because I'd be devastated to think that a priest would betray my trust, although being a good guy doesn't necessarily mean you are innocent. Harrison was the easiest going, fun boyfriend I'd ever had and look how that turned out. He tried to kill me; he massacred my family then he went after you.'

A chill crossed Morgan's shoulders, this case was bringing forward all those terrible memories that she'd worked so hard to push to the back of her mind. Unaware she was doing it, her fingers reached for her neck, to where he'd tried to hang her.

Bronte said, 'It's horrible, isn't it? The memories? They come flooding back when you least expect them to, and sometimes, they are so crippling that you can't focus or perform even the most basic functions. I drive my aunt mad; I know I do with my constant fear and insecurities, but I never used to be this way. I didn't care about anything much apart from how many likes my Instagram posts were getting and my clothes. Look at me now, I don't give a crap about any of that; I can't remember the last time I looked on any social media and now... Well, now I prefer to wear black; I like to blend into the background and not draw attention to myself...' Bronte paused, and Morgan could feel herself getting too hot; the room was too small and stuffy, and she wished she hadn't worn a turtleneck, a long-sleeved top. She felt as if she was suffocating in it, and she knew her cheeks must be a deep shade of red.

'Is that why you always wear black?' Bronte asked thoughtfully. Not waiting for an answer, she continued. 'You know you're kind of a role model for the group, your name gets mentioned every single meeting.'

This made Morgan feel very uncomfortable, and she wanted to run out of this room and forget she'd ever met Bronte Potter, but she couldn't do that because not only had she met her, but she'd also saved her life, and they were connected on some deep level that neither of them could describe. The fact that they'd both survived the same killer had forged some kind of unspoken bond between them, even more so than the others in the group.

Bronte was staring at her. 'Are you okay, do you need a glass of water or something?'

She snapped herself out of her thoughts. 'No, I'm fine thanks. What time should we meet? Sara will need a couple of hours to get here, won't she?'

'We normally meet between five and seven thirty, we mix the times up too because' – she shrugged – 'Well, you know why. It's precisely this. It looks as if our biggest fears that have haunted us since the time of our attacks have come true. Are you sure Lexie was killed because she's a survivor? If she was then that means we're all in danger until you catch whoever did it.'

'I can't say for sure, but to me it seems that way. The way her body was displayed.'

Bronte's jaw slackened and her eyes looked as if they might pop out of her head, making Morgan realise she was giving far too much away.

'*Displayed?*'

'Forget I said that; it's not public knowledge.'

'But she was. How did she die?'

Morgan knew that the teenagers last night would no doubt have told their friends, parents, siblings what they had discovered, even though they had been asked not to. It was human nature, once they got over the shock, they would no doubt thrive off the gossip and story they could tell about the body on the park shelter roof. Bronte was going to hear about it sooner or later, so it was pointless not telling her.

'She was attacked with a sharp instrument, and her body was found in the park by a group of teenage kids.'

Bronte pushed her chair back. She looked devastated and sick, and Morgan felt awful. 'I have to go, I'm sorry. I'll let you know what time we're meeting so you can come speak to everyone.'

She walked out, leaving Morgan feeling terrible. She needed fresh air and lots of it to clear her fuzzy head.

TWENTY-FOUR

By the time Morgan got back up the stairs, Ben took one look at her and said, 'My office.'

She followed him towards an untidy desk, and he closed the door behind her and pointed to a chair.

'What's going on? You look ill, do you need to go home, Morgan?'

Unsure if she should be telling him about the feeling of dread that had lodged itself deep inside her bones, she shook her head. 'I just feel a bit off, it's nothing major.'

'Does it have anything to do with Bronte Potter?'

She realised Cain would have told him where she was. 'No, well maybe. I feel bad that they're being dragged into a murder investigation all over again. It's so unfair, they're struggling enough to get on with their lives as it is and now this.'

He took a perch on the corner of his desk and looked at her.

'You are not responsible for those women; you are not the evil bastard who decided to kill Lexie White. You saved her, who knew we'd need to save her twice?'

She had to blink away the tears. 'I know I'm not, yet I feel as if I am.'

He reached out, squeezing her shoulder. 'Morgan, listen to me; you are responsible for no one but yourself. At this present moment you are my priority, okay. I know you won't let me take you off the case, and even though I'm going against every instinct in my body, I think that I need you more than ever to work this because of your connections and everything that has happened to you. However, I will not put you at risk, and if I tell you not to do something you better bloody listen to me. I've talked to Marc, and he's agreed to put patrols outside of everyone in the group's houses for the next seventy-two hours, when we have their addresses. Can you get those for me? He's also contacting GMP to arrange the same for Sara Fletcher.'

She nodded and felt the pent-up breath she'd been holding release, and her shoulders sagged a little.

'There is also going to be a patrol outside of our house when you're off duty. Don't argue with me, it's non-negotiable. I won't let you work this if I don't think that you're safe. Do you want to come to the post-mortem with me or should I take Amy?' He rolled his head gently around and she knew he was trying to release some of the stress that must be building up inside.

Morgan did not want to go and watch Lexie have to go through this final indignity, but she knew that she had to; she owed it to her to be there for every single step of her last journey. 'I'll go.'

'Good, now from this moment on we are all to carry CS gas, radios, cuffs – I don't want anyone going anywhere unequipped to deal with an emergency. I've already told the others, though Cain is exempt because he's working from the office. He's too vulnerable at the moment with not being up to full fitness. I've managed to draft in an extra pair of hands from Barrow. Chris Marshall is old school, I've worked with him a few times over the years, and he knows his stuff.'

'Good.'

'The Murder Investigation Team are also going to be

joining us but from HQ, as they're short staffed, but Claire is going to work alongside us.'

Morgan knew then just how serious Ben was taking the threat level to not just her, but to all of the women in Bronte's support group.

'Are you good to go to the mortuary?'

'Yes, and that's good, about Chris and MIT.'

'It is, we want to catch this bastard before anyone else gets hurt, because we're not doing too good on the evidence front. I've just heard back that the newsagents CCTV cameras are faulty; they don't record the footage. The youths from the park weren't able to give us anything other than the circumstances they found the body in, and we know that both Lexie's and Milly's attackers are still behind bars.'

He cast his gaze downwards, and she knew he was thinking specifically about her. She was wondering if she'd be back in time for the meeting with the group at St Martha's; there was a chance she may not.

'Ben, we need to go now. Is Declan ready? I have an appointment later on that I can't miss.'

'What kind of appointment?'

She lowered her voice, even though they were in his office with the door closed. 'With the support group that Lexie attended. They've agreed to have an emergency meeting I can attend, so I can warn them and get all their current details, addresses, phone numbers and anything else we may need.'

'I'll come with you.'

'I don't think that's a good idea.'

'Why not, I'm a copper? I'm here to help them.'

Shrugging, she felt bad, but she had no choice. 'Ben, I know that you are, and they know that on the surface, but I think they'll talk more openly about any concerns if it's just me. I'm sorry, you're a man and they might see you as a threat. Plus, this way we might draw the killer out... I want to catch him.'

'Okay then, can I at least drive you there and wait for you, if I can't speak to them? But you're going to have to make it clear to them that at some point I might have to.'

'I'm sure it will be fine in a one-to-one situation, just not going into the group space. They're going to be upset enough as it is about what's happening, and I don't want them to clam up and not talk to me.'

'I get that, are you okay going in on your own?'

'Yeah, fine.'

He leaned forward and kissed the top of her head. 'I love you; you better be extra vigilant.'

She wondered if now was the time to tell him about the silver car. Cain can't have mentioned it, or he would have been grilling her for every little detail. Despite her good intentions she decided not to; if he thought she'd been followed, he would never let her go anywhere on her own, and it could have been a coincidence. Was she seeing silver cars because she was on high alert looking for them? It could well be that and the poor guy could have been going about his business. This made her feel marginally better, but there was still a tiny niggle inside her head that wouldn't be placated so easily.

Ben drove them to Royal Lancaster Infirmary, and she spent the whole time searching through her junk mail for an email from Bronte. About to give up before she got car sick, she found one from months ago, from a BPotter13. She opened it and read the short but succinct message.

Hi Morgan,

It's Bronte Potter, I hope you get this message. I'm starting a support group for survivors of, well you know what, I don't need to spell it out to you. I wondered if you'd like to be a part of it, especially after everything you've been through. Anyway, have a think about it and let me know, then I'll send you the details.

B. x

She read it again. Would she have gone along if she'd seen this when it arrived? She wasn't sure that she would. It sounded like a great idea, and she got that it would be nice to talk about stuff with people who had been through similar situations, but would she have actually walked through the door and told them how she felt? Probably not, she found it hard enough talking to Ben about any of it and he was her best friend, her lover and the guy who had been there for her through all of it. She realised that preferring to block it all out and live her life pretending she hadn't been battered, bruised and almost died several times over at the hands of violent criminals was the only way she could cope with it and still function like a normal human being. The car had stopped moving and when she looked up, she saw they were in the car park.

'Already, did you speed?'

'Only a little. What were you looking for? I glanced down, and you were just scrolling through your emails like an unhinged woman.'

She smiled at him. 'I was looking for my invite to the support group.'

'Did you find it?'

'Unfortunately, yes. I don't know whether I feel bad about missing it or relieved.'

He released a long, drawn-out breath. 'I'll leave that with you. I'm not sure either, though I don't think you'd have gone if that's any help.'

She laughed. 'Nah, I don't think so too, but I kind of feel

bad as if maybe I should have put in an appearance or at least answered Bronte's invitation.'

'I'm sure she knows you were busy; you rarely have anytime to yourself as it is with the caseloads that seem to just keep growing.' He reached out to stroke her cheek, and she clasped his warm hand to her face. 'I know we do a vital job, but do you ever just think how nice it would be to have a job without such heavy responsibilities?'

He nodded. 'After Cindy died, I wished I could take back every hour that I'd worked over the end of my shift. I wished that I had a job in BAE or maybe Sellafield, one where I could work my eight hours then go home and not have to think about work until I clocked on for the next eight hours. The gut-wrenching guilt I carried with me, still carry, made it hard to go to work let alone put my all into it.'

'Then why did you? How did you?'

'I realised that if I didn't care about the victims of some of the heinous crimes we work, then who would, and then I met you and selfishly forced you to come join my team. I was smitten with you from the moment I set eyes on you, Morgan. You're so beautiful. I love your hair that matches your fiery temper, I love the ambition, the strength you show even after everything you've been through. You lifted me out of my self-pitying downward spiral and gave me a whole new reason to carry on with this job. Without you I probably wouldn't still be here.'

She stared into his eyes; she knew he was saying that without her he had no reason to carry on living.

'Not that I'm saying you are tied to me for the rest of my life, I'm not trying to make you feel as if you are and no, I wouldn't do anything stupid or reckless if you came to your senses and decided you wanted a different life than the one I can only offer you. I'd still carry on, heartbroken maybe and in a whole different world of self-pity, but I'd be okay.'

'Why do you always think I'd be off at the first opportunity that came along? Can you not accept that I love you and want to be with you for the rest of my life?'

He held his hand across his heart. 'You do?'

She nodded. 'I did from the moment I met you, although I wasn't sure if I was scared of you or starstruck by your reputation.'

Ben laughed. 'I have a reputation?'

'Oh, yes. You do know that most of the females in the station have a crush on you, don't you?'

'Get out, why on earth?'

She shrugged. 'No idea to be fair; I mean you can be a right grouch at times.'

'I suppose I can and I'm still not sure how I hit the double jackpot or what you see in me, but thank you for putting up with me.'

'My pleasure.'

'Come on, we better get on with this before Declan comes out looking for us.'

A warm smile spread across Morgan's face at the mention of Declan's name. She loved him dearly but wished they didn't always have to meet this way.

Susie, the mortuary technician, greeted them both with open arms and the most vibrant peacock hued head of hair.

Ben beat her to it. 'Nice hair, you look like a peacock about to shake its feathers to all the birds.'

Morgan looked at him in horror, but Susie laughed. 'Funny you should mention that, I actually got my inspiration from a fantastic picture of a male peacock off Pinterest. You're getting good, Ben.'

She turned to Morgan. 'Hey, what happened with the book club? Did you ever get there?'

'Not yet, I'm hoping to. I desperately want to read something out of my usual genre and need some motivation as to why and to finish the book.'

'Should we go to the next one for sure? I'm up for it. What about you, Ben?'

He held up his hands. 'Absolutely not, ladies, you have fun without me. I did read a great book though last week.'

Both Morgan and Susie stared at him in wonder. 'You did?' asked Morgan.

He nodded. 'Yep, can't remember the name but it was a good one.'

Susie rolled her eyes at him.

'Guys, are you ready?'

Declan's head was sticking out of his office door, the cap on his head stretched far too tight for it.

Susie whispered, 'He's grown his hair even more; I wish someone would write to Ryan Reynolds and tell him to shave it all off. He faffs around with his quiff more than I do with my curling tongs.'

All three of them headed for the changing rooms, splitting and going in different directions as Susie headed straight into the mortuary. Morgan's heart felt too heavy for her chest as she tied the plastic apron around her waist.

She didn't want to do this but knew there was no choice.

TWENTY-FIVE

Bronte stared at the open visiting order on the table in front of her. Why had Sara taken it upon herself to write to him of all the people? The thought of it sent tiny shooting pains into her heart; it felt like the worst kind of betrayal she'd had since that day. There was nothing that would ever compete with that, knowing that the guy you liked and trusted, thought might have your heart, wanted you and your family dead. Who does that kind of thing? She was alone in her aunt's house again; she was always alone these days.

It hurt her to think about the times as a teenager she'd wished she was alone, that Beatrix wasn't the most annoying sister in the world, that her mum and dad weren't the most annoying parents that ever walked the planet – and now look at her. She got that wish all those years ago, didn't she? She felt awful, had wondered if it was her fault – had she ever said anything to him to make him think she wanted to be on her own? She had spent hours, days, going over the conversations they'd had, to see if she had complained one too many times about her irritating family. She would give anything to see them again and be back in their home, arguing over what was for tea and whose turn it was to pick a film off Netflix.

The front door shut with a bang loud enough to make her throw the mug of tea she was drinking all over the visiting order. 'Shit, shit.' She jumped up to grab some kitchen towels and mop it up before her aunt saw it. She'd have a complete meltdown if she thought that she was even entertaining the idea of going to see him in prison.

'Hey, what are you doing?'

She turned to see her aunt's boyfriend leaning against the kitchen doorframe, staring at her and relaxed.

'Oh hey, nothing, just spilled my tea over a letter from the college.'

He walked past her to the fridge, not even glancing at the sodden piece of paper in her hand.

'What's for tea?'

She shrugged. 'No idea, whatever you want to make. Michelle never said I had to cook so I haven't.'

He turned to her and rolled his eyes. 'How old are you now? Twenty, twenty-one? I don't think you need to be told when to make the tea. If there's nobody home but you, wouldn't you want to do it anyway? I mean, are you not hungry?'

'Not really.'

'Jesus, Bee, I am, I'm starving. Where's Shelle?'

She hated the way he shortened her name to Bee, because he was too lazy to say her full name, but other than that he was okay she supposed. He didn't cause arguments, he hoovered, and he was nice to her most of the time considering she was always there and only went out to meet the support group and college.

'Do you want pasta?' he asked her as he was pulling open cupboard doors, looking for the ingredients to throw something together.

'If you do.'

He shook his head. 'If you don't tell me, you don't. We need to toughen you up a little or you're going to get eaten alive in this big bad old world.'

In her head she screamed at the top of her voice. *No, I don't want fucking pasta, we had that yesterday and the day before.* Then she heard her voice say, 'Pasta's fine, do you want me to make it?'

'Nah, not after the last time. I'm not sure how you can mess up mac and cheese, but you royally screwed it up. I'll do it, you can wash up instead.'

'Okay.'

She left the kitchen with her soggy letter sandwiched between two sheets of paper towels and headed to her bedroom to dry it with her hairdryer. He was right, she did need to toughen up. Maybe she should go and see Harrison tomorrow and tell him exactly what she thought of him. As she sat on the edge of her bed, the letter clamped between her fingers and thumbs, gently wafting warm air from her Dyson over it, she felt better, if that was the right word to describe the crippling anxiety that made her shy away from everyone and everything. Maybe the time was right to get it off her chest.

Her phone pinged with a series of beeps, and she looked down at the WhatsApp group; everyone but Sara had replied. They would be at the hall for eight fifteen, which was late for them, but it was a time they hadn't met before so anyone watching wouldn't be expecting it. One-handed she tapped out a message to Morgan, confirming the time. She wasn't sure if the detective would come, but she had a feeling that she might be compelled to put in an appearance, to see what they were about and hopefully to give them some information about what had happened to poor Lexie, so they could keep themselves safe.

TWENTY-SIX

'Morgan, Morgan.' Declan's gentle voice, with a touch of an Irish lilt to it, was calling her from above. She was lying down horizontal, and he was peering down at her, waving a thick magazine over her face. Her eyes felt heavy, and the inside of her ears were buzzing loudly.

'What happened?'

'Bejesus, you scared the life out of me and Ben. You went down like a sack of potatoes and hit the deck with a loud crack. I thought you'd knocked yourself out and given yourself a concussion.'

Horror made her push herself onto her elbows as she realised she was on the worn leather sofa he kept in his office for emergency naps. 'I didn't?'

'Uhuh, you most certainly did.'

She lifted her fingers to her head where a large lump had formed above her right ear. Prodding it resulted in an, 'Ouch.'

'Yep, it's a good egg is that one, but I think you're okay. How many fingers am I holding up?' He waved his hand in front of her.

'Three.'

'Good, you can still count. What year is it?'

'It's 2023.'

'Who is the current reigning monarch?'

'Charles.'

'No, that would be King Charles to you, but it's near enough.'

'Where's Ben?'

'Sent him to the canteen to get you a can of full fat cola and a Mars bar. He almost passed out himself with shock. Next time, could you give us some kind of warning that you're going to hit the deck, kid, because I'm too old for this much excitement.'

'Sorry.' She couldn't think of a more embarrassing situation than fainting at a post-mortem in front of everyone.

'I don't want you to be sorry. I want you to tell me what happened.'

'It's the whole situation, Declan. I guess it's affected me more than I realised, and when you started up the bone saw...'

He flopped down next to her, wrapping an arm around her shoulder and pulling her close to him.

'You, my precious child, have been through too much; you knew the lovely Lexie and I surmise that you liked her more than you care to admit, and it's hit you harder than you ever imagined. It's a hard one, knowing that she survived only for another sick person to kill her; and you couldn't save her a second time; it's hard for anyone. It makes me so angry. I could honestly punch a hole in that wall and not feel bad about it, only I'm a wimp and need my knuckles so I won't. Don't feel bad, don't torture yourself either. I'm a little annoyed Ben dragged you here, so he has to take some of the blame. An autopsy is too personal, too intimate. He should have realised this was never going to be easy for you.'

'Thanks, Declan.'

He kissed the top of her head, mimicking what Ben had

done an hour earlier. 'You're excused for the rest of this post-mortem; I need a new outfit for a hot date with Theo on Saturday night, so if you want to do a bit of browsing on ASOS for men for me and add stuff to my basket it would be greatly appreciated.'

Morgan smiled at him. 'You don't need fashion advice from me, unless you want to look like a Goth dude.'

'Maybe I fancy a whole new look. Black looks good on you; it might make me look younger. I'm not into chains or anything too extreme though, well not unless it's in the bedroom but that's too much information.' He winked at her and stood up. 'You are not allowed back in my mortuary today, so don't argue, take the fizzy pop, eat the chocolate and have a good old online shop for me, surprise me. My wallet is in the top drawer. I'm a large on top and a medium on the bottom, size 11 shoes.'

Ben opened the door, and Declan stood up, taking the drink and chocolate from him. 'Shoo, give her some space. She's good, aren't you, Morgan?'

'I'm good.'

Ben opened his mouth, and Declan chased him. 'Away with you, can't you see she needs a bit of freedom and a change of scenery?'

He turned to wink at her and then closed the door behind him, leaving her feeling a little out of herself and one hundred per cent mortified that she had passed out in front of an audience. She felt terrible: her hands were trembling, and her head was still spinning a little.

She popped the tab on the cola and took a couple of huge gulps, the sugar hit instantly making her feel a little less spacey. Standing up on legs that felt as if they belonged to someone else, she walked to Declan's desk and sat in his chair. His office was cosy, if you ignored the posters on the walls and framed photographs of different stages of a post-mortem, but they weren't too graphic. She looked at his computer and realised she had no idea what the password was to get onto it. There was a pink Post-it note stuck to the corner, with a password written on it, and she smiled to herself. He was a brilliant pathologist, an amazing human being, who was clearly very intelligent, yet he had to write his own password down, which made her feel a lot better about herself. As she sipped at the fizzy drink and nibbled on the chocolate bar, she began to feel a little more human; the ringing in her ears subsided but the pain from the lump on her head persisted. She thought about going back into the mortuary, then decided not to. If they could manage without her for once, why would she willingly put herself through all that heartache and pain?

Instead, she logged on to Declan's computer and went on the internet, noticing he already had several shopping sites open. She browsed them, glad to have something to take her mind off what was happening next door.

Her phone was on silent, but she took it out and checked she hadn't broken it into a million pieces when she'd fallen. Thankfully it was still intact. She rarely used WhatsApp but stared at the green icon before tapping it, to see if she had a message from Bronte. She had been added to a group called *Survivors Anonymous*. She hesitated for a moment, knowing that her life was about to change when she joined the chat. She knew she needed to join, to find Lexie's killer, and keep Milly safe, if he was indeed targeting them, but joining had personal consequences for her too. She would no longer be a loner, who could hide her thoughts and feelings about her past... what could she call them? *Incidents* was too blasé: they had been life-changing, even if she wouldn't admit that to anyone. *Attacks* seemed a more appropriate word, but even that didn't feel right. Whatever they were once she joined the group, if she wanted anything from the women who were a part of it, she would have to reciprocate, to share stuff with them, and that was harder for her than anything, because she just didn't talk about it to anyone but Ben and that was the minimum details she could get away with, in case it upset him too much. But she knew she needed to speak to the women urgently, so if talking about herself was the price she had to pay then so be it.

She tapped her finger on the screen and watched as the message from Bronte appeared. Telling her the group were meeting tonight at eight fifteen. Now, it was almost four. She should be good to make it in time, so she typed out a response.

Thx for the invite, see you all later. M x

Then she turned her phone over so she couldn't see if they replied. She might lose herself in the world of WhatsApp. Her priority was to make sure they were safe, had their current addresses so they could provide officers to watch over them, and warn them to be on the lookout for a killer who drove a silver or white car.

TWENTY-SEVEN

Morgan gave up on shopping for Declan and soon phoned Cain. Her head had stopped throbbing, and she could feel her legs again. She wanted to dive back into the case and figure out where all of her clues had led the team.

'Hey, how's it going?'

'I wimped out.'

'You did? That's not like you.'

'Well, I passed out but don't tell anyone, and I'm currently waiting in Declan's office for them to finish.'

Cain paused for a moment. *'Do you want me to come get you?'*

'No, I'm good, I'll hang on, but can you do me a huge favour?'

'Certainly can.'

'I need you to print out all the files on each victim's attack for me. We already have Lexie White's; can you make me a copy? There is Milly Blake, Bronte Potter, Sara Fletcher, Ava Rigg, Evelyn Reynolds, and there's also Macy, but she's on holiday and I swear to God, I will find him before she gets back so there's no chance she is in danger. Then can you put them in a folder? You can leave it on my desk, if you finish before I get back.'

'*Should I be asking why?*'

'No, it's so I can work on it at home. Don't mention it to Ben. I wish I'd brought my laptop with me. I could have been doing something useful, instead of sitting here twiddling my thumbs.'

'*Make the most of it, doesn't happen very often.*'

'Thanks, Cain, can you check the other victims' attackers are still in prison, just to be on the safe side?'

'*Do you want me to trace them all? I don't know where to start?*'

'Go and speak to Tracy in the offender management team, she will be able to tell you which prisons they're currently in, then if you could check with them to make sure everyone is accounted for that would be a big relief, and at least you can tell the boss you've already done it when he asks at some point, because he will ask.'

'*Morgan, I keep saying it, but you should be the one with the stripes on your shoulder and running this spot. No disrespect to Benno because he's a great boss, but you're always one step ahead of them all, and you could run rings around Marc because most of the time I don't know which planet he's on.*'

She laughed. 'No, thank you, I don't want that kind of responsibility just yet. It's bad enough doing our job. Will you let me know once you've confirmed they are all still incarcerated, and if any of them have had any visitors that have never been before? It's worth checking.'

'*I will.*'

She hung up, not sure what to do until her phone beeped with a message from Cain.

Tracy sending list ASAP, will get started.

Smiling to herself she began to do the only thing she could, trawl through Facebook, checking out each woman's profile to see if they had any unusual activity on there or odd comments. Although she did think to herself it was a fruitless task, it was better than doing nothing. She could check if they had any mutual male friends in common.

Morgan was deep into Ava's profile when the door opened.

Ben looked tired; he stepped inside.

'Declan is just cleaning up.'

'Sorry.'

'Don't be, how do you feel now?'

'Okay, you?'

'Weary of this for a start, angry too. I have this simmering rage inside my chest that feels as if it's bubbling away ready to explode. How dare he do this to her. It was brutal, savage, and uncalled for.' He flopped down on the sofa and loosened his tie, then undid his top three buttons.

'You scared me, scared all of us.'

'I didn't know it was going to happen, it just did. I mean there was no warning. I woke up with ringing in my ears, but it didn't happen before.'

Declan walked in. He smelled like a tropical fruit cocktail.

'You smell good.'

He grinned. 'I do, isn't it divine? It's like showering in a bottle of Malibu. How are we all?'

They both shrugged their shoulders at the same time.

He nodded. 'I know, it's terrible. Did you give Morgan a rundown?'

'Not yet.'

'I'll do it then. I've established that Lexie's cause of death was caused by major blood loss due to the severity of the injuries she received. The weapon had to have been something like a machete, with a blade size of between sixteen to eighteen inches. I would say it had been professionally sharpened too, because it sliced through her skin like butter.' He glanced at Morgan's face. 'Too much, sorry, I know.'

'Where do you get a machete?'

'The internet, you can buy anything and there are lots of online shops selling them for hunting, gardening use, and survivalists buy them in case they need to chop down trees and build a shelter in the middle of an apocalypse.'

He sat down at the desk and typed in *machete UK*; nine different sites loaded immediately. 'Let's not forget good old Amazon either; you could have one posted through your letter box less than twenty-four hours after buying one. The good news is that if you locate the weapon, and we haven't yet, either at the park or near the house, I'm positive I can match it up to the wounds.'

'Sounds like it should be easy, find the machete-wielding killer before he attacks again. This reminds me of something.'

Declan nodded. '*Friday the 13th* and Jason Voorhees. I'm pretty sure he used a machete, or it looked like one in the posters.'

Morgan felt something inside of her brain snap, as if an elastic band had been twanged inside of it. '*Friday the 13th*, is this some kind of sick joke? Does he think that it's funny, did he do it on purpose, chose a horror movie monster to copy and kill Lexie? Oh God, do you think he wore a mask when he attacked her?' Morgan stopped, realisation dawning. She remembered that movie. What the women were called. 'Oh my God that's what Milly Blake referred to them as. They're all final girls, every single one of them just like in the movies.'

Ben furrowed his brow. 'I don't know, Morgan, unless we get some footage of the actual attack we're going to struggle to say if he wore a mask.'

'Sick bastard, what if he did though? Can you imagine how scared Lexie must have been? Did she scream? Have any of the neighbours reported hearing a woman screaming around the time of her attack?'

'I don't think so, apart from the one kid who lives a couple of doors up.'

Declan leaned forward. 'Final girls? There's more?'

Morgan shook her head; she couldn't process her thoughts coherently enough to answer him.

Declan continued. 'I think he took Lexie by surprise and delivered the fatal blow to her neck area first. Rendering her unable to scream or call out for help, she would have bled out in a matter of minutes, yet he still continued to stab her here and here.' He pointed to his abdomen and his left side. 'He wanted to make sure that she bled to death and fast. His car must be a real mess inside. If you find it, there is no way he would have managed to get all the blood out of it, no matter how many car washes he's taken it to, and we all know how good they are at cleaning cars.'

Morgan felt as if the inside of her brain was swimming through thick treacle it felt so strange. 'We have to warn the girls. What if he's going to kill each of them dressed up as some horror movie monster?'

Ben glanced at Declan, and she saw the look of concern they gave each other; they thought she was freaking out, and she was but she didn't care. She had spent all night thinking about possible suspects. She didn't believe that Natalie White would hurt her daughter this way or Jasper either: there was no motive. Milly's neighbour, Jack, could have followed her in his Picasso and, in her panic, she may have got the colour of the car wrong, but she would have known him, and she'd have recognised him, surely.

Then there was Theo, bless him. Poor Theo, who somehow ended up in the middle of their investigations. He knew about the support group, but what did he have to gain? What motive did he have for committing such a heinous act? The last people on her list were the teenage boy and his dad, a couple of doors up from Lexie's house, but the dad had been at work and the boy was online gaming – or so he'd told them. He had been cool and calm when he'd answered the door. How could he have got Milly to the park, though? He wasn't even old enough to drive. Her head was spinning, and she had to squeeze her eyes shut momentarily to try and clear it.

Ben stood up and reached out for her hand to tug her off the chair. 'Come on, Brookes, let's get back, there's lots to do.'

Declan was staring at his computer, and he looked up. 'Good taste, I like it a lot.'

'I ordered a couple of tops and trousers for you, plus a pair of jeans and a pair of Dr. Martens because all the cool kids wear them.' She winked at him, and he laughed.

'When you get fed up with chasing the bogeyman, you could set yourself up as a personal shopper for guys who haven't got a clue.'

'Declan, you don't need my help. You dress impeccably, well except for that faded Springsteen T-shirt that needs to go in the bin.'

'Ouch, I love that tee.'

She shrugged. 'I suppose you can't be perfect.'

They left him laughing to himself.

Out in the corridor Ben took hold of her hand. 'Am I supposed to even know what that was about?'

She shook her head. 'Nah, he wanted some clothes for a hot date. Seriously, Ben, what if I'm right, what if the killer is going to go after the rest of the women, dressed as Freddy Krueger, *Scream*, Michael Myers, even bloody Pennywise, because he's taken his inspiration from these horror movies.'

'I think we're getting way ahead of ourselves. I can't imagine how you're feeling, when I feel so torn up about this, but we have to look at the cold, hard facts. There is nothing to suggest what he is up to now, all we have is that Lexie was viciously attacked by a guy with a machete outside her house. We need to go speak to her mum too; it's time we got a statement from her.'

'Yes, we do. Then I have an appointment I have to make at eight fifteen. Have you got the addresses of the women from the group yet?'

He shook his head. 'A couple of them, but not all, some of the women have moved from the time of the attacks, which I don't blame them for at all. I don't know how you managed to stay in your apartment as long as you did.'

'I'll have them for you by the time I leave the group.' She hadn't moved because she had nowhere to go and not much money to be able to do it with. Ben had been her saviour in more ways than she could ever repay.

'That would be great. Are you up for a quick visit to see Natalie?'

'Yes, I think we should. We need to get her statement and make sure she's safe.' She couldn't miss the meeting, but she felt there was a little time to spare, so she should still be able to see Natalie.

He nodded. 'You are as always absolutely right.'

Neither of them spoke all the way to the beautiful house where Natalie used to live before she left her husband, and where she was currently stopping until she could face going back home.

TWENTY-EIGHT

His entire shift he kept screwing things up because his mind wasn't on the job like it should be, and he knew why. All he could think about was the girl; the look on her face had been priceless. It was as if she'd known that it would end like this. There had been the wide-eyed look of fear but also a look of resignation that had drawn him in deep.

'Jesus Christ, you dipstick, will you pay attention? That's twice you've almost scalded me.'

He jerked his hand back from the huge vat and glared at Miranda. 'Sorry.'

'What the hell is wrong with you today?' she shouted over the racket of the machinery. 'You should see if you can clock off, you're not much good to anyone and I don't want to die of third-degree burns. It's a painful way to go.'

He stared at her but gave her a half smile as if he was apologising, which he wasn't. He'd have quite liked to see her skin peeling from her body, but she had given him an idea. He knew the cops would be on the lookout for him, they would be on high alert, which they bloody well should be. He knew what he did was bad, he knew that, but he didn't care. It had been the most thrilling thing, apart from sex with the slut in the office who wore tiny crop tops and shorts so short you could see the outline of her arse. He'd had her in the stationery cupboard at the Christmas party. It had been hot, sweaty, and fast – but it had been awesome. She was wild, she had also been drunk and had never even acknowledged him the next day; he didn't think she remembered their intimacy at all. She probably took half of the office staff in there that night. He wouldn't complain about it though because it had been good, and he lived in hope that one day she might feel horny enough to drag him back in there for a second time.

He knew they met, had some kind of support group, his final girls, which was how he fondly called them. He had hung around that church often enough; he quite liked the peace and serenity it offered him and the opportunity to see them coming and going. He knew he could have done something much sooner, but he'd wanted it to be dramatic, impactful, and scare the shit out of the girls. Sending them in a spiralling panic that they might stop paying attention to what they were doing and let things slip. He'd watched them long enough to know that they were good, cautiously good at taking care of themselves and each other.

Now he had an idea, thanks to Miranda. It could either pay off spectacularly or be a complete disaster, but he was willing to take that chance.

He heard his name being called by Gary, his supervisor, and he sighed; he was as much of a dick as Miranda.

If he managed to finish what he started, he could carry on forever and even begin to rid the world of every arsehole he came across. He stepped away from his machine and headed towards the office. Trying to hide how upbeat he was now feeling by trudging slowly towards Gary and his stinking office not much bigger than the stationery cupboard. He went inside, removed his ear defenders and safety glasses, and stared at Gary whose trousers were far too tight, and his shirt buttons were straining so much against the polyester, cotton blend of the Tesco special he was at risk of losing an eyeball if one of those bad boys pinged off. Maybe he should keep the glasses on.

'Something's off with you today. Miranda has a face like a slapped arse, and I've heard her screaming at you twice. Want to tell me why you're not feeling it?'

He shrugged. 'Feel a bit rough, Gary, got a pounding headache.'

'Self-inflicted? Were you drinking last night when you knew you had a full shift?'

He wanted to step forward and punch him right between the eyes. 'You know I don't drink when I'm on shift. I have a headache that's all.'

'Tried paracetamol?'

He nodded.

'Well, I'd rather you went home than fucked up my shift by causing an accident. You look like shit, get some sleep and be back here tomorrow with a clear head.'

'What about Miranda?'

'What about her? She can work on her own; it's not like she needs you to hold her hand, is it?'

'Suppose not, thanks.'

He turned and walked out Gary's stinking office with a grin on his face, which he had to remedy in case anyone saw him. He could go home and figure out the best way to put his next plan into action. He needed some petrol cans; he didn't have any. Where was he going to get those? He supposed a garage would be best. If he bought a couple, he could fill them up and *boom*. All he had to do was wait around long enough to get the chance to use them. It wouldn't be as up close and personal as last night, but it would give him the same kind of thrill, which was good enough.

TWENTY-NINE

Lexie's dad, Jasper, opened the door and he looked as different as Natalie had the first time Morgan set eyes on her yesterday. He had lost weight, but his face looked drawn, and he looked as if he was ill more than on some kind of health kick. The separation and divorce had clearly taken its toll on both Natalie and Jasper, and now they were grieving the loss of their only child, and it was devastating to see the pure grief that was so clearly etched into his face. Morgan had never particularly liked the guy standing in front of her looking so broken, but she felt sorry for him.

'Detectives.'

He held up a hand. 'I know who you are, I remember you. Come in.'

Morgan stepped inside first, Ben behind her. Classical music drifted down the hall; it was muted, and it had a sombre tone to it. Morgan didn't really know anything about the classics. Sylvia, her adoptive mother, used to listen to Classic FM in the run up to Christmas, and she'd play it in the kitchen on the ancient Roberts radio as she made the Christmas dinner each year, up until the year she decided to end it all. A wave of sadness rushed over her, for the loss of such a kind, caring woman, for Lexie, for every single victim she'd dealt with and their families. She heard Ben talking and realised she'd zoned out, lost in her own world of grief.

'How are you both?' he said.

'How would you like me to answer that, truthfully or give you some bullshit story that we're coping and are quite happy living without our daughter in our life as if she never existed?'

Ben squirmed, and Morgan gave Jasper a sad, half smile.

'We can't imagine how painful this must be for you both, and we are very sorry for your loss. Lexie was so beautiful and full of life, this is just awful.'

Jasper was watching Morgan's face, scrutinising her every expression, but she didn't blame him. She would be the same. He wanted to know if her condolences were genuine, and they were.

'Thank you, she is.' He paused for a moment, turned away from them and wiped his eyes before turning around. 'She was the most beautiful and precious thing in my life. I miss her, I can't cope with the hate I feel inside of myself that I wasn't there to protect her when she needed me.'

'That's to be expected, but you didn't know what was going to happen, and I'm pretty sure Lexie wouldn't have let you pick her up and drop her off every single time she left the house.'

He let out a gruff, barking laugh. 'No, she wouldn't. The last couple of months, but before she left with Natalie, she would quite happily have let me drive her to the end of the driveway. So you see, I feel this terrible guilt...' He sniffed and paused. 'Because... quite frankly, if I hadn't been screwing around and Natalie hadn't left me then there is a real chance that Lexie would still be alive... I'd have still been chauffeuring her around.'

'Morgan, have you any news?'

Natalie appeared at the doorway to the kitchen down the

hall, and Morgan wondered at how she had aged so much in the space of twenty-four hours; she had shrunk in on herself and looked tiny.

'I'm afraid not at this moment, we have leads that we're following up on, but it all takes time.'

Jasper composed himself quickly and glared at her. 'Leads, you don't have a name or anything that's useful? Why is the monster not behind bars?'

Caroline appeared from behind Natalie and waved them in. 'Come on, guys, let's sit down and talk about this. They know how much you're both hurting, and they want to help it go away as much as is possible.'

Jasper looked at her and his shoulders stooped, his jaw unclenched a little and he nodded. 'Sorry, I'm just so angry with the world right now.'

Ben reached out and squeezed his shoulder. 'And so you should be, there is nothing that can stop the pain you're both going through, but we are working hard to find the person who did this to Lexie.'

They both nodded. Caroline already had the coffee machine on, and the pot was brewing, the smell so good Morgan realised she was desperate for caffeine. It would perk her up and make her brain begin to function again. They all sat at the stools along the huge marble breakfast bar, and Caroline poured their drinks. She put the milk and sugar on the table, so they could help themselves. Ben took his black so did Jasper, the rest of them added milk, and Natalie two heaped spoonfuls of sugar.

Morgan didn't want to tell them this, but they had a right to know.

'We've just come from Lexie's post-mortem.'

Natalie let out a huge sob, burying her face into her hands. Jasper nodded. 'What do you have to report?'

Morgan paused, hoping Ben would take over, and he took the hint.

'Lexie died of massive blood loss due to the catastrophic wound to her neck and side; she bled out relatively quickly.'

'*Relatively*, how long was my baby girl in pain and bleeding to death?'

Ben looked him in the eye. 'Between two to four minutes.'

Natalie groaned, and Morgan was surprised when Jasper reached out to take hold of her hand. The words hung in the air so heavy she imagined she could see them dangling and wanted to reach out with a finger to push them away.

'Natalie, do you know about the support group that Lexie went to?'

She lifted her head. 'Yes.'

'Were you asked if you wanted to attend?'

She nodded.

'Was there a reason you didn't? You went through a terrible time. Jackie Thorpe tried to suffocate you as well as Lexie.'

'I didn't want Lexie to feel as if she couldn't talk about it in front of me without upsetting me. I wanted her to have some freedom and the chance to have friends who knew how she was feeling. I wouldn't want my mum attending something like that with me.'

'What about you though, do you not feel as if you could do with the support?' Morgan was genuinely curious to know how she felt about what had happened to her.

'I'm not really one to dwell on the matter. I pushed it to the back of my head and was just grateful that you turned up when you did to save us both. If I thought about it all the time, I'd end up a nervous wreck. You can't let them win like that, can you? We survived so we owe it to ourselves to carry on the best we can and not let the bastards win, or they would be gloating forever in prison if it got too much and we topped ourselves.'

'Did you ever feel like that?'

Jasper glared at her. 'What the hell has that got to do with Lexie?'

She didn't answer, and Ben stepped in. 'Natalie, did you see a silver or white Picasso type car hanging around near your house the last few days?'

She shook her head. 'It's a busy street, there are always cars coming and going. You wouldn't believe how many of those people live off takeaways; there are always Uber Eats cars and bicycles coming and going. Why? Did he drive a Picasso?'

'We believe so, and we also know that Milly Blake saw it outside her house, which is why she came to yours. It scared her enough that she didn't want to go home.'

Natalie stared into Morgan's eyes. 'Milly brought him to my home?' The anger was radiating off Natalie in waves. 'Stupid cow, why didn't she go somewhere else? If she hadn't come to my house, Lexie wouldn't be dead, that's so unfair. She should be the one in that fucking mortuary not my Lexie.'

Natalie was standing up now; her fingers were curled into two tight fists. She picked up her mug and threw it at the sink, where it exploded into a thousand pieces, spraying hot coffee and pottery everywhere. Then she ran out of the room. Jasper stared after her, but it was Caroline who stood up.

'I'll go see if she's okay.'

Morgan looked at Jasper. 'I'm sorry, I don't think Milly would have gone there if she'd known he'd followed her. But it's also possible they were both being targeted. We think everyone attending the support group should be taking extra precautions.'

'It's all too much.'

'We'll leave you to it. If you have any questions, Caroline will get in touch with us.' Ben was standing up; he'd clearly had enough of being the bearer of terrible news.

As they walked towards the door she turned to Jasper. 'Did you know about the group? Did Lexie talk about it?'

The laugh that left his lips was more of a bark. 'Lexie didn't talk to me about anything these last couple of months; she hated me for cheating on Natalie, and I don't blame her. I have to live with the knowledge that my daughter was murdered not knowing how much I loved her and how sorry I was that I messed everyone's lives up.'

He buried his head in his arms, and Ben beckoned for Morgan to follow him. She wanted to offer Jasper some words of comfort, but what could she say to ease the guilt and pain he was feeling?

Instead they let themselves out, quietly closing the front door behind them.

THIRTY

'That was a decent cup of coffee,' Ben stated. 'Pity we didn't get to finish them.'

She looked at him, but still smiled. 'Yes, that could have gone a lot better than it did.'

'Don't blame yourself, is there any easy way to explain to someone's parents how their child was brutally murdered?'

'Absolutely not. Can you drop me off at the church hall, please? I want to get there early and hang around a bit to make sure no one is watching.'

'I'd rather you didn't. I'm not comfortable with you going there.'

'Well, it's not really a question of what you're comfortable with, it's a matter of necessity.'

'I'm going to have officers watching.'

'No, you are not. If you do that, you're going to scare the women who attend and draw so much attention to the place you might as well get a neon sign with a big red arrow pointing to the building.'

'Can I watch then? I can park up further up the street or in the car park of the retirement home opposite.'

'Or you could go see Theo and ask him if he knows anything about a Picasso hanging around. See what he knows about the group while I talk to them, if he knows what they are meeting for and their routines. Then you'll be close by.'

'Do you think he's a suspect?'

She let out a loud sigh. 'I feel bad, but don't you think we need to consider him and get an alibi at least? He knows that Bronte wanted to use the hall and gave her a key so she could come and go as she pleased, which kind of made me think that he has some kind of inkling of what they get up to. He could easily have looked her up on the internet, and who knows who he could have talked to about them.'

'I'm not sure we want to be doing this, but I'll ask him if he knows anything, if it means I can be close by while you're there.'

He drove onto the main street.

'Drop me here, by the florists, and I'll walk down.'

'Morgan.'

'Please, Ben, you can park up and watch to make sure I get in there okay, then go park in the nursing home and call on Theo. Whatever you do, promise me you won't come into the hall unless you are invited in. I don't want to betray their trust before I've even spoken to them.'

'When did you get so bossy?' he said, jokingly, and reached out and stroked her cheek. 'Got your CS in your pocket, radio and phone?' She nodded. 'Good, any funny business and you call for backup. I will come in there if I think there is a chance you are in danger regardless of whether you want me to or not.'

She leaned over and brushed her lips against his cheek. She didn't reply but she felt better knowing he was going to be close by.

She walked down the street not turning around once to look back at him. It was pretty quiet, the church grounds were floodlit, which was a relief. The hall was at the rear of the church, and it was all in darkness. She flicked her wrist to check the time on her watch and jumped when a voice whispered, 'Morgan, it's you, it's really you?'

She turned to see Ava, dressed from head to toe in black. 'Hi, Ava, yes it's me.'

'Follow me, it's a bit eerie tonight, isn't it? and it feels a bit strange knowing that Lexie isn't ever going to be coming here again.' Her voice broke and she stifled a sob.

Morgan followed the teenage girl around to a small door, attached to another room at the rear of the church hall, where a muted yellow light shone through the windows. Ava did a double tap in quick succession, and the door opened just wide enough for a pair of eyes to peer through.

'Ava, Morgan, come in.'

Bronte opened the door wide enough for them to step inside then slammed it shut again, turning the key in the lock. Morgan felt as if she'd just been admitted into a top security prison, not a church hall storeroom. The room smelled of old books and coffee; she saw the stacks of old hymn and prayer books, and she smiled. There were few things in life that made her truly happy, and books and coffee were at the top of that list. She smiled at Milly, Sara was also there, and she felt terrible that she was about to turn their worlds upside down all over again. Morgan looked at the two empty seats in the semi-circle, not wanting to take Lexie's but Bronte smiled at her.

'Please, we never sit in the same chair each week, we swap around. It's kind of like a thing, we never meet at the same time, but we do always leave together and make sure that we all get into our cars safely.'

Morgan returned the smile, and she sat on the chair closest to Ava. 'Thank you.' She paused. 'I'm so sorry about Lexie.' The women all looked to the ground. 'I'm devastated, so I can't imagine how you're all feeling. You must be so angry and scared. I'll let you ask questions, and I will answer as frankly as I can. This is an ongoing police investigation, so there may be answers that I can't give to you, but only so I don't jeopardise the investigation in any way. I'm not being difficult.'

Sara nodded. 'Hi, it's great to see you again, Morgan. How are you coping with everything?'

Morgan smiled at her. 'This case or life in general?' She could feel the heat begin to rise up her chest as the skin underneath her roll-neck top began to itch and burn. This was the worst question anyone could have asked her, because it was too personal, and she hated talking to anyone except Ben about this kind of stuff. But it was just like Sara to think of other people.

'Both? It must be so hard doing your job after everything you've been through, yet you still go to work and never know what the day will bring. How do you concentrate enough on the cases you have to work?'

Bronte was staring at Sara. 'That's a bit personal for a first question, Sara.'

Sara turned to her. 'Might as well get it out of the way then. I'm fascinated how Morgan can still carry on despite the trauma she's endured. I'm a fucking nervous wreck going anywhere on my own, even out to my car. I have to talk myself into it, yet she's still out there, chasing sick bastards.'

'Thank God she is,' said Ava. 'Thank you, we don't know how you do it, but we are truly grateful.'

Everyone was staring at her, their eyes full of unshed tears, full of grief and anger about Lexie.

Morgan could feel the crippling anxiety turning her face pinker than the neon trainers Ava was wearing. She couldn't believe they didn't blame her for not saving Lexie. She glanced down at their feet and realised they were all wearing trainers; she was the odd one out.

'I, erm, honestly, it's hard but on some level I know that someone has to do it, and it helps me to feel in control knowing that I'm involved, if that makes any sense. Also, because I'm so busy at work most of the time I don't have a lot of time to dwell on the different...' She paused, what did she call them? 'Attacks. I think a lot of them were associated with the investigations, so I try not to take it too personally. If it had been someone else, it would be the same.'

'But would it or do you think you're one of the few unlucky ones? Do you know what percentage of people survive an attack by a serial killer? Because that's what they have been, what we've all been through.'

Ava shook her head. 'Sara.'

'I'm curious, that's all.'

Ava continued. 'Well, I'm scared about what happened to Lexie. She's my best friend and I feel terrible about what happened. That I wasn't there. How bad was it for her? Because Milly said there was so much blood.'

Morgan glanced at Milly, who had the courtesy to look embarrassed. She had been asked not to come to the group while she was being guarded, but she'd insisted, and it looked as if she'd been talking to them after being asked not to. Milly was staring down at Morgan's feet.

'There was a lot of blood, and yes, it was a very brutal attack,' she said, cringing. 'But it was fast and, thankfully, Lexie would have bled out quickly. She wasn't in pain for long.'

Ava began to cry, and Sara nodded. 'How did he make her bleed out so fast? Did he cut her throat?'

Bronte looked as if she wanted to be anywhere but here. She was sitting on her hands and visibly squirming.

'She sustained a deep wound to her neck area as well as two others.'

'Outside her own fucking front door. What kind of person could do that to a kid?' Sara's hands were balled into fists. 'I wish I could get my hands on them.'

'So do I,' whispered Morgan. She gave them a minute to

gather themselves before continuing. 'Milly told me she saw a guy in a silver car watching her house. Have any of you noticed the same?'

They all shook their heads.

'It's vitally important that you are on high alert, and if you notice anything strange you call us. Keep an eye out for what we think is a light-coloured Picasso, it could be silver or white, in the area of your houses or places of work. The driver has a shaved head. Call the police on 999, don't mess around or try to approach him. If you could get the VRN that would be brilliant, but get inside a safe place, lock the doors and wait for the police to arrive.'

Ava looked at her. 'VRN?'

'Sorry. It's the vehicle registration number. The number plate.'

She nodded.

Sara smiled at Morgan. 'I don't know about you, but it seems as if we are permanently on high alert. I don't understand how Lexie didn't notice him or the car, she was just as freaked out as the rest of us by what happened to her.'

'We haven't found her phone yet, but it's possible because she was about to enter her house that she may have been distracted or just felt that she was safe.'

'Which is the real kicker. She was inches away from safety, from going inside of her front door, yet she was still murdered right outside of it and her body left...' Sara's voice finally cracked, and she began to cry, whispering, 'I can't believe it.'

Morgan nodded. 'It's sick and it's beyond cruel. I'm worried and my team agree with me that because Milly had noticed the silver car too that he may have been watching you all. That he knows about this group.'

Ava was glaring at Milly. 'What if the person only wanted to kill you, Milly, and you led them straight to Lexie? It should be you who is dead not her.'

Milly began to sob as Bronte's mouth fell open and she shook her head. 'Ava, you can't say that.'

'Why not, if he couldn't get her and she went to Lexie's house, it's her fault.'

Bronte gasped. 'But we're so careful, we don't talk about it to anyone, it's just us. How could they know about the group?'

'If he's been following you then he could easily have followed you here and watched as you all walked in. I'm really sorry to tell you this, but I think for your own safety it might be better not to meet in person until we catch him.'

Sara glared at Morgan. 'What, and show him that we're scared and he's winning?'

'It's not a case of showing your fear; it's a case of putting your life at a higher value than what he believes it is and by not making yourselves an easy target. I would like to get all your current addresses and if it's okay with each of you, have officers stationed outside, it would be safer for you all if you didn't leave the house.'

Bronte nodded. 'Won't that make it even more obvious if there's police outside?'

'I hate to tell you this, but there is already a good chance he knows where you all live. If he's been watching Milly and Lexie – and you can't say that he hasn't – I'm working as hard as I can, the whole team is working flat out to catch this guy before he tries to do it again.'

All of them sat in silence, staring at her, and she felt bad, but Morgan knew she would want to know, if she was in their shoes, if there was a chance she was being stalked.

No one noticed the fine tendrils of smoke that had begun to seep under the door to the church hall; they were all too consumed in their own worlds of fear.

THIRTY-ONE

Father Theo had grinned with pleasure as he'd realised it was Ben who was knocking at his door so late.

'Ben, my friend, it's so good to see you even if it is late.'

Ben glanced at his watch. 'Sorry, Theo, I'm waiting for Morgan and thought I'd come pay you a visit. Are you busy?'

He laughed. 'Not busy enough that the tail end of *East-Enders* comes before you, come inside. Actually, I'm relieved it's you and not some weary parishioner with a strange request.'

'How often do you get strange requests?'

'Too bloody often.' He laughed. 'Can I get you a coffee or are you off duty and want something stronger?'

'I would love a triple vodka over ice, but I'm on duty and still will be for the foreseeable.'

'I heard about the murder, poor, poor girl. It's so sad, what is the world coming to? I keep saying it, but this quaint, small town surrounded by the beauty of the Lakeland fells and mountains has more darkness to it than a busy inner city.'

Ben was so weary he almost fell down onto the chair. 'It does, it never used to be this way. There were murders occasionally that were mainly domestic or drunken arguments gone wrong, but this is something on a whole different level.'

'Has anyone checked if there's a group of devil worshippers out in the woods lately?'

Ben glanced at Theo to see if he was being sarcastic, but his expression was serious.

'For real?'

He shrugged. 'It's crossed my mind that there could be someone or a group of people that might have one time messed around summoning dark forces to the area, which could explain why there is so much violent crime now.'

He passed a mug of freshly brewed coffee to Ben, who sipped it and let out a long sigh. 'Thanks, I needed this. I'm not sure about the whole devil worshipping thing though. I've never had reports of anything like that going on.'

'It's just a theory, maybe Rydal Falls is on a fault line. There is a lot of stuff that happens along fault lines too, paranormal activity, killings.'

'Theo, have you been binge-watching Discovery Plus and all the paranormal shows on there?'

He threw back his head and roared with laughter. 'Guilty as charged, my friend, how did you know? It was Morgan who told me about it, so you can blame your good woman for filling my head with it.'

'Phew, I thought you had been privy to information that Satan had been summoned, which to be fair would kind of explain how crazy this place has been the last few years. I'm not sure I'd be the right person to pick a fight with him though, I'd have to recruit you for that.'

Theo sat opposite Ben. 'I guess that would be fair, it's kind of part of my job description though, thankfully, I've never had to face that battle yet. Where is Morgan, by the way? It's late; is she at the nursing home visiting Evelyn? She's not been too well; I saw her this afternoon and she looked so frail.'

Ben didn't want to lie to Theo, but he wasn't sure how much he knew about the support group. 'No, she's doing a talk at the church hall. That's so sad about Evelyn, I'll let her know, she will want to go and see her. She really likes Evelyn; they bonded so well after what they went through when her grandson tried to kill them both.'

'A talk this late, there's nobody at the church hall. Do you mean the little group that meets in the storeroom?'

'You know about the group?'

He nodded. 'I do, such a lovely bunch of women who have had a terrible time. I leave them to it, gave Bronte a key so they could come and go as they pleased. I offered them the hall, but she wanted something more low-key, not as noticeable. I almost offered them my front room; I never use it and it's a lot warmer, but I didn't want her to think I'd be here, hanging around listening to what they were talking about. I didn't realise Morgan attended too, that's probably a very good thing for her. It can't be good keeping all that bad stuff bottled up inside.'

Ben lifted the mug to his lips and sipped at the hot drink to give himself a little time. He'd never thought too much about Morgan not talking about the stuff that had happened to her, and now he felt dreadful; she was so good at locking it away and pretending she was fine, but what if she wasn't and, deep down, she was crying out for someone to listen to her? He set the mug down on the table.

'She's there on work-related stuff. She wouldn't go to something like that; she doesn't talk about anything much.'

'I can imagine she doesn't. It's a shame though, maybe you could suggest it to her, or she could always come talk to me. They say confession is good for the soul, not that Morgan needs to confess anything, but I'm here anytime if she ever feels she needs to talk. Why is she there then?'

Ben knew that Theo was dating Declan. And Declan would likely mention he'd performed Lexie's post-mortem. 'We're worried about the women in the group; there was a murder last night.'

'Horrific.'

'Exactly.'

Theo looked devastated, and Ben felt bad. How had he become so hardened to the terrible, brutal crimes he dealt with? For him, although it made his blood boil with the injustice of it all, once he'd seen the body, he could detach himself from them as a person so he could concentrate, and he sometimes forgot just how traumatic the things he dealt with were to anyone else.

'Have you ever noticed a silver or white Picasso hanging around this area, male driver, shaved or bald head?'

Theo closed his eyes momentarily, then shook his head. 'I can't say that I have because I don't drive. I don't really pay much attention to cars unless they are ridiculously expensive and then I might give them a second glance. Why? Do you think whoever did this has been hanging around watching the women?'

He shrugged. 'I can't say for sure, but it's a possibility. Did you ever get CCTV at the church?'

'We're waiting for it to be installed; the powers that be agreed after everything that has happened here that it might be a great time to invest in some. Little did I know it would take forever to get the funding and permission. I might just go out and bloody buy my own cameras. Declan could help me install them; in fact I'm going to do that tomorrow. I'm not having those women put at risk by anyone. I wish I'd thought of this sooner. I'm sorry, Ben, it's like bolting the stable door after the horse escaped.'

'It's not your fault, you weren't to know but that's a good idea. It wouldn't hurt for you to get a camera above your front door either.'

'Do you think? Show me where you think it would be discreet enough not to get me in trouble.'

They both walked to the front door of the vicarage, which Theo opened. Ben wrinkled his nose. 'Can you smell burning?'

Theo nodded, then shouted, 'The church hall is on fire.'

Fear froze Ben to the spot for a moment and then he was running across the grass towards the hall, calling for the fire service and backup to St Martha's. His heart was in his mouth as he watched the orange flames that licked against the curtains inside the hall. And soon they were a burning mass of flames. The door was well ablaze; there was no way anyone could get out that way.

Theo was running to the side of the building where the door to the storeroom was. Ben could hear the screams coming from inside, and he had never felt terror like it for Morgan and the women she was with. He watched as Theo lifted his foot and kicked at a large plank of wood that had been jammed under the door handle then grabbed it, thrusting it open as the women burst through, crying and screaming.

Ben scanned each woman until he saw Morgan come out last. She was coughing but she was okay. She wasn't hurt. He turned around, the sensation he was being watched so strong the hairs on the back of his neck had prickled, and then he took off running towards the nursing home car park.

He was scanning the street for a Picasso, but couldn't see one. They may have had the same idea and parked over at the nursing home. He expected to get run over by a car speeding away, but there weren't many cars parked and none of them had a driver inside.

The grounds of the home were vast, so they could be on foot and hiding anywhere, and he knew that he was because he would have wanted to watch this show; he would have wanted to hear the screams of the women he'd trapped inside as they burned to death.

Ben could feel rage build inside him. He was so angry he was shaking; he didn't know what he'd do if he got hold of whoever had done this, but he knew it would make him feel a whole lot better. Lifting the radio to his lips he whispered, 'Control, I need a dog to my location now; I don't care if there isn't one on duty get me one ASAP. We have a suspected killer still in the area.' He slowly turned in a circle, scanning the bushes and trees to see if there was any indication a person was hiding. Planting his feet wide apart and crossing his arms, he could wait as long as it took; they would move at some point, and he would be waiting.

THIRTY-TWO

Morgan had been the first to smell the acrid smoke as it had begun to seep under the door. She had called the control room for the fire service ASAP and officers to attend. Probably around the same time as Ben first noticed the flames and began to run towards the church hall. For a moment she wondered how horrific it would be if they'd all succumbed to smoke inhalation, but after she had touched the interior door handle with the palm of her hand and felt her skin sear, she had opted to block the gap under the door with handfuls of books. They would not die here, not like this.

Even with Milly and Ava shoving against it, Bronte couldn't push open the exterior door; it was jammed. The other women had stood crying and shaking, not much use to her, except for Sara who had helped stack the books. Then they heard muffled voices from outside and the door was thrown open, and Morgan had seen Theo's face and felt a sigh of relief it hadn't been a machete-wielding killer, waiting for them, to chop off their heads one by one. Once she knew they were outside she followed them out, just as the flames began to burn through the small adjoining door.

She'd caught a glimpse of Ben then he'd run off. Turning to Theo she asked, 'Can you take them inside your house until the police come? I need to help Ben.'

He'd nodded then gathered the women around and herded them in the direction of the rectory, while staring after Ben. He'd called after her, 'Morgan, let me go. You stay here.' But she'd ignored his request. Theo was a good man, a gentle soul, and she wasn't about to let him chase a killer who might hurt him. She wouldn't let anything happen to him because she liked him and because she loved Declan.

The skin on the palm of her hand had blistered and the pain made her eyes water, but she kept on running; she had to find Ben. As she flew through the gates, she saw him standing at the side of the old mansion with his arms crossed, staring into the grounds. Sirens were getting nearer, and she felt glad that she had backup.

He didn't turn to her but whispered, 'I think he's hiding out here somewhere. He didn't leave because he'd want to watch you all burn, and now, I think he's probably a little scared that it's all gone horribly wrong, thank God. Are you okay, is everyone else?'

'Shocked and upset, but we're all good.'

He nodded, not turning his attention away from the huge expanse of grounds that lay in front of them. Two vans drove into the car park, lights blazing, sirens blaring, and the front door of the nursing home opened. Two nurses were standing watching the show with their hands on their hips. One of them called out, 'What's going on?'

'I need you to get back inside and keep the doors locked. There's a violent fugitive on the loose,' Ben yelled back.

The door slammed shut, and Morgan felt better hearing the key turn in the lock. The officers joined them, but Ben waved them all back.

'We need a dog to search the area, I can't risk you scaring

him off or him staying put for the rest of the night; he may well be up a tree hiding. Spread out along this path though, and keep your eyes peeled.'

'Boss, should we go get a couple of dragon lights out of the vans?'

'Not yet, I want the dog to do its thing first. As soon as it gets here then you can light up the area like a flaming disco. Morgan, can you go back to Theo's? I don't want you out here at any cost.'

She was torn; she wanted to be out here searching, but she also wanted to make sure the rest of the women were okay. The palm of her hand was painful, and she should really run it under some cold water, so without arguing she turned to walk back and heard Ben say, 'Smithy, walk Morgan to the vicarage and stay with her.'

She wasn't going to argue because there was no point, and the other women needed protection, although what good Smithy was against a homicidal killer was anyone's guess.

He caught up with her and whispered, 'This is some mad shit, were you almost burned alive? It's like some kind of witch hunt.'

She turned to look at him, they'd already had someone hunting down modern day witches and now this, although she didn't think it was anything to do with witches. What she thought was that the killer had taken an opportunity to try and kill as many of the women in the group at the same time as possible. Had he known she'd turn up? Was she on his list? She had so many questions.

The front door was locked so she walked around to the back door, letting herself in through his broken side gate. She could see Theo in the kitchen passing around mugs. There was already a huge teapot on the table, and she smiled. He was such a good man; a kind man. She knocked on the window, and he started a little, but then smiled at her and threw open the door almost dragging her inside.

'Am I glad to see you, that was close.'

She glanced back towards the church where the fire service had put out the blaze and were damping down the building. He pulled her in and hugged her. She wrapped her arms around him and clung on to him fiercely; it was the equivalent of a hug from God, and she needed all the help she could get. When he finally let go he grabbed her hand, and she yelped, snatching it away. Picking it up he turned it over. 'That's a nasty burn, Morgan, let me run it under the tap and dress it for you.' She nodded, relieved he hadn't mentioned a trip to A&E.

Bronte looked shell-shocked; the others had tear tracks through the soot on their faces but were all okay, no burns, nothing major physically. Mentally, how do you recover from knowing someone is purposely trying to kill you? It was Sara who spoke first.

'What the hell is going on? Why would some sick bastard try and burn us all to death?'

The cold water felt good against the blistered skin on her palm. 'I wish I could answer that, but I can't.'

'Well, what are we going to do? He tried to kill us all, and I'm scared enough of my own shadow as it is; I don't know if I can go home now. He could be waiting for each of us to kill us.' There was a quiver in Ava's voice that hadn't been there before.

'We will take you to somewhere safe until we catch him, but no more going out when you're there. You have to stay there until we have him in custody. I will have armed officers front and back at all times.'

'Is that supposed to make us feel better?' Sara laughed.

Theo was trying to blot Morgan's hand dry, and she winced as he pressed a little too hard, but in a way the pain was good; it cleared her mind and made her focus.

'Look, I'm sorry you are going through this, and I'm devastated about Lexie, but I don't know the answers to everything and I'm just as worried about it as you are.'

'Yeah, but you're a copper. You have stuff to protect yourself with and lots of friends to look after you. It's not as hard for you, as it is for us.'

Bronte snapped out of the trance she had been in, turning on Sara. 'Stop it, who gave you the right to be such a bitch? Morgan has been through more than any of us and she's trying to help. We're all terrified, but it's not fair to take it out on her. None of this is her fault, if it wasn't for Morgan, we'd probably all be dead anyway so have a bit of respect.'

Morgan smiled at Bronte; she liked this tough version of her. 'Thank you, Bronte, I'm scared for you all too, and I'm scared for myself, but there are lots of officers out there searching for him. We will find him, I promise you.'

Milly crossed her fingers in the air. 'I hope so. Are you coming to the safe house with us, Morgan? I'd feel better knowing you were also stopping there.'

'I can't, Milly, I have to work this investigation and I can't do it from the safe house. I need to find him fast and I won't have access to the information from there.'

'But aren't you scared he'll get you? If he can't get to us then he's going to come after you probably. I mean he might not but there's a good chance he will.'

She closed her eyes momentarily; she could be the decoy. She could force him to come after her and she would be ready and waiting for him. Ben would never agree to it in a million years, but she could make this work if she figured out what it was he wanted and how he was going to get it. He might think he's clever, but he'd just confirmed what they feared might be happening. He went after all the women with the intention of killing or seriously harming them, but what he'd actually done was given them concrete proof of his intentions, which could not be denied in a court of law. He had also just taken away his potential victim pool. She turned to stare out of the kitchen window into the darkness of the night and thought to herself *you might be hiding now, but you'll show yourself soon enough and when you do, I'll be waiting for you.*

THIRTY-THREE

Cassie let Caesar off the long leash. He wasn't quite as good at searching as Brock, but he wasn't far behind, and Brock had injured his leg, so he was technically on the sick while it got better. Plus, there was the added factor that to a stranger Caesar looked scary as hell. Ben liked dogs, but he was a little bit wary of the huge Italian mastiff that Morgan adored. He felt bad; she would have loved to have given him a cuddle, but the guy had important work to do. Before Cassie had unleashed him, he had patted the top of his head and whispered, 'If you find him, take a chunk out of his leg for Morgan.' The dog had barked once and set off running down the gentle slope towards the wooded area Ben had been watching. Cassie followed behind.

'Do you want officers to follow?'

She shook her head. 'Nope, he's good at detaining suspects. In fact, he's probably better than all of us put together.' She had a huge torch with her, the beam illuminating the trees and bushes. The dog was barking but it was nothing overtly exciting. 'Probably a rabbit, that's his happy bark,' Cassie yelled back at them. Ben wanted to follow her, as he was so nervous letting her go down there alone, but she wasn't in the least bit fazed by the fact that she was tracking a violent killer.

Ben wondered if the guy had scared himself. He obviously hadn't expected Ben to be in the area, so they must have missed each other somehow. It made him furious to think that he could have been in reaching distance of the man he wanted to lock up so badly for what he'd done to Lexie White and now the rest of the women, including Morgan. The dog made its way up to the old mansion and began to sniff around the perimeter of the old slate building then he sat down by the conservatory door. Cassie, out of breath, caught up with him, and Ben headed in their direction.

'What's that mean?' He pointed to the dog.

'I'm afraid it means that he didn't find your guy. This place probably has so many different scents, he won't know if he's coming or going.'

Ben nodded but scanned the windows and doors. 'Do you think he could have gone inside?'

She shrugged. 'I can't say, probably not. Wouldn't the staff or residents have noticed a strange man climbing in through the window?'

Ben patted the dog's head. 'I really wanted you to find him and rip him to pieces, you know.'

Caesar looked him straight in the eyes then bowed his head, and Cassie rubbed his ears.

'Good boy, you did good.' Then she looked at Ben. 'I'm pretty sure he'd have enjoyed that as much as you.'

'Thank you anyway.'

'No, problem. I'm going to have a walk around the area with him, just in case he took a different route. He may not have come this way.'

He nodded. 'Good idea.' He didn't tell her he was almost a hundred per cent positive that the guy had come through here;

instead he went to the front door to talk to the staff and see if they had any unexpected visitors.

He pressed the intercom on the wall adjacent to the door and waited for a voice to answer. When it finally did it was quiet and there were crackles making it hard to hear.

'Who is it and what do you want?'

'Hi, sorry to bother you, my name is Detective Sergeant Ben Matthews. Can I speak to you for a moment?'

'I'm not sure, we had a phone call from someone from the police telling us to keep the building locked down and not to let anyone inside. Can you prove you're a detective?'

He took out his warrant card and held it in front of the video doorbell camera for them to study his picture, then he lifted it so it was next to his face for them to compare.

'Okay, I'll come let you in.'

The line went quiet, and he waited patiently for someone to come open the door. A woman with icy-blue hair opened it and smiled at him. 'Sorry, can I see your badge again?'

He passed it to her and wondered how many US detective TV shows she'd watched. She stared at the photo on the card then scrutinised him. Passing it back she opened the door.

'Sorry, but I've never been so scared. First of all, we saw you run through the gates, then noticed the smoke coming from the church, then the sirens and well, all hell broke loose.'

He smiled at her, stepping inside the huge entrance that smelled of boiled cauliflower and roast beef, which made him hungry despite everything that was happening. 'Are other entrances to the property locked?'

She nodded. 'Yeah. The first thing we do is check all windows and doors when the evening shift come on duty. Good job we did.'

'It is, you aren't worried that anyone could have got inside the building?'

'Nope, it's secure. What's happening?'

'Someone tried to burn down the church hall with a group inside of it. They're very dangerous.'

'Shit, oh sorry.'

He smiled at her. She was so young, too young to be in charge of a building this size and all the residents. 'Are you in charge?'

She laughed. 'God, no. I just answer the call bells, make the tea, and clean up after the residents. The supervisor is late. She had to go to a meeting at her kids' school or something, so she won't be here for another thirty minutes.'

'How many staff are on duty now?'

'Three.'

'Are you sure you don't want officers to come in and check the building?'

'Positive, we've just got the patients settled after their tea. They'll never go to bed if they think there's something exciting happening, they'll get too excited.'

'I understand. If you have any concerns, ring 999 okay? Although there is going to be officers on scene guard at the church for the foreseeable. We're just checking the grounds to make sure no one is hiding out and then we'll leave you in peace. What's your name?'

'Tasmin.'

'Thanks, Tasmin.'

She shrugged, and he walked out of the building, waiting for her to turn the lock after him and keep it secure. As he walked towards the gates, he still couldn't shake the feeling he was being watched, and he turned one last time to take in the grand Victorian mansion that had belonged to one of the wealthy Rydal Falls families at some point. He still thought that the killer was hiding out somewhere, but he didn't have any evidence to back up a full search.

Ben went back to Theo's. Daisy and another armed officer had arrived to protect the women who were inside of the rambling old vicarage. Seeing her gun made him feel a lot better; hopefully it would scare the killer off. He heard Marc's voice from over the church wall as he spoke to the fire officer. Subtlety wasn't in Marc's nature, but he was grateful to have a full team here, working to try and find the killer.

THIRTY-FOUR

He had crept into the room he'd visited a couple of days ago, where he'd left the window unlatched. It didn't shut properly because he'd broken it purposely. He knew the old woman insisted on having her bed facing the large picture window, because he'd seen her staring out at him many times. She'd had a stroke and couldn't speak much or use her left hand, but she was still sharp as a button. He would smile and wave at her as he walked past, and she'd nod her head curtly at him. He'd been coming past this window a long time. Wanting to make himself familiar to her so that when the time came, he could slip in without her causing too much of a fuss.

Tonight, he had panicked and had come running over here, hoping he could get into her room to hide. Thankfully she was asleep, dozing in her chair, when he'd cupped his hand over his eyes and peered into her bedroom. He managed to let himself in. She'd stirred at the cool evening breeze as he'd opened the window and climbed inside, but hadn't woken up. The sound of gentle snores was coming from her direction, and he wondered how easy it would be to hold a pillow over her face and end her misery. She had no family that visited, and he knew she had once owned a grand house herself. How sad she must be to have been reduced to this. Living in a nursing home, where strangers who didn't care one little bit about her tended to her daily needs and wiped her backside for her. He couldn't leave this room; he'd heard the staff outside calling to each other about checking the windows and doors were secure, so he'd scrabbled underneath the bed in case they came in here. He literally just made it, pulling his foot under as the door opened and he saw the long, slender legs of a girl wearing black tights and white shoes walk past the bed towards the window. The woman had stirred at her entrance and let out a grunt.

'Sorry, lovely, I'll be right back to help you to the toilet and get you into bed. I just have to check the windows are shut, won't be long and then I'll get you a nice cup of tea.'

He lay there thinking she sounded nice, that was good. He hoped that if he ever ended up in one of these awful places, he'd get nurses who gave a shit. He lay there trying not to sneeze as the dust and smell of stale urine tickled his nostrils, making him feel sick. Who said he didn't go all out for his cause? There was nothing he could do about anything while the cops were outside patrolling the grounds. He'd heard the deep barks of a dog and hoped it didn't lead the handler to this window.

He closed his eyes and heard the screams for help as they fluttered around like trapped butterflies trying to escape. It had almost worked. It had been so satisfying, then that vicar and copper had come running out like a pair of middle-aged superheroes, and he'd had to leg it across the road. It didn't matter, he was safe for the time being; there were worse places he could be hiding out, although he wasn't sure about the smell. It was warm and he felt safe despite the threat of coppers surrounding the place. They would give up eventually.

He must have drifted off because he woke up with a start. The night sky was blacker and denser than when he'd come in here. She didn't like her curtains closed, and if he turned to the right he could see out of the window. The coppers must have left because there were no shadows from the flashing lights in the night sky, and he couldn't see any torch beams moving around the grounds. He couldn't feel his leg or his hand; they felt numb, and his hand had swollen to three times its normal size. He began to gently move them, trying to get his circulation going without making too much noise and scaring Evelyn, whose gentle snores he could hear directly above him.

He wondered what she'd been like as a mother. He knew a lot about her thanks to her grandson. He'd read that he'd tried to murder the people who had worked for Evelyn back in the day. He'd even tried to kill her, but she'd stabbed him in the eye with a pen, which was pretty good for a woman who could only use one hand. He knew that her daughter had been a drug addict who had overdosed. She died and left a kid and, for all her wealth, she had still managed to raise a screwed-up family that were no better than anyone else. He wished she could talk; it would be an interesting conversation about her family. Once he could feel his fingers and leg again, he slipped out from underneath the bed and stood still, watching her from the darkness of the shadows.

THIRTY-FIVE

Theo had loosely put a cotton gauze pad on the palm of Morgan's hand and was wrapping a crepe bandage around it when Ben's voice called down the hall.

'It's me. Is everyone okay?'

'In the kitchen, Ben,' Morgan called out to him; she was relieved to see him unharmed. 'Did you find him?'

Ben stepped into the kitchen to see six sets of eyes all staring in his direction. 'Unfortunately, not, but he's close by. I'm pretty sure he's hiding out somewhere. There are officers searching the entire area, and Caesar is here too.' He glanced down at Morgan's hand. 'Do you need to go to the hospital?'

She shook her head. 'No, I'm good for now. I want to go see Caesar.'

Ben smiled at her. 'He's a little preoccupied, but Cassie said she will bring him to see you when he's finished.'

'Thank you, how did you know?'

'I had a feeling you'd want to see him.'

Sara was staring at the pair of them. 'Who the hell is Caesar?'

'The best police dog in the world.'

She shrugged but had no answer much to Morgan's relief. She found her a little too intense and intimidating. 'So, what's the plan. Are we waiting here or are we being moved to a safe house?'

'I think I would like to see you all moved out of this area as soon as possible. However, I'm not sure about the logistics of putting you all in the same place, and we don't have that many safe houses available.'

'He's not going to come after us all again. He tried that and fucked up. I think he'll go back to taking us out individually.' Sara was staring at Ben, daring him to argue with her. Morgan didn't think he was brave enough.

'I'd rather not take that chance; we might have to split you up to be on the safe side.'

Ben walked outside to find Marc so they could figure out what to do.

Theo's kitchen was big, but it was still too hot inside with that many people crowded into it. Marc had arrived and had taken Ben into the lounge to talk to him. Theo's phone began to ring.

'Hi, where are you?'

'*Outside this police cordon, what on earth is going on, Theo? I can't get through. Are you okay?*'

'I'm good, hang on, Morgan is here. I'll send her to come get you. Too complicated to talk about over the phone.'

He hung up and turned to her. 'Declan can't get through.'

'I'll get him.'

She left, relieved to be outside in the cool night air, where she could think a little better; the noise was deafening inside of there. She saw Declan's white Audi parked up and him standing there chatting to the officer on scene guard.

'Smithy, it's okay, the doctor can come through.'

Smithy turned to Morgan and nodded. 'Sorry, had to get authority you know.'

Declan nodded. 'Absolutely, no problem.'

He ducked under the tape, and his eyes fell onto the bandage on her hand. 'What happened?'

'I burned it trying to get out of a burning building, but it's okay, just stings a bit.'

He wrapped an arm around her and pulled her close to him. Morgan breathed out a heavy sigh of relief, he kissed the top of her head. 'What are we going to do with you? What a crap day you've had, you've passed out and burned yourself, got trapped in a burning building and it looks as if you're not going to be finishing work anytime soon. It's a good job you're Superwoman.'

'I don't know about that; I'm worn out and I can't see an end to it. We're running around chasing our tails with no clue whatsoever as to what's going on.'

Declan stopped and turned to face her. 'Hey, none of that talk, especially not from you. You're not a defeatist, you will find him, I know you will, you always do.' He'd cupped her chin in his fingers and lifted her face to look at his. 'I wish I could do more, but you're the experts and I know that you and the team will find something that will help you to find him. He will make a mistake, leave some forensics behind, something that will lead you to him because he's not some superhero like you; he's human, he's the scourge of society and probably not that bright. I'd say he's been very lucky up to now, but his luck won't hold out and then you'll be there to stop him.'

She smiled at him, and he pulled her close for another hug. She didn't have the heart to say at what cost would they find him? How many more would die? Would she? Was she on his hit list? Instead, she melted into his arms; his cologne had faded but it still lingered, and his body heat was soothing the aches and pains she felt deep inside of her bones.

'Hey, put her down. You're just greedy.'

Ben's voice had humour in it, and Declan hugged Morgan

even tighter giving his friend the middle finger. 'No, I'll hug her all I want and if you want to fight me for her then come on.'

Ben laughed. 'I don't think I could. Can you please get inside? I'm worried that you might be being watched.'

Declan released her and whispered, 'He's jealous of his gay best friend, well I never.' He grabbed Morgan's unbandaged fingers and they walked hand in hand into Theo's. Ben followed them with a smile on his face. 'Why are you here, Declan, there's no body, thank God. Did the control room call you out?'

Declan looked around the bustling kitchen filled with women, Theo and Marc then turned to Ben.

'I came for some supper and to watch a movie with my man. Who invited this lot along?'

Theo waved at him and mouthed, *sorry*. Declan winked at him then said to Morgan, 'Should I take a look at that hand for you, and tell you if it needs medical treatment?'

'I'm good, Theo did a great job and it's too painful to keep touching. Thanks though.'

All the women were staring at him, he was incredibly hand-some, and Morgan smiled at them. 'This is Doctor Declan Donnelly. He's okay, and has nothing to do with tonight; he's only just finished work and drove here from Lancaster.' She didn't tell them he was a forensic pathologist; they'd had enough upset for one night, and she didn't want them to start asking him lots of questions about Lexie that he couldn't answer.

'Good evening, ladies, is everyone okay? Any injuries that I can look at?'

They shook their heads, and Sara said, 'Nothing physical, but now I wish there was, thanks.'

Declan's cheeks flushed a little, and Theo snorted then turned away.

Ben came back in the room. 'I have a van coming to collect you all and take you to the station. I think it's best we get you to a secure, safe place where we can decide with yourselves what you want to do about the situation. Is that okay with you all?'

They nodded. 'Thank you, I don't suppose we have any choice in the matter?' Bronte asked.

'You do, of course you do, and if you would rather go home then that's up to you, but I need you to know that at this point in time I have no spare officers to go with you. We are stretched to the limit while they're out looking for the suspect. You would be doing so at your own risk; all I'm asking is that you give me a little time to draft in some more staff to help protect you, but you are free to do what you want.'

'Thank you, we appreciate your help. I know you're trying your best; we'll come to the station and see what's happening. I suppose I don't want to die tonight.'

Morgan noticed Theo exhale a sigh of relief and felt a little bad for him. His church hall had been set on fire, and his house had been taken over by a group of women who were all on some killer's hit list.

Ben's radio came to life.

'Outside, boss.'

Morgan recognised Cain's voice, and she looked at Ben, but he shrugged. 'Right then, your ride is here, follow me.'

Ben went first, Marc second and Morgan waited until the last woman stood up and she followed behind. They all filed out of the vicarage to the huge waiting carrier van that only a handful of officers were permitted to drive and was nicknamed *the party bus* because it had colour changing lights inside and a radio. Cain was one of the permitted drivers. Amy was standing by the sliding door ready to help the women inside. Once they were all in, she slammed the door shut and turned to Ben.

'We'll take them to the canteen, get them drinks and wait for you there.'

'Thanks, Amy.' He gave Cain a thumbs up, and he grinned at him. Amy turned to him.

'Cain said the breakfast buns are on you tomorrow, Ben, and he wants double sausage and egg, said you owe him big time.'

Ben grinned at her. 'No problem.'

They watched as Cain managed to complete a five-point turn in the bus-sized van and then drove down main street until he was out of sight. It was Ben's turn to sigh. 'What a huge mess this all is.'

He echoed her feelings exactly, and she reached out to squeeze his hand. Morgan was also furious, a deep down kind of anger was bubbling away inside of her stomach at the thought of the injustice and audacity this person had. Just what gave him the right to do this to a group of women who had already been through so much in their lives was beyond her, but she knew one thing. The hunt was well and truly on. She was going to grab the files Cain had printed out for her, and once Ben was asleep she would study them to see if they were missing something, or if there was any hint of a clue hidden inside them.

THIRTY-SIX

Lara was running late; she'd slept in because her stupid alarm hadn't gone off, and her car wouldn't start, so she'd had to phone for a taxi which had taken forever. She rushed through the doors of the nursing home where she worked just in time to catch the tail end of the briefing.

'Glad you could join us, Lara, you're covering the Bayview unit with Mary once she arrives. Not sure what's going on with everyone this morning, but make sure this doesn't happen again.' The staff nurse didn't give her the chance to explain or apologise, so she nodded and tried to keep the annoyance she felt inside of her. She was bloody here, wasn't she? and Mary was even later than she was.

'Now, last night was a bit of a nightmare. Someone tried to set fire to the church hall over the road, and the police were all over the grounds looking for the guy. Luckily no one was hurt, and the fire service managed to put the fire out before it got a real hold and burned down the church. Apparently, it was chaos according to the night staff. They scared the crap out of them by telling them to make sure the building was secure, and nobody could get inside.'

Lara shuddered, the thought of someone sneaking around inside the nursing home, it gave her the creeps.

'Anyway, enough excitement. Lara, there is nothing of any concern to report for your unit. Evelyn had a late night; I think she got caught up in the excitement as she had a bird's eye view, so night staff have left her in bed to have a little longer. She finally dozed off in her chair and had to be put to bed around eleven, which is late for her. Alan has a hospital appointment today, but it's not until after lunch and the ambulance service are collecting him at one, so if you can make sure he's showered and dressed in time that would be great, because he was adamant he wasn't going and stopping in bed. Apart from that there's nothing much to report.'

Lara nodded and smiled. She needed coffee, and as if reading her mind Shelly, who was standing behind the staff nurse, mimicked lifting a coffee cup to her lips, and she nodded at her. Shelley walked into the lounge, where there was a kitchen area to make hot drinks, and she followed her. There was only Edna sitting in front of the television nursing a cup of tea. She glanced at the two carers and waved a hand in their direction, then turned back to watch GMTV, which she never missed.

'Morning, Edna,' they both chimed, and then turned away. Shelley took two mugs out of the cupboard and spooned coffee into both. She kept the tone of her voice low.

'We missed all the fun by the sounds of it.'

'Thank God, imagine how scary that would be, having to check the entire building for a weirdo who likes to burn places down. It would be like something out of a horror film,' replied Lara.

'Be a bit exciting though for a change.'

'You're crazy, why would you want to be a part of that?'

'Because this place is driving me batshit crazy; it's the same old, day in, day out. Wash, dress, feed, toilet, feed, it's like some horrible time loop that repeats itself every day and we're stuck in it.'

'Someone got out of bed on the wrong side this morning.'

'Wrong side, I'm fed up with this life.'

'Then look for something else. Have you got any idea what you'd like to do?'

Shelley took a sip of her coffee. 'Anything that doesn't involve cleaning up poop and scraping it off walls would be a start.'

Lara spat a mouthful of her coffee all down her clean white tunic as she laughed.

'What a glorious job we have, but someone has to do it. Where do you think Mary is? She's later than me.'

'Hungover to shit and can't get out of bed probably.'

'Am I keeping you both from your jobs?'

The staff nurse was standing with her arms crossed, glaring at them both.

'Sorry, just needed a quick slurp,' replied Shelley, who didn't care about anything. 'I can't really get started without Mary; can she not help me?'

'I suppose so, get cracking. You're not getting paid to stand around complaining.'

Lara grinned at Shelly as the nurse turned and walked away. 'Oops, I guess she heard our conversation.'

'Snotty cow, it wouldn't hurt for her to pitch in now and again. Come on, let's go see Evelyn and get the gossip if she watched it all first-hand.'

Lara smiled. 'You do know Evelyn can't talk, don't you?'

Shelley rolled her eyes. 'Duoh! We can ask her questions though, and she can knock her answers to us, and she can write with her good hand; I've seen her do it when the detective woman comes to visit.'

They rinsed out the mugs and left them on the draining board, to go and wake Evelyn up.

Shelly knocked gently on Evelyn's door. It was the last one at the end of the hall, and she had a large corner room with French windows that opened onto the gardens.

She opened the door and whispered, 'Morning, Evelyn, better get you up or you'll never sleep tonight.' She was hovering outside. She liked the old woman; even though she couldn't speak she gave off an air of being well to do, and she imagined that she would be a fascinating woman to talk to.

Shelley shoved her hard from behind. 'Get in there.'

Lara stumbled forwards and pushed the door wide open. There was a cool breeze blowing in through the open window, and the room was freezing cold. Lara glanced at the chair and whispered, 'Oh, you're already up. It's freezing in here.'

She went to close the window and jumped at the loud scream that filled the room. She turned to see what the hell Shelley was screaming at, and then felt her knees give way as she fell to the floor.

Evelyn was in her chair, her hands were tied in the prayer position, but it was the black, gaping holes where her eyes should have been that pushed Lara over the edge. She joined Shelley and let out an even louder screech, which brought the staff nurse and several other nursing assistants running to see what was happening.

THIRTY-SEVEN

Bleary-eyed and in desperate need of coffee, Morgan had offered to run into The Coffee Pot for breakfast on the way into work. She had tossed and turned all night, unable to settle after going through all of the case files and finding nothing of any use, drifting off only to be jolted awake by a nightmare. It hadn't helped that her hand was painful, it was pulsating, and she knew she should go to the hospital to get it professionally cleaned and dressed. If they got a little downtime this morning she would nip through, but if not, she could go and see the custody nurse, who might be able to sort it out for her, which would be easier than a trip to A&E. She was nibbling her breakfast roll when Marc burst through the door, his face a mask of horror.

'Body at the nursing home, staff found her this morning.'

Morgan felt herself falling forwards, and this time she reached out, grabbing hold of the desk to stop herself from going any further. She knew, deep down in her heart, she knew he was going to tell her that it was Evelyn. Why hadn't she thought of her sooner? Why hadn't she protected her? She was a final girl too. He hadn't been able to get them the way he'd wanted and so he'd gone after her instead: frail, vulnerable, elderly, lovely Evelyn. Morgan felt the blackness begin to rise inside of her chest. She was seething with pain and fury, and she pushed herself away from the desk.

'The bastard, he went after Evelyn.'

Ben glanced at her; Marc was nodding frantically. 'We left him in a nursing home to run riot.'

'No, boss. I spoke to the night staff, and they assured me all the windows and doors were locked. They said it was the first job they did when they came on shift. How, what did he do?'

'It's terrible, the two staff that found her have had to be sedated.'

Cain stood up. 'Nah, not happening on my shift. You do not hurt kids or old people; I'm feeling much better today. I want to be back on active duty.'

Ben nodded. 'If you're sure.'

'I'm positive, I liked that old lady, she was feisty and funny.'

Morgan nodded. 'I can't believe she's gone.'

'Well, you better because he did; the log is just getting put on now. I want all of us to attend. There's something else you should know...' He paused and winced. 'He cut out her eyes.'

Cain's huge fist slammed down onto the desk he was standing by, sending shockwaves to Morgan who was next to him.

Morgan wanted to cry, scream, do something, but she couldn't speak because the shock had taken away her voice. All four of them rushed out of the office to get in the carrier, which Cain still had the keys for. She could feel hot tears pooling in the corner of her eyes, which she swiped with the sleeve of her jumper.

Ben was sitting next to her, and he reached out for her hand, but she flinched as he touched the palm of her burned hand.

'Sorry, are you okay?' he whispered, and she shook her head because she wasn't. She had no idea how she could even begin to work the crime scene, but she knew that deep down inside she would find the strength. She had to see what he'd done to her friend and see how much he'd made her suffer. So that she knew when it was time to face him, she would have the power to take him down like he deserved.

They suited and booted before going inside the home, where a fraught looking nurse met them at the door. 'It's terrible, I don't know what to do. We've kept all the residents in their rooms and told them we have an emergency. They are being looked after the best we can, but some of them wander and we don't have enough staff to watch each one individually.'

Marc asked, 'Have you informed her next of kin yet?'

Morgan knew that Evelyn's only next of kin was her murderous grandson, who had intended to kill his grandmother and her, though between them they had thwarted his attempt. Evelyn had used her good hand to stab him in the eyeball with a ballpoint pen and saved her life.

The nurse shook her head.

Ben stared down the long, empty corridor that led to Evelyn's room. 'It's okay we'll deal with that side of things. We're going to need to deal with the hallways first so the residents can leave their rooms; once CSI have documented them you can move them into the lounge, so they don't see the police activity. Is that okay?'

She nodded. 'The nursing director is on his way in, it's his day off.'

'Morning, guys.' Wendy's voice was like music to Morgan's ears. 'I'm going to need a hand if you could find me another CSI, boss.'

Marc looked at her. 'Where's that new guy?'

'Dentist.'

'You're kidding me. He's not anymore.' He stormed off outside, asking the control room for the mobile number of Ian, the crime scene manager.

Wendy rolled her eyes. 'May as well crack on with it because he's neither use nor ornament. Have you guys been in yet?'

They shook their heads, and she tilted hers quizzically but didn't say anything. Cain, who hadn't suited up, stood at the reception desk. 'I'll handle enquiries from this side, and CCTV if you want to.' He pointed down the corridor.

'Cheers, can you ring Amy? I know she was going to work a late today but see if she can get here earlier. I'm going to need her.'

Ben turned to Morgan. 'Ready?'

She bowed her head; she couldn't ever be ready to face something so terrible. Wendy led the way, and they all kept to the left-hand side of the wall. Morgan felt as if the corridor was growing and getting longer the closer they got, like something out of a fun house you'd find at the fair.

The door was closed, and Morgan had an overwhelming urge to knock out of politeness. Whenever she'd visited Evelyn, she always knocked twice the few times she'd visited and without thinking, she stepped forward and tapped twice, gently.

Wendy whispered, 'I'm right here, quick look then get out again, okay?'

Morgan knew the score; they just needed to see for themselves. She pushed the door open and took a step in; Ben was right behind her. Morgan fixed her gaze on the chair that Evelyn favoured over the bed and felt her heart miss a beat. She stared at the empty eye sockets, cupped a hand across her mouth and whispered, 'I can't, I'm so sorry, Evelyn.' She turned around and stepped back into the corridor.

Wendy let out a low whistle. 'What the hell...?'

Ben nodded, the shock and grief etched across his face, as he whispered, 'I should have come in and checked myself, but I trusted the staff when they said the place was secure. This is my fault.'

He followed Morgan out of the room.

'He wanted to shock us, scare us, Ben. Let us know that we didn't get away unharmed. This was not your fault. If the staff told you the place was secure what else could you do? There was little point in you storming inside to search on your own when he could have been outside still. You weren't to know he would do this; I don't think he knew he was going to do it until he did. He was so angry that we didn't burn to death, he came straight over here; he must have already had a way to get inside. We need to check if Evelyn had any visitors, check the camera footage. See if anyone came out of her room after we searched the area. Where are her eyes? I didn't see them.'

Wendy was uncapping the camera, and she whispered, 'He might have taken them with him as a trophy.'

Morgan felt a pain so intense in her heart she clutched at her chest. She wanted to smash her fist into something, preferably whoever had violated her friend this way. Instead, she marched down the corridor to the reception desk, where Cain was studying a bank of monitors. He pointed to the nurses coming out of Evelyn's room around ten thirty, then fast-forwarding it so they could still see movement but not waste hours. Nobody else entered or left the room until a nurse opened the door a little at seven, though she didn't go inside, just turned her head to listen then closed it quietly and carried on to the next room. The next movement was the two nurses who must have discovered her body. They watched as one of them paused at the door, the other pushed her inside, and seconds later they were running from the room screaming.

'Well, that makes life a little easier, knowing that he didn't go on the prowl around the entire building; he must have come in and left through the window.'

Morgan was devastated. 'I wanted him to walk out of the door, into the corridor, so we could see his fucking face on camera though.'

Cain looked up at her. 'Sorry, yes, me too. I was just thinking logistically, not practically. Is it bad?'

She nodded; how else did you describe what she had just witnessed? It was bad, it was horrific: it was beyond horrific. The doorbell rang and a nurse scurried to open it. She saw Declan there with his heavy silver case.

'I stayed over at Theo's; after all the excitement I thought he needed a bit of company, and I always have my trusty case in the boot of my car.'

That made perfect sense. She tried to smile at him, but it physically hurt both her heart and her face, so instead she nodded. 'Glad you're here, it's—' She stopped. 'It's the worst.'

He tilted his head. 'I'm sorry, Morgan, today is no better than yesterday and it's only just begun.'

She couldn't answer him because it wasn't, and she imagined it was only going to get a whole lot worse. Ben walked down the corridor towards him, and Morgan saved him the trouble of asking. 'He was at Theo's.'

Ben reached out and shook his hand. 'Glad to see you, thank you.'

'You know, one of these days I might not answer you with: you're welcome, my friend. This is getting tiresome for us all.' Declan glanced at Morgan, and Ben nodded. She knew he was trying to politely tell Ben to cut her some slack, but she didn't need it. Now that she had seen Evelyn's desecrated body, she had dug as deep as she could and channelled some inner strength. She would work until she dropped, if it meant catching the killer before anyone else got hurt. If the other women were out of his reach and she made it obvious she had been in the church hall when he set it ablaze, he would have no choice but to come after her. She could taunt him and get the newspaper to write an article about how Detective Morgan Brookes defied death again. His ego would never let him ignore her. He would be the one to try and track her down, when in reality she was the one hunting him. As long as she didn't let Ben know, it could work, she was sure it would.

THIRTY-EIGHT

The house was safe, Bronte supposed, but it was so secluded and not to mention overcrowded she felt as if she was being suffocated. She needed to get out of here. She had the urge to go home and get the visiting order to go and see Harrison. Who was going to follow her to Manchester prison? Nobody in their right mind. Everyone else was still sleeping. She was still wearing the clothes she had on yesterday, as in their panic nobody had time to go grab fresh clothes and toiletries.

She opened the front door and spied the car on the drive with a young woman sitting in the driver's seat, her head bowed. Bronte wondered if she was asleep, then realised she was looking down at a book. She was reading. Bronte didn't blame her: she couldn't exactly stare at the front door of the ex-council house all night. She tapped on the driver's window, making her jump, and she wondered just how safe they'd been last night if she had managed to approach her without being seen and scared her. She put the window down.

'Is everything okay?'

Bronte looked to see what she was reading and smiled at the book she was holding: *The Housemaid* by Frieda McFadden was on her to be read list. 'Yes, fine. What's that like?' She pointed to the book.

The undercover officer laughed. 'Good, too good as you can tell; you made me jump.'

'I love it when I get lost in a book, it's the best place to be. Far better than this crappy life that's for sure. Look, I need to go do some stuff and I know you can't leave, but I'm okay. I don't think he knows where we are yet, and my aunt and her boyfriend will be home. I'll come back as soon as I'm done, but I have a hospital appointment in Manchester, so it won't be until later on, is that okay?'

The woman bit her lip. 'I'm not sure, can I check it's okay?'

'How long will that take?'

She shrugged. 'There's been an urgent job come in, all the staff have been diverted so it could take a while.'

'I'm sorry, I can't hang about. I can sign something if you need me to?'

She picked up her notepad and flipped it open to a blank page. 'Would you mind writing your name and where you're going, so I don't get in trouble, then sign it?' She passed her the notebook, and Bronte did as she asked, glancing back at the house to make sure the others weren't watching her because she knew they would try and stop her. She passed the book back to her and smiled. 'Thanks, when do you get relieved?'

She shrugged. 'No idea now this sudden death has come in. You be careful, okay, and if you think someone is following you, you need to ring 999.'

Bronte lifted a hand and waved at her, then hurried out of the garden gate onto the front street in the small cul-de-sac. She could be home in twenty minutes if she walked fast.

By the time she reached her aunt's house she was sweating and out of breath. Her aunt's car wasn't parked outside but her boyfriend's was. She let herself in the house, hoping he was still in bed. He walked out of the kitchen in his boxers and a faded T-shirt. 'Where the hell have you been? We were worried sick about you.'

She snorted. 'You were, really? I thought you'd have enjoyed having the house to yourselves.'

'We did, but you kind of put a damper on the whole mood because she couldn't settle and kept checking her phone to see if you'd messaged.'

'Sorry, stayed at a friend's.' She stopped, realising that she owed him no explanation of what she'd been doing, she was an adult. The only person she needed to apologise to was her aunt, and she clearly wasn't that bothered because she'd gone to work. He tutted at her, she ignored him and rushed up to the room to grab some stuff and the visiting order she'd hidden. She filled a weekend bag with underwear, clothes, and toiletries, grabbed her diary and the brown envelope containing the papers she needed, and her purse. As she rushed downstairs he was still there, staring at her.

'What you up to? You're a sneaky little bitch at times.'

'What I do is none of your business. You stay here and welch off my aunt's kindness.'

He snorted and pointed to her. 'Look who's talking.'

'It's different, I'm family, she got money for taking me in. What do you give her?'

He arched an eyebrow. 'I give her a good time, baby, that's what.'

Bronte turned away; she hated him but wasn't about to get into a huge argument with him. 'Tell Michelle I'll ring her later.' Then she was out of the door, hoisting her bag over her shoulder and walking as fast as she could to the train station to get away from him. He really was a creep, and she had no idea what Michelle saw in him.

THIRTY-NINE

The director of the nursing home arrived in a whirlwind of confusion and full of bluster as he tried to take charge of the situation. Morgan kept out of it; he was ordering his staff around then he came for them. 'Who is in charge of this?' His arms were swinging wildly in the air as he spun around looking for someone to come forward. Marc had disappeared outside to greet Ian and tell him he needed to work the perimeter, which had put a smile on Wendy's face. Ben, who had been talking to Wendy and Declan outside Evelyn's room, came sauntering along the corridor.

'Detective Sergeant Ben Matthews.' He reached out a hand, and the flustered guy with far too much hair for someone in his late fifties, that was sticking up all over the place, took it and gave it a limp shake.

Morgan turned away; she knew Ben would find him lame, if he didn't even have a firm handshake.

'I can't be having this.'

'Can't be having what?'

'This, I have other residents to consider. I can't keep them locked up in their bedrooms all day while you lot are messing around.'

'We are working as quickly as we can, and I understand that. We're happy for you to let them out of their rooms as long as they don't go past Evelyn's door.'

'Oh, we can?'

'Yes.'

'But how long do you think it's going to take? The residents get family and friends visiting – we have an open door policy. I don't want them to experience any of this, we are supposed to be a safe place.'

Ben had tucked his hands into his trouser pockets, a sign that he was getting annoyed and didn't want anyone to see he had curled his fingers into fists. 'As long as it takes to find Evelyn's eyeballs, which were brutally cut out of her eye sockets, is my guess. I'm sorry, I didn't catch your name.'

The man was shocked by Ben's words. He was full of nervous energy and hadn't stopped running his hand through his hair, but he stopped moving for a few seconds.

'Erm, Brian Heywood.'

'Well, Brian, I said we need to locate Evelyn's eyeballs, they are missing from their sockets.'

'I heard you, shh. I don't want anyone hearing that.'

Morgan wanted to trip the guy up or something, he was an arse.

'Why are they missing?'

'I wish that I knew, the same way I wish that I knew which sick individual has done this. Unfortunately, I don't, so my team have to investigate her murder properly. By the way my CSI said that the catch on her French windows is broken and doesn't shut properly, so you might want to worry about the possibility that poor maintenance of the building led to her murder. There could be a huge lawsuit. In my opinion you should get someone in to check all of the windows and doors can be secured when we've finished.'

The man's face paled even more, and he turned and walked towards a door with a sign on that read Director's Office. He went in and closed the door, leaving Ben staring after him.

'Is that true?' Morgan whispered.

He nodded. 'Unfortunately, there is a faulty catch; and Wendy got some great partials off the glass.'

'She did?'

'Yep.'

Morgan grinned at him. 'I'm going to pray that he's on the system.'

'Me too.'

Declan beckoned them both outside into the car park, away from anyone who might be listening in. It was cloudy, but the sun kept peeking through, offering them hope that it might warm up a little. The air still smelled of woody, burning smoke as if someone was having a bonfire. It made Morgan uneasy when she thought about how lucky she'd been that it also didn't have the smell of burning flesh lingering in it too.

'Smells, doesn't it? Although I quite like it, reminds me of bonfire night back in the day. We could build bonfires as tall as a two-storey house and watch them go up like a towering inferno. While letting off rockets and bangers so loud it sounded as if an air strike was happening. Now, those were the days.'

'We used to build a huge bonfire on the common. It would take us weeks going round gathering everyone's old wood in a wheelbarrow. My dad was a gardener and he'd let us use his two barrows to collect it all in. They were dangerous though, once it almost got lit with Jonny and Debbie inside it; they were snogging and had gone in there so nobody could see them.'

Morgan had never seen a huge bonfire and had no idea what they were talking about. 'The good old days, eh? You're showing your age, the pair of you.'

'And you, you cheeky young whippersnapper, have no idea what fun being a feral child was. I bet you only got to go on those tiny slides in the park that didn't make your hair stand on end or question your own mortality. We had one back home that took nerves of steel and balls of fire to even contemplate climbing up.'

Morgan said, 'I'm pretty sure you've told me about the size of the slides before.'

Ben laughed and then coughed when he realised where they were and why they were here.

'What's your verdict?'

Declan lowered his voice. 'Unless Evelyn had the urge to cut her own eyeballs out then it's homicide. There are bright red handprints and bruising around her neck, and the lack of blood when they were removed tells me they were taken post-mortem, thank God. There's a fair bit of rigor mortis, so I think you're looking at time of death somewhere between ten and twelve, but as you know, my friends, this is a rough estimate. I prefer not to speculate but sometimes it's pretty obvious. I also heard that prick talking to you. If you want to take him down a peg or two maybe you should show him the body and let it sink in that this happened on his watch. Your call obviously and I'm being petty, but I don't think he's thinking about poor Evelyn and more about himself. Some people need a reality check, just saying.'

'Would it have taken long, the strangulation?'

Declan looked to Morgan. 'I don't think so, she's very frail, her bones will be very brittle and weak. I should imagine it wouldn't have taken much. You, for instance, you're a fit, young thing with lots more muscle around your neck, so it would take longer. I think when it comes to the PM we'll find that her hyoid bone is cleanly snapped in two; it could have been pretty instantaneous.'

'I hope so, I can't bear the thought of her being terrified and suffering. Who in their right minds kills an old lady and takes her eyes?'

'A very sick individual, that's who.'

'At least this time we have some prints,' Ben reminded her, and she smiled at him, not wanting to put a damper on his enthusiasm. But they both knew that the prints could belong to any one of the nursing staff as well as the killer.

FORTY

Morgan's radio began to vibrate, signalling she was getting a private call.

'Hi.'

'Is this Morgan?'

'Yep.'

'It's Blake, I'm on scene guard at the safe house.'

'Is everything okay, Blake?'

'I think so, one of the women came out earlier and said she had to leave, she has a doctor's appointment in Manchester. I didn't know what to do. Mads said they're free to come and go at their own risk.'

'Who was it?' She knew Blake was going to say Sara; it made sense as she lived in Manchester and seemed the least perturbed by it all.

'Hang on.' There was the sound of rustling pages. 'Bronte Potter.'

Morgan let out a small, 'Oh, wow.' The shock at it being Bronte threw her off guard a little.

'Did she say how she was getting there or which hospital?'

'No, sorry, I should have asked. It was all going on over the radio and I didn't want to disturb any of you. I know that you're up to your neck in it.'

'Don't worry, thanks for letting me know. I'll swing by the train station to see if she's around.'

She ended the call, perplexed as to why Bronte had the sudden urge to go to Manchester, unless she was thinking she'd be safer there, which she possibly would. When the news was broken to them about Evelyn, they would all be freaked out and scared even more. It might be a good idea to get them out of the county, as far away from the killer. As she stared across the grounds at the trees, she realised that if they were out of the equation and he had no idea where they were, he would have to come after her and she would be ready and waiting for him.

Ben was still chatting to Declan; she relayed the information to him. 'Bronte has left the safe house to go to Manchester.'

He closed his eyes for a few moments, and she felt bad – he was tired. 'When? Do we know where she's going?'

She shook her head. 'I was thinking that it might be a good idea though.'

'What, having her running around on her own?'

'No, we could get the rest of the women moved out of the county, Manchester, Liverpool, Blackpool even. Somewhere that he won't be able to reach as easily, and then we can concentrate on finding him without worrying about them all the time.'

'I think.' He looked around the expansive grounds, across at the spire of St Martha's over the road and then back at her. 'I think that may be a great idea. We can get them to a much safer place and leave it with GMP. We wouldn't even have to know the address, so there is no chance it could get leaked from our end.'

Declan was staring at Morgan; he opened his mouth to speak, and she gave the slightest shake of her head.

'Leave it with me, I'll speak to Marc and get the ball rolling.' He wandered off to find Marc, leaving Declan glaring at her.

'You little minx.'

'What do you mean?'

'You can't do this to him, don't you think you should tell him?'

'Tell him what?' She was doing her best to feign innocence, but acting wasn't her strong point.

'Tell him that if the other women are out of the way, then the only one left your man can come after is yourself.'

'He might not be interested in me.'

He crossed his arms. 'Were you in that church hall when he decided to burn it down?'

'He didn't know I was going to be there; he was going to do it whether I was there or not.'

'Hmph, possibly but I don't like it and, to be fair, Ben can't be thinking straight because I'm sure he wouldn't agree to that if he was.'

'Look, the stress of worrying about all those women is having an effect on us both. If we don't have to worry about their safety, then we can put all our efforts into hunting him down and, Declan, I am going to hunt him down.'

'I suppose that's a fair comment, but it's what scares me the most.' He reached out his hand, letting his fingers brush the soft skin of her cheek. 'I worry about you both, but especially you. I have this fear deep down inside me that one day your luck might run out, Ms Brookes, and you will end up in one of those awful body bags in one of my fridges, waiting for me to cut you open. I can't bear it. If that ever happened, I'd give up my job, it would be the end of me for sure.'

Morgan reached up to clasp hold of his hand. 'I'm sorry, don't say that. You're the most amazing pathologist, and I will do my utmost best not to end up dead, Declan. I don't particularly want to die just yet, I have you and Ben, I love my job most of the time, although I'm partly scared and angry that this guy can just think he can kill innocent women who have already had a terrible time and get away with it. His audacity is beyond my comprehension, and I have to stop him.'

He gave her the sweetest smile, bending down to kiss the top of her head. 'And that's what I'm afraid of. Can you not carry a gun?'

She laughed. 'I don't think they'd trust me with one. Thank you though.'

He squeezed her fingers then walked towards the gate, where his car was parked a little further up the street. Morgan inhaled deeply. She was putting herself at risk, but there was no other choice to draw him out. She had messaged Tom, a journalist she knew at the *Cumbrian News*, and asked him if he would run an article about the fire. She would be ready when it was published tomorrow, but first she wanted to find Bronte Potter and find out what the hell she was doing.

FORTY-ONE

Ben agreed Morgan could take Cain and go have a look for Bronte. She'd forgotten that they had arrived in the carrier and muttered, 'We can't search in this.'

'Not if we want to be discreet, we can't, it's an all singing, all dancing, sparkling riot van.'

She smiled at him; that's what it was. The riot van, it had plastic shields and the hard helmets the cops wore for public order at football games if the fans began to get out of hand. Luckily Rydal Falls only had a team in the bottom of the county league, so there wasn't much chance of a full-scale riot going on, but it was there should they ever need it. Rydal Falls didn't have much in the way of rioters, but what it did have was its fair share of killers, which unsettled Morgan way beyond a few mouthy drunken louts, angry at their team losing a match.

'Let's go swap it for something a little sexier.'

She laughed, shaking her head. 'You're terrible.'

'I know, but I dare you to say I'm not funny.'

'Sometimes, you are.'

'Was the old lady bad?'

Morgan turned to him: he hadn't shaved, and his usually

smooth face was covered with a five o'clock shadow. 'Horrifi-
cally bad, I really liked Evelyn. I've visited her a few times, you
know, not as often as I would have liked but I'd pop in whenever
I could. Last time I took her some of my aunt Ettie's Sleep Well
tea.' Grief formed a lump in her throat that made it hard to say
anything else, and she turned her face to stare out of the
window. Cain must have sensed how upset she was because he
didn't ask any more questions. Leaving her alone with her
thoughts. She watched the houses as he drove slowly past and
saw the tail end of a silver car the same shape as a Picasso turn a
corner into a street.

'Turn down there, I saw the car.'

He looked at the narrow road she was pointing at. 'You're
kidding me, right? I can't get this beast down that one-way
street.'

'Then let me out.'

He slammed on the brakes, and she threw the door open
bolting towards the street. He looked in his rear-view mirror to
see a line of traffic backing up behind him. 'Shit, Morgan.'
Pulling the van as close as he could to a row of parked traffic, he
jumped out, locking it and followed her as best as he could. The
car had disappeared, but it was a long street and there was no
way it had got away from her unless it had sped up when seeing
the van. If it had it meant that whoever was driving didn't want
to come to the attention of the officers in the van. Out of breath
she stood in the middle of the street with her hands on her hips,
leaning forward.

Cain joined her. 'What the hell?'

'It was him; it must have been. Why did it speed off so
fast down here? We need to see if there are any cameras that
we can get a number plate from.' She began to pace up and
down, looking up for CCTV cameras or doorbell cameras.
She found a business further up the street with a camera and
crossed her fingers: *please be working, please be working,*

please be working. She knocked loudly on the door, and a guy opened it.

'Hi, Detective Morgan Brookes. Does your camera work?'

He nodded. 'It does, it's got motion detection and records everything.'

'Cars?'

'Cars, cats, people, bratty teenagers.'

She wanted to leap forward and hug the guy. 'Can you work it?' This was the golden question: whenever most people were asked they said no, it needed some manager or supervisor to access it.

He arched an eyebrow at her. 'Be pretty useless if I couldn't. Do you want to take a look at it?'

She stared up into the blue sky and thought. *Whoever is looking down on me, I owe you big time and if you could keep it up until we have this guy in handcuffs that would be great.* 'That would be amazing, thank you.'

Cain had joined her, and she grinned at him. 'We have a working camera that picks up cars and someone who knows how to use it.'

Cain nodded at the guy. 'Wow, I guess it had to happen at some point.'

The guy laughed. 'I take it you don't get this very often.'

She shook her head. 'It's like getting all six numbers on the lottery, the chances are so rare you kind of give up hoping you'll win.'

'Oh, man, that's really sad. Why do people have cameras if they don't use them for what they're intended?'

Cain shrugs. 'Beats me, pal.'

They followed him into the open-office area space. 'What is it you do? This is a nice place.'

'Graphic design, web design, IT stuff mainly. I'm Glyn by the way.'

Cain was eyeing up the huge iMac desktop computers;

there were three of them. He waved them over and they watched as several views of the front street loaded on the screen.

'What time?'

'It was five minutes ago; I'm looking for a silver Picasso driving past.'

'You are? My colleague drives a silver car, but I'm not sure it's a Citroen though. I don't really do cars; I cycle everywhere.'

Morgan could feel the skin on her arms begin to rise with tiny goosebumps, and she tried to keep her voice calm. 'Has he been in work this morning?'

Glyn shook his head. 'No, he's taken a week's annual leave.' He loaded the footage, and they watched as he slowed it down and the silver car drove down the street, its number plate in full view. Morgan grabbed a pen off the desk and scribbled it onto her hand: J34 XUN. She walked outside and asked control for a vehicle PNC and waited, holding her breath for a reply.

'That comes back to a silver Citroen Picasso, registered to 101 Fenton Street. Named drivers are a Mr William Dent and Elizabeth Dent.'

She wanted to whoop for joy, cry, scream and wave her hands in the air. She went back into the office and smiled at Cain.

'It's not Glyn's colleagues' car,' he said with a hint of sadness in his voice.

'No, but it's registered to Fenton Street.' She turned back to Glyn. 'Thank you so much for your help, do you think you could download that for me?'

'I can email you a link to view it if that's quicker.'

She grinned at him. 'Glyn you are a superstar.' Taking a Post-it note off a pad on the desk she wrote down her email in block capitals. 'I really, really appreciate this.'

He smiled at her. 'Glad to help, you certainly brightened

my morning up.' His gaze met hers, and she felt her cheeks begin to turn pink.

They left him and went back to the carrier, which was causing carnage on the street. Cain had abandoned it.

'Oops, but worth the bollocking and complaints that are probably winging their way to the boss as we speak.' He waved a hand in thanks at the row of cars behind him and climbed in.

'He fancied you, bet you a fiver he asks you out.'

'He did not.'

'He bloody did, good work, Brookes.'

'That car is registered to the same street Lexie lives in.'

'I knew it sounded familiar, what are the chances of that?'

'Exactly, which is probably the reason why she wasn't spooked by it being outside her house if she was used to seeing it. She may even have known the driver, so would let him get close to her without realising she was in danger.'

'What an arsehole.'

'We can't go there in this though, we'll scare him off.'

He nodded. 'Right then, my observant little friend, let's go find an invisible car to do a spot of our own stalking in.'

Morgan laughed and for the first time since she'd seen Lexie's desecrated body, she felt a little lighter. It didn't mean that this was their man, but it was a very real possibility he could be, and she would take that over the nothing that they'd had fifteen minutes ago. They were closing in, and it felt good, but in their excitement at the possible connection they both forgot all about what they were supposed to be doing: searching for Bronte.

FORTY-TWO

Bronte left the train at Manchester Victoria station; she had looked on Google Maps and it was only a ten-minute walk to the prison. She had been nervous the whole journey, staring at every male who got on at each stop. One poor guy had asked if he could sit next to her, and she'd almost screamed no at him, but the look on her face must have said it for her because he carried on moving up the carriage.

She wished she hadn't brought the overnight bag with her; it was heavy and weighing her down. She felt like a teenager running away from home, and maybe that's what she was doing, trying to escape her fate – it certainly felt like it. It felt to her as if somehow her fate had been preordained in the stars. She was supposed to die young, had survived against the odds and now she was being chased by death through the streets of Rydal Falls and possibly Manchester. Only she didn't think he looked anything like the grim reaper; he probably looked like a nice, normal guy. One who opened doors and smiled at strangers to throw them off the track of the monster that lived inside him. She wondered if he felt any regrets about what he'd done to Lexie, or whether it just fuelled him to continue stalking and killing them off, one by one. She clenched her fists by her sides, so absorbed in her thoughts she stepped off the crossing onto the busy road and almost got hit by a taxi that blared its horn so loud her feet left the floor, she jumped that high. A hand reached out for her coat, tugging her backwards, and she turned to see a man smiling at her, a little older than herself, wearing a pair of Bose headphones and a trench coat.

'Too close, lady, these roads are unforgiving.'

She nodded, then smiled at him. 'Thank you, I was in a world of my own.'

He shrugged. 'Man, I wish I was.'

The pips began to beep, signalling it was time to cross the road, breaking her trance, and she watched as he hurried past her. As she reached the other side he stopped, turning back to look at her. 'Have a good day, whatever you're doing and be safe.' Then he was gone, sucked into the crowd of people all walking in the same direction, before she could even reply.

That had been too close, and she made sure she paid attention the rest of the way, until the red-brick building came into view, with a row of flags outside waving in the breeze. She felt her stomach begin to churn and whispered, 'What the hell are you doing here?' She looked around, there were a few women queuing to go inside, and she wanted to throw up all over her new Nikes. She put the heavy bag down on the pavement and stared at the entrance.

'First time, love? Don't worry, you'll get used to it. Not that you want to, but you know if your fella's a wrong 'un there isn't much you can do about it.'

She turned to the older woman with short, bleached hair and two ginormous hooped earrings that were swaying in the breeze. 'It's hard at first and you ask yourself what the hell you're bothering for, but if you love 'em, then you got to accept that this is your lot in life. Some of my mates gave up on their fellas after the third or fourth time.'

'How many times has yours been in prison?' Bronte didn't want to know, but felt she owed it to the woman to be polite to her, as she had bothered to be nice to her.

She let out a loud cackle. 'Too bloody many to count. Still, I love the daft sod so here I am. Why don't you follow me? I'll show you the way in, and don't get too offended by the screws either, they look hard as nails and like right bastards but it's just their job. They don't mean nothing by it.'

Bronte picked up her bag and followed the woman who led the way. Turning to her she waved a visiting order at her, and Bronte took the one she had out of the front pocket of the bag, her palms sweating. She kept asking herself what the hell she was doing here, but still she kept on walking, hoping that if nothing else she could tell Harrison what a complete and utter arsehole he was.

She got through security and had her bag searched and then she had to put it in a locker. She was led into a large, open visiting area where there were lots of tables and chairs. There was a snack bar along one side of the wall, with the metal shutters down and a sign that read, *closed due to sickness.*

She looked around and couldn't see him, so went to the nearest table and sat down. She had no idea what he looked like now. He could come and find her, if he was the one who had booked the visit. She didn't look that different. Maybe once she'd faced him, she would do a Milly and book herself in at the hairdresser, have a complete change of cut and colour. Bronte felt hot, too hot even though the room wasn't overly warm, and she could feel her heart racing. She couldn't believe she was doing this and thought that she must be mad, completely off her head.

'Bronte.'

She looked up to see a man with a shaved head standing opposite her. Not the skinny, spotty teenage boy she had been expecting to see.

'Yes.'

'Damn, it's good to see you.'

Her eyes narrowed as she stared at him. This couldn't be Harrison; this guy was all ripped, with muscles that made the T-shirt he was wearing look as if it could burst at the seams if he flexed his bicep. He had home-made tattoos on his knuckles; they were new, but she recognised the skull and cross bones on his arm.

'Harrison, you look...' She couldn't say good, because she was supposed to hate him, but seeing him like this had taken her by surprise and now, she didn't know how she felt.

He lifted his hands, which were handcuffed, and pointed to a chair. 'May I?'

She looked around at the people at the other tables, chatting, smiling and then looked back at him. 'Yes.'

He sat down, keeping his hands under the table out of sight. 'I can't believe you came; I was shocked when your friend wrote to me and asked if you could.'

She couldn't move her mouth; she felt as if her throat had closed, it was so dry.

'It's okay, it must be hard for you. I get that. How are you?'

Cupping a hand over her mouth she coughed, and her eyes began to water, and the woman who had walked her in glanced over to see if she was okay. Then she stood up and went to get her a plastic cup of water from the cooler. Bronte nodded at her in thanks, and she smiled, patting her back before going back to her guy. Bronte took a sip of the cool water then cleared her throat.

'This, is a bit difficult.'

He nodded. 'I get that.'

All the words she'd promised she'd say to him were clogging her throat, blocking the words she so desperately wanted to say to him. She inhaled deeply. 'You killed them, you almost killed me. Why?'

He had the decency to cast his eyes downwards, and his face looked flushed. Then he shrugged. 'I don't think you want to know.'

'Yes, I do, of course I do.' She worried that he might get up and leave. She had thought she might be able to make small talk with him, be a little polite before setting on him, and she'd failed miserably.

'Truth is, I fancied your mum; I hated your dad, and your sister was a cow, and you were in the way.'

She lifted her eyes and stared at him. 'You killed my entire family because you fancied my mum?'

He shrugged and began picking at a hangnail on his thumb. 'I told you, you wouldn't want to know.'

She felt a burning hot rage begin to boil inside of her stomach that was pushing to rise higher. 'Are you even sorry for what you did?'

'Course I am.' He didn't look her in the eyes, and she realised that he wasn't in the least bit remorseful.

'If things were different and you could go back in time, would you do it again, live through it again knowing how it ended for you?'

This time he did lift his face, and there was a sly grin on his face. 'Yes, every single minute of it.'

It all happened in slow motion. She stood up so fast that the cup of water spilled all over the table, and she flew at him with such force it knocked him off his chair. The guards ran at her, their rough hands grabbing her arms and dragging her away, but not before she managed to rake his cheek with the nails of her right hand that she'd sharpened into points with an emery board on the train here. Blood began to pool at the top of the marks she'd made on his skin, and she grinned at him.

'You're a fucking arsehole, a murdering arsehole and I hope you die in here.'

She felt herself being dragged backwards. She was being

carried and dragged, and she glanced at the woman who had been kind to her and mouthed, 'Sorry.'

The woman grinned at her, and standing up she began to applause her.

She felt better. She felt powerful.

And then he spoke again.

As she reached the door, he called out to her, 'Bronte, you're still going to die like your friend did... and the rest of them too.'

FORTY-THREE

Morgan ran up to the office and logged on to the computer to do a quick search on the intel systems for William and Elizabeth Dent. There was nothing for William, but Elizabeth had a string of shoplifting offences from ten years ago. She sat back in her chair and sighed; this wasn't what she'd been hoping to find. She'd wanted William to have a string of violent assaults on his record, not to say that it had to be him; it could be his wife. God knows women were just as violent if not more than men but did a petty shoplifter go from stealing cosmetics out of Debenhams to violent murder and arson? Plus, if it was a woman, who was the man she had thought was following her in the silver car? She wasn't feeling it, not that it meant anything about William either. He could be a clever guy who had managed to keep off the police radar. She did a quick Google search of his address on Maps and saw he lived on the next block up from Lexie. It was still too close for her liking. She wondered if anyone had already spoken to the Dents and looked at the pile of clipboards stacked on the spare desk in the corner. There was one with a few sheets on it and *No Answer* scrawled across the top of the sheets. She flicked through them and saw that 101 had been no reply. Taking the clipboard with her she went back to find Cain, who was loitering by the brew station eating digestives out of a packet that someone had left lying around. He offered them to her, and she shook her head.

'No reply at 101 when the PCSOs did the house to house.'

He nodded. 'Might be just as well if there's a killer living there. We have a legitimate reason to go pay them a visit then, don't we? How many others didn't answer?'

Morgan flicked through the forms. 'Seven in total, they did a pretty good job actually. Let's go finish it off.'

'Erm, do you think the boss will want us doing this?'

'Probably not, but it needs to be completed anyway and besides, just because I keep seeing a silver car doesn't really mean much except to me, so it wouldn't hurt to do the house to house.'

'I have a bad feeling about this. You better let me knock on their door because I'm not going to be held responsible for your blatant disregard of your own safety.'

She couldn't help the laugh that escaped.

'What's going on here then? Far too much hilarity for this place.'

They turned to see Mads standing there, and both grinned.

'Seriously, what have you two got to laugh about? I'd have thought you were up to your neck in it.'

Morgan shrugged. 'We are up to our neck in it, but you know how it is, a good laugh away keeps the doctor away.'

He shook his head. 'Seriously, don't become a poet. I have no idea how it is with you, Brookes, and I don't want to either. Glad you're not still on my shift; I couldn't keep up with the paperwork.'

He turned and walked towards the duty sergeant's office, and Cain whispered, 'Do you think he's having a bad day?'

Not sure why it did, but this tickled her even more and she laughed even louder. Cain grabbed her elbow and the remainder of the packet of biscuits and steered her towards the car park exit. He'd managed to secure a set of car keys for a plain divisional car, and he clicked the fob to see which car unlocked, because some dimwit had wiped the reg off the key ring and not written it back on.

Cain drove down the full length of Fenton Street, but there was no silver car parked outside the Dents' house, and Morgan felt a little deflated.

'It doesn't mean there's no one home. They might not be both out in it.'

'Are you psychic? You read my mind all the time.'

He shook his head. 'Nah, just perceptive. I don't believe in all that kind of stuff.'

He squeezed the car into a tiny space, and she grabbed the clipboard. 'Should we split up?'

'No. I'm not letting you out of my sight. Benno would kill me.'

She sighed. 'Okay, be quicker if we did though.' She didn't say it, because she knew he meant well, but she was sick of being treated like a child. 'We'll save the Dents for last.'

They began to knock on the doors that hadn't replied on the initial round of investigations and got answers from two out of the seven. Morgan's eyes kept glancing down at Lexie's house, and it was hard to get the image of the girl out of her head.

'Anyway, I don't know why someone would do that, poor girl she was so sweet.'

She turned to the woman who had been talking to Cain, and she nodded. 'She was, it's very sad. Sorry, I didn't catch your name?'

'Debbie. Have you lot not caught him yet? How are we supposed to sleep at night knowing what happened on our own doorstep? Although I work nights at the nursing home, so I wouldn't have been here anyway.'

'Which nursing home?'

'Aldingham Manor.'

'Were you at work last night?'

She nodded. 'There was a right fuss at the church, some bloody kids set it on fire.'

'Have you spoken to anyone from work this morning?'

'No, I don't answer my phone when I'm not at work if the number flashes up. I give them my pound of flesh every shift I work; they're not taking it when I'm off as well.'

'So, you haven't heard about Evelyn.'

'No, what about her?'

Morgan looked around, wishing the woman would ask them inside, but she didn't budge.

'They found her body this morning. She was murdered.'

The woman stumbled backwards; her hand clasped across her mouth. 'No.'

'Yes.'

'Did you check on her last night?'

'How? Who would murder her?'

'That's what my colleagues who are at the home are trying to find out. Did you look after her last night?'

'No, I was on the other unit, Woodland Walk. I can't believe that. It must be why I have seven missed calls from there and an unknown number.'

'You might be better ringing back; someone will want to formally interview you.'

Debbie nodded. 'I will, shit.'

Then she closed the door on them.

Cain sighed. 'What is it with this street? It's like the hub that connects everything to everyone. Yet nobody knows anything.'

'I wish that I knew.'

They walked towards 101, and she whispered, 'Let's hope we hit the jackpot.'

Morgan did her police knock, firm and loud, to show it was important. There was no reply, Cain stepped closer and hammered on the door with his fist.

'I'm here, there's no one inside.'

She turned to look at the guy who had crept up on them, who had just spoken. He was wearing a beanie hat and a black jacket. She couldn't tell if it was the driver of the car because she'd only seen fleeting glances of them.

'Is there a problem? Or are you selling double glazing, because I'm not interested in it if you are.'

'Police. We're finishing off the house to house. I assume you've heard about what happened?'

He arched an eyebrow at her. 'You better come inside then.'

Cain glanced at her, and she felt bad. He'd only just returned to work after being stabbed going into a similar situation. The guy opened the door, and they followed him inside. He pointed to the sofa.

'Sit down, I can't really tell you anything though. Neither my wife nor I saw or heard anything. Isn't that what you usually ask?' He was smiling, and she got the impression he was trying to be nice.

'What kind of car do you drive? We're also checking out all the vehicles in the area.'

'I used to drive a Picasso, but we sold it last month. It was getting too expensive to run so it had to go, and we've been trying to walk more so haven't bought another yet.'

Her shoulders slumped, and she felt as if they had hit another dead end, but she continued.

'Do you have the name and address of the person who bought it?'

'Liz will, somewhere. He's local, we only put a sign in the car that day and he knocked on the door later that night.'

'Would you be able to describe him?'

'White, probably around forty, possibly younger, clean-shaven, shaved head. That's about it, really, he had the cash in his pocket, so you know, we gave him the keys and off he went. The DVLA will have his details if he's sent off the new keeper form.'

She shook her head. 'Unfortunately, he hasn't, it's still registered to you.'

'Is that why you're here? Do you think he had something to do with what happened to that poor girl down the road?'

Cain stood up. 'Hard to say, we're just following all leads and hoping they give us something back. When will your wife be home to get the details from her?'

'In a couple of hours.'

Morgan asked, 'Where were you last night between the hours of eight and ten?'

His eyes opened wide; his lips parted a little. 'Oh, I was here watching TV with my wife. We rarely go out of an evening; everything is too expensive around here.'

Morgan smiled at him, nodding in agreement.

He continued. 'Do you have a phone number? I could ring you as soon as I've spoken to Liz and give you them.'

Morgan passed him a card with her work number on. 'If you ring that and leave me a message, I'll get in touch as soon as I can. Thank you for your help.'

He walked them to the door, then closed it softly behind them.

FORTY-FOUR

Morgan's phone began to ring as soon as she got into the car, and she looked down to see the area code 0161. She didn't know anyone in Manchester and was about to divert it, when she slid her finger across at the last minute, wondering if it could be Bronte.

'Hello.'

'Hi, is this Detective Brookes?'

'Speaking.'

'I'm the assistant governor at HMP Manchester, Donovan Price. We have a bit of a situation here and I'm hoping you might be able to help.'

She put the phone on loudspeaker so Cain could listen.

'I'll try my best, but I'm not too sure how I can be of any assistance.' For an awful moment she thought that it was something to do with her murderous brother Taylor; and if that was the case then she didn't care one little bit.

'Thanks, I have Bronte Potter here in my office. She asked that I contact you. I hope this is acceptable?'

Cain looked at her wide-eyed, and she didn't know whether to be relieved or concerned.

'Yes, of course it is. Is Bronte okay?'

'A little shook up and agitated, but generally she's okay. Maybe it might be better for you to speak to her direct. I'll pass you over.'

A thousand questions were running through her mind.

'Morgan.'

'Hey, what's up?'

'I came to see him; I don't know why I just couldn't stop thinking about if I did it might make me feel better.'

'You went to visit Harrison?'

'Yeah, he got me so mad that I attacked him and pushed him off his chair. I scratched his face too. The guards had to drag me out. I wanted to kill him.'

Cain high fived Morgan, his face lit up with a huge grin, and she felt her own face break into a smile.

'Are they pressing charges?'

'Don't know. Hang on I'll pass you back to Donovan.'

'Hi, Morgan, no we don't think it would be in the best interest to pursue an assault charge after what Bronte has endured. However, we will need someone to come and collect her. I feel responsible to make sure she is in safe hands. She's told me about her friend and the arson attack. Mr Williams also seemed to know about this and found it highly amusing. He made a veiled threat towards Ms Potter about how they were all going to die. I know there is a murder investigation ongoing, and you must be very busy, but I think it might be worth someone talking to Mr Williams about what he knows. Just my observations, I understand if there isn't anybody free at this present time.'

'I'm on my way, tell Bronte I'll be there as soon as I can. Oh, and thank you, Donovan, for phoning, it's very kind and considerate of you.'

'I thought it best under the extenuating circumstances. Drive

safe, Detective Brookes, I'll still be here when you arrive, to make the necessary arrangements.'

'That's very kind of you.'

'My pleasure.'

He hung up, and she looked at Cain; he was shaking his head.

'You have to run this one by the boss. There is no way I'm running off to Manchester prison with you and not telling him. He'd have a heart attack on the spot.'

'Come on, let's go find him and see what he thinks.'

'Morgan, what if he says no?'

She shrugged. 'Someone has to go pick Bronte up.'

'Suppose.'

She rang Ben. 'Where are you?'

'On my way back to the station with the boss.'

'Good, I'll meet you there.'

Cain nodded. 'You don't need a colleague; you need an Uber driver.'

Morgan smiled at him. 'I need both and you fit the role perfectly.'

There was a briefing due to start imminently so Morgan and Cain made their way to the blue room, which was packed with everyone from task force, CSI, uniforms and CID. Amy was there with a pad and pencil ready to take notes. Ben was talking to Marc, their heads bent so close to each other they were almost touching. He didn't even look their way or acknowledge their arrival, so they squeezed in at the back of the room next to Al and Daisy, who were sipping coffee from chipped mugs. Al whispered, 'Where's the biscuits, Daisy?'

'Dunno, I left half a packet of digestives by the kettle earlier and someone swiped them.'

Morgan glanced at Cain with a smile on her face, and he blanked her.

Ben stood up. 'Thanks, guys, for coming at short notice, this is not an easy case. We have the murder of Lexie White two evenings ago, and last night there was an arson attack on the church hall, where a number of women were holding a meeting, which thankfully was caught in time before any real harm was done to anyone. The suspect then made their way to the nursing home across the street, where he hid out until we'd left the area and killed one of the elderly residents, Evelyn Reynolds. Evelyn has only been at Aldingham Manor four months. She transferred from Saint Quentin's because of differences with the nursing staff and being moved out of her room to one that didn't have a garden view.'

One of the coppers stuck their hand up. 'Are we thinking one of the staff bumped her off because she complained?'

Morgan watched Ben's face to see if his eyes would roll to give away his train of thought, but ever the professional he didn't. He shook his head.

'Not at this moment in time we're not. Now, some of you may be familiar with Evelyn; her grandson was arrested after he committed murders and intended to kill her.'

Morgan felt relieved he didn't bring her into it.

'Evelyn managed to stop him by blinding him in one eye, which was an extremely heroic thing to do given the circumstances and the fact that she only has the use of one hand. Morgan has a theory that the person who killed Lexie White has also killed Evelyn. I agree with Morgan that whoever killed Lexie, on all counts of probability, also killed Evelyn and tried to kill the women in the meeting. Which leads us to a suspect pool which at the moment is non-existent. By the end of today I want that changing and some names added to it we can focus on.'

Morgan held up a hand. 'Boss, while me and Cain were on our way to search for Bronte, we saw the same silver car that I think Milly Blake saw parked outside her house. House to house on Fenton Street gave us a witness who saw a similar car the night of the murder. It disappeared down a one-way street, but after some CCTV enquiries we got a hit and have a numberplate, name and address.'

A cheer went around the room, followed by a round of applause which made Morgan's cheeks turn a deep, fiery red. She held up her hand. 'Don't get too excited, the keeper enquiries led us to 101 Fenton Street, and the registered owners are William and Elizabeth Dent. We spoke to William who confirmed they sold the car a month ago. But they did confirm a male, with a bald head, who matches the description we have of the man in the silver car.'

There was a collective sigh that whispered around the room. Meanwhile Ben was staring at her with a look of admiration on his face.

She continued. 'William is going to ring me later when he's spoken with Liz, his wife, who dealt with the guy who bought it, but for now, we are looking out for a silver car with the number plate J34 XUN. It has to be a local buyer because he said that they only stuck a note in the car earlier the same day it was bought.'

Marc was also staring at her, only he wasn't quite as dumbstruck as Ben. 'Good work, both of you. I'll get a marker put on it so if it passes any ANPR cameras we'll know where it's travelling to and get it pulled over. Wendy also had some luck at the nursing home earlier this morning. She got a couple of partial prints off the window we think he gained entry through. Have you had anything back, Wendy?'

'Unfortunately, they don't match any prints we have on the database, but when you do apprehend a suspect, we can see if they're a match.'

Ben was looking down at the sheet of papers clutched between his fingers. 'I want to speak to Al and Daisy separately, if that's okay with you two. For now, I want everyone out looking for this car. All the women who we believe are being targeted are all at a safe house, except for one, but they should be being moved shortly somewhere else, but that's not for you to worry about.'

Al asked, 'What about the nursing home, is it likely he'll go back there?'

Morgan shook her head. 'I don't think so, there is no one else living there who has already survived a previous attack from a killer.'

Daisy was shaking her head. 'This is like some terrifying horror film where the killer is targeting final girls who survived the first time they should have died. You couldn't make this stuff up. Morgan, do you think whoever this is has you on their list?'

All heads turned to look at Daisy and Morgan, and her already inflamed cheeks felt as if they were on fire.

'Who knows?'

She had been about to tell them about Bronte but had stopped herself, preferring to talk to her team alone in their office. The room was too full of people, and she felt as if it needed to be kept between them for the time being.

Ben began to talk about the patrol strategy he wanted on a loop around the previous attack sites and murder sites, and she couldn't help glancing at her watch. They needed to get a move on and get to Manchester before it got too late.

When he finally dismissed everyone, she grabbed his arm and whispered, 'I need to talk to you urgently.'

'Really, I was thinking the same thing.'

He was angry with her for going off with Cain on enquiries. Everyone filtered out of the room except for Daisy and Al, who were hanging about for Ben. He held up his hand. 'Two minutes, just need to speak to Morgan.'

Al nodded. 'Don't you two be having a domestic in works time. I can't be bothered with the paperwork.'

Ben ushered Morgan out of the blue room and into the corridor. 'What were you thinking?'

'That it was too much of a coincidence to ignore it and now we have an address and numberplate.'

'You should have run it past me first.'

'There was no time and Cain was with me. It's not like I was on my own. There's something else you need to know. I got a phone call from the assistant governor at HMP Manchester. He has Bronte there. She went to visit Harrison and attacked him. She needs picking up, and he needs speaking to because he made veiled threats to her that they were all going to die, and I need to interview him to see how he could possibly know this.'

'Fuck my life, why, Morgan, why you?'

'I don't know, I'm sorry, but who else is there to go? Cain will come with me; I won't be on my own. We cannot ignore this; he might know something.'

'And you think he's going to talk to you? Do you even want to look at him after he tried to hang you?'

'If you send Amy or someone else, he might not talk at all or refuse to see them. If he wanted to see Bronte, there's a good chance he will see me even if it is only to relive his twisted memories.'

He turned and slammed the palms of his hands against the wall and groaned. 'Fuck me.'

Marc was striding down the corridor towards them. 'Are you two okay?'

Ben shook his head. 'Tell the boss what you just told me.'

Morgan repeated herself and to give Marc his due he didn't seem as disturbed by it as Ben.

'What's the problem, Ben? I know we can't really spare two officers to go on a jolly to Manchester, but we can't not send someone, and she has a point: there's no point sending anyone all that way if there's not a cat in hells chance he won't see them. I can't spare Cain as well as you, though. Are you okay to go there? When you get off the motorway on the way back, if you let me or Ben know I'll send a patrol to meet you both and escort you back the rest of the way.'

She didn't even look in Ben's direction because she could feel the heat and fury radiating from him, sending waves of hot anger her way.

'What if she gets followed on the way there?'

'Morgan can take my car, it's fast and if he has been stalking Morgan as well as everyone else, he won't recognise it.'

'He's not some kind of superman. He won't be driving around now. He knew that I saw him, and he drove away before we could follow him. I think he's going to be lying low and re-evaluating his plans. Maybe we're giving him more credit than he's due. He was panicked, angry and frustrated last night, and he left a print behind. If we find the car, then we'll have a wealth of forensics to nail him with.'

Marc dug his hand into his trouser pocket and passed her the Porsche key ring. 'She's my baby, she's all I have so be kind to her, Morgan.'

She grinned at him. 'Of course, I will.' She passed him her car keys, and he laughed.

'No offence and it's not that I'm a snob, but have you seen the state of that car? I had a VW Golf like that years ago. I'd rather use a div car, thank you.'

She tutted at him. 'You are a snob; my trusty car always starts even on the coldest days, and it's never let me down yet.'

She walked off before either of them could stop her. She knew Ben was teetering on the edge of a cliff and would be thinking that Marc had just handed her a loaded gun. She heard Marc remark that he better get her added onto his insurance, and he disappeared back to his office.

She ran down the stairs, not turning to look back because

she felt as if she was betraying Ben by doing this, but she also knew that she had no choice. There were too many lives at stake, and if there was a chance Harrison Williams knew something then she had to go and face him one last time.

FORTY-FIVE

Morgan felt a little dubious about driving Marc's car. It still smelled of that new car scent. The seats were soft leather, and she had to wipe her boots on the tarmac several times before she was brave enough to put them on his pristine car mat.

She ran her hand along the deep red paintwork and made a silent promise to look after it, not sure if she was telling the car or herself. She didn't wait long before giving herself a little pep talk that she could drive this with no trouble, plus she wanted to leave before Marc changed his mind, or Ben came running after her to beg her not to go on her own.

She knew the way to the prison, had unfortunately been there before. After a quick prayer to the universe to help her have a smooth, uneventful drive she left the car park as slowly as she could. She knew that Marc would be watching her out of one of the huge glass windows out the front to make sure she wasn't driving like a maniac.

Once she was on the A590 it was all smooth driving from there. She kept an eye in the rear-view mirror to make sure she wasn't being followed, but it was busy, and she had to pay attention to the road. It seemed like she reached the car park near to the prison in no time. She did worry about leaving Marc's nice car in such close proximity to a place full of convicts who no doubt may have some associates that were unsavoury too, but figured she wouldn't be in there too long. She showed the guards her warrant card and she was immediately taken down to a room further along, where Bronte was sitting sipping a plastic cup of hot chocolate and flipping through the curled up pages of one of those celebrity magazines.

'Hey, how are you?'

She smiled at Morgan. 'I'm sorry for this mess, I don't know what possessed me.'

'How do you feel now?'

'Like a fucking boss bitch!'

Morgan began to laugh. 'I bet you do, feels good to get that off your chest, eh?'

She nodded. 'It was hard though, he looked so different, and I had this rush of emotions, because you know back then he was the love of my life before he screwed it up for good.'

'I bet, well you're okay at least.'

There was a knock on the door, and the man that walked in was a lot younger than she'd expected.

He held out his hand. 'Donovan Price, thanks for coming so swiftly. I've spoken to Harrison and he's willing to chat with you. Bronte, are you okay to wait here a little longer and then I'm sure you'll be glad to get out of here with Detective Brookes.'

She smiled at him and nodded. 'I'm fine, thank you.'

He turned to Morgan. 'Shall we?' Then opened the door and waited for her to follow him. When they were out of Bronte's hearing he continued. 'She's a brave woman, feisty too. You should have heard him complaining like a baby about his face. He wanted her arresting.'

'I bet he did, it's very kind of you not to do that.'

'Well, technically we're supposed to, and I did seek advice

from the sergeant at the local station who deals with prisoner assaults, but when I told him the circumstances, he agreed it was not in anyone's interest to pursue an assault charge. He said because Bronte had never been in any kind of trouble that she could write him a letter of apology that would no doubt get lost in the post.'

'Has she written a letter?'

'Not on my watch, like he said it probably got lost in the post.'

Morgan smiled at him; he was a good man and she liked him a lot.

'Don't get me wrong, I'm all for prisoners being treated fairly, but the man killed her entire family and left her for dead. How does he even have the gall to want to get her charged with a minor assault? Some days my brain can't cope with human beings and how their thought processes work.'

She smiled to herself and thought *me too, on a daily basis.* He stopped outside a room and opened the door.

'If you go in and take a seat we'll go and fetch Mr Harrison. There will be two guards with him, and he will be wearing arm restraints because I'm also aware that he attempted to kill you too, Detective Brookes. You are also a brave woman. I'm not sure I would want to be in a confined space with a person who tried to take my life. I read his file thoroughly after the incident with Bronte, and I'm aware I may have put you in a difficult situation by asking you to come here for which I apologise, but I can see you are a lot tougher than you look.' He winked at her and left her staring after him not sure if she should take that as a compliment or not.

She tried to control her breathing and not fidget so she looked relaxed as Harrison was led into the room, flanked by guards at each side. She stared at him. If she passed him in the street, she would never have recognised him; he did look so different. He was no longer that gangly teenage boy. He was a man and one that worked out daily judging by the muscles and broad chest. She felt an oddly satisfying feeling at the deep laceration across the length of his cheek that was crusted with dried blood. He was smiling at her, and she smiled back, waiting for him to take a seat before speaking.

'Harrison, it's been a while.'

'Morgan, it has. How are you?'

She paused, was he asking her a genuine question or was it all a game she could play along nicely when it suited her. 'Busy, always busy.'

He nodded. 'You are, I read the papers.'

And she realised that he might have been bluffing when he'd threatened Bronte, and she may have just wasted an entire afternoon chasing after him for no reason other than to feed his ego.

'How are you?'

He pointed to his face. 'Have you come to arrest her for assaulting me?'

'Not my jurisdiction, I've come to escort her home.'

He stared at her, and she could feel his eyes taking everything in from the messy bun that fine wisps of her copper hair were escaping from, to her lightly freckled face, her eyeliner, then her black T-shirt and her tattoos, which she'd purposely left on show by removing her jacket.

'Nice tattoos, I had no idea you had so many.'

She glanced down at her almost finished sleeve and shrugged. 'They're kind of addictive and I have the best tattooist.'

'Not in here they're not.'

'I can imagine they're not. It's painful with a tattoo gun, not sure how it would feel without one. I'm not here to talk about tattoos though, and I think you realise that. I want to know why you said to Bronte that they were all going to die.'

He pushed back in his chair, folding his arms as best as he could, and smiled at her.

'Didn't mean a thing by it, just came out in anger.'

'I get that, but if you were angry with her why not say she was going to die? Why did you refer to them as a collective?'

'I'm not sure what you're saying, who is a collective? Do you think you're clever, Morgan? Do you think that you're not involved in this in any way?'

'Why should I be? I'm just doing the job I'm paid to do, nothing more or less. It's nothing personal, it's how I earn the money to pay my bills at the end of each month and pay for these if any is left over.' She held her arm up so he could see the tattoos again.

'What is your job to you? Do you enjoy it? I think you must, it suits you very well.'

'My job is to catch evil people like yourself and get them off the streets away from the nice, normal people who don't deserve what people like you think is okay to inflict on them.'

'People like me?'

'Killers.'

He grinned at her. 'He's coming for you too; you know that right? Take this as a friendly warning to be very careful out there. I wouldn't trust anyone, not even your colleagues.' He winked at her.

She leaned forward, putting her elbows onto the white plastic table in front of her. 'And why should I take any notice of you? You're full of shit and know absolutely nothing about what's happening on the outside world, except for what snippets you might hear in the news or in the paper.'

'He drives a silver car, he tried to burn you all to death but failed and so he will have snuck into that nursing home and killed that old woman who also shouldn't have survived but did. God knows why, there was no point. She'd have been better off dead. I wonder what he did with her eyeballs though? I bet that's got you guessing.'

Anger tore through her, and she had to force herself to contain it. She couldn't afford to lunge at him like Bronte did or they'd both end up getting arrested.

'Who is he?'

'I can't say, but he writes very nice, graphic letters. I bet if you asked all your other loyal fans if they'd had a fan letter from him, they'd tell you yes.'

'Why would he want to write to you losers? Have you asked yourself that? Is he not gloating about finishing the jobs you so spectacularly failed at because you're all just messed up mother's boys who weren't brave enough to stand up for yourselves in the first place.'

She was grinning at him, and she could see a muscle in the side of his cheek begin to twitch, along with his left eye. He was getting angry with her, and she didn't care in the slightest. She wanted him to slip up and if this was the only way then so be it.

'I'll tell you what I think: he isn't seeking your approval. He's rubbing it in that you're locked up and he's out there roaming around free, taking all the glory that you had taken away from you. Did he ask you for details about the crimes you committed that weren't public knowledge, so he could use them to his advantage and make him look like a far superior killer than you amateurs ever were? I bet he did, and you spoon-fed him everything because you were so grateful for a bit of attention from someone.'

Harrison's chair scraped back with such force it tippled over as he rushed towards her, and the two guards who were standing close by scrambled to get to him. Morgan pushed herself away from the table seconds before he reached her and stood up, watching the guards wrestle with him.

'I'm done, thank you, Harrison, you told me everything I

needed to know. I really hope I never have to set eyes on you again.'

This time he did try to get to her, kicking the overturned chair he'd been sitting on flying across the room. The guards were on top of him, and she slammed her hand against the red emergency call button on the wall. Seconds later more guards burst through the door and had Harrison in arm and leg restraints, dragging him out of the room. She watched them go and blew out a long breath.

Donovan appeared. 'Wow, that wasn't quite what I was expecting. Are you okay?'

'I'm fine but could you do me a favour and search his cell for that letter? He'll have hidden it away. It might have forensics on it that we could really do with.'

'Absolutely, we'll keep him out of his cell and do a search now.'

'I can't tell you how much I appreciate your help.'

He nodded. 'Glad to be of assistance, Morgan. Come on, I'll take you back to collect Bronte and you can head back home.'

She couldn't wait to tell Ben that their suspect had written to the killers who'd failed at killing the women in the support group. Whether to gloat or to commiserate and make them feel better she had no idea. Her heart racing, she was glad to be escaping the prison unscathed.

FORTY-SIX

Ben was struggling to concentrate. Not only was he worried about Morgan going to speak to Harrison Williams, but she was also driving Marc's bloody Porsche to top it all off. Amy came rushing into the office, waving frantically at him. He banged his thigh on the corner of his desk running to see what was wrong. His heart in his mouth.

'Ben, they found the car.'

'What car and who did?'

'That silver car Morgan mentioned at the briefing. Amber and Scotty on patrol. She thought she'd go check all the car parks to see if it had been abandoned, and it's at Pelter Bridge car park. She said it's not even locked up and the keys are in the ignition.'

'Right, wow. Well, I guess that's amazing.'

'Amazing, it's a bloody gift from the gods.'

'It would be if there was a dead body inside.'

'What another?'

'No, the killer. Be great if he'd decided he could no longer live with himself and ended it all.'

She laughed. 'You live in a fantasy world, but I suppose it

would be pretty fab. Killer dead, a confession in ink, case closed, everyone safe. Talking of everyone safe have you heard from Morgan yet?'

As if by magic his phone vibrated with a message.

On my way back, see you soon.

He turned the screen around to show Amy.

'Well, I guess that's a good start. Are you coming to see this car?'

'Yep, give me a minute, I'll meet you downstairs.'

The five-minute drive to Pelter Bridge car park was uneventful. The car park wasn't busy and there, sitting in the far corner as if waiting for its driver to return from a brisk fell walk, was a silver Picasso. There was a marked van parked near to it with Amber leaning against it. Ben jumped out of the car and grinned at Amber. 'Nice work.'

She laughed. 'It wasn't exactly hard, just a thought.'

'Take a compliment, you did good.'

For the first time he noticed that she had a pink glow to her cheeks and wasn't full of herself. Maybe she was losing her bad attitude, or had he caught her on a good day? He didn't know, but he thought she was a good copper, or would be if she could get over her dislike of everything.

'Most people park here if White Moss is too busy so they can go up to Rydal Caves.'

Ben nodded. 'They do; how do you and Scotty fancy a wander up there to check our suspect hasn't gone up there to cause mischief?'

She sighed. 'I knew you'd say that. I guess so, but you can tell Scotty because he's so bloody lazy and I'm not arguing with him.'

Ben tugged on a pair of blue gloves and opened the passenger door. The stench from inside hit his nostrils making him gag. It smelled of decomposition. There were a couple of blue bottles that had found their way inside, and he knew it wouldn't be long before the whole car was alive with them. He hadn't cleaned away the blood from Lexie properly – unless there was a body in the boot. But all the women were accounted for and had been taken to a safe house on the outskirts of Lytham St Annes. The only one missing to his knowledge was Bronte and she was with Morgan on their way back from the prison. He slammed the door shut.

'Did you take a look inside or the boot?'

She shook her head. 'Nope, I could see it wasn't locked so I called it in. I didn't want to mess with forensics.'

He was a little impressed and nodded, then walked around to the boot and pressed the button. The sound of buzzing filled his ears as a cloud of flies and the stench of decomp hit him so hard that he gagged and slammed it back down. There was a body in there, but he couldn't see who it was because of the flies crawling all over their face.

Amber groaned; her face had turned a shade of green that Ben thought his own must echo. He staggered away gulping in mouthfuls of fresh air. Scotty, who was watching from the opposite side of the van, called, 'I'll go check the caves. Amber, you wait here and scene guard.' He was striding away before either of them could call him back, and Ben heard her say 'Arsehole' under her breath.

He leaned against the van, trying to compose himself. He had not expected that. If everyone from the support group was accounted for, who the hell was in the boot of that car? They'd clearly been there days by the state of the body and the flies. Had he been driving around with that body in the back of the car the whole time? The audacity, not to mention the smell. How did he do it? Had he not been afraid he'd get pulled over?

He leaned against the tree and wondered how they were going to manage to run this many cases with so few staff. Then he rang Marc.

'Sir, we have a huge problem. There's another body; it's in the boot of the car Amber found.'

Even cool, calm, collected Marc swore loudly down his ear, making him hold the phone away so as not to deafen him. Amy had been watching from afar and came closer. Pulling the neck of her shirt over her nose she pointed at the boot of the car.

'How many days do you reckon that body has been in there? It's got to be at least three or four? Maybe he killed this one first. If we can figure out who it is we might have a better idea of who he is?'

Ben couldn't take his eyes away from the trunk. 'Do you want to search their pockets for ID? Be my guest.'

'Can't, I'll throw up all over. Where's Morgan when you need her, I bet she'd do it.'

He didn't doubt that she would, but he wouldn't wish that on her. 'I guess we'll have to wait for CSI. Maybe when we get it moved Wendy will check them for us.'

As if he'd summoned her, the CIS van turned into the car park with Marc sitting next to Wendy. She waved at them, before getting suited and booted. Marc joined them and was staring at the car.

'I guess we don't need Declan to confirm there is no proof of life?'

'Nope we can call it. He's aware and said he'll see whoever it is at the mortuary. Once Wendy is done, we can get the undertakers to move the body.'

'Any idea who it is?'

'Well, it's not the killer because he drove it here and left it. It's not a long walk back to Rydal Falls or Ambleside if you're a walker, or I suppose he could have got picked up, but surely he would have started to smell. It would have begun to seep into the interior of the car, so how the hell he could drive around with that is beyond me. It's only been a couple of hours since Morgan saw the car, so unless he got picked up, we could have him walking back into Rydal Falls captured on CCTV. We need to get someone to go around checking the camera footage on the main routes in. He could also have gone up onto the fell.'

Marc was staring at the back of the car. 'What's the plan then?'

Wendy's phone began to ring. 'Ian.'

She began an animated conversation with her crime scene manager that lasted a little longer than Ben expected. He was waiting for her to hang up but to give her credit she didn't.

'He's happy for us to process the body in the boot the best that we can.'

'So is Declan; he said there is nothing he could do anyway and if you can get all the samples before we move it.'

She smiled at Ben. 'Job's a good one then, glad I haven't eaten my tea yet.'

'Yeah, you will be when you look in the car.'

'Being killed is bad enough but to be dumped in the boot of a car like a discarded bag of rubbish is just awful. I could really do with a hand to process the body. I'm going to take some samples of fibre tapings off any exposed areas of skin, swab under the nails using crime lite for possible body fluids then I'll swab them if I find any. First though have you determined if the murder happened in the boot of the car? If it did then we're going to need a blood pattern analysis scientist to process it before I can even get started.'

Ben shook his head. 'No, sorry. I opened the boot then slammed it shut again pretty quick.'

Wendy grinned at him. 'Come on then, you can be my assistant and we'll take a look together.'

'Why me?'

'Because your footprints are already around the vehicle, and

I need a hand.' As she walked towards the car she whispered, 'And because you're the best out of a bad bunch.'

He smiled at her. 'I won't be if I throw up all over though. Do you not want to wait for Ian or Claire to come and help you?'

'Claire is at a commercial break-in. I already phoned her on my way here to see if she could give me a hand. Ian is as much use as a chocolate fireguard. Sorry, Ben, but you're my last hope.'

He stared at the boot of the car and felt a wave of nausea begin to rise from his stomach. 'God help you then if I'm your last hope.'

'You'll be fine, just do what I say and try not to think about the smell or the flies.'

'You're not helping.' He was worried about the sadness that was about to consume him dealing with yet another horrific, pointless death in such a short space of time. His heart felt physically heavy with the burden of it all, and he had no idea how Morgan was still functioning.

'I just want you to take the samples from me and label the bags. You can do it and probably have many times before.'

He nodded, he had but it felt like forever since the last time he'd marked up his own evidence bags. Wendy was placing footplates down as she walked one in front of the other for them to stand on, in case there was any evidence around the car. 'Just follow my lead and you won't go wrong.' She handed him a face mask.

He could think of many other things he would rather be doing, but realised if she was able to do this, then the least he could do was assist her the best he could, even if he did feel way out of his depth. And it would take his mind off Morgan driving home.

FORTY-SEVEN

They didn't talk much, both of them lost in their own thoughts, until Morgan's phone began to ring. She didn't recognise the number. She pointed to it. 'Can you answer that, please, and tell them I'll ring back?'

Bronte picked it up. 'Hi, Morgan's phone, she's driving right now. Can I take a message?' ... 'Okay, yes I'll let her know, thank you.' Bronte replaced the phone on the charging pad. 'Some guy called William Dent said his wife is home in five minutes, if you want to pop by and speak to her about a car.'

'Amazing, we'll call on the way to the station and I'll nip in. I don't know where you're supposed to be, so you're going to have to come with me if that's okay.'

She let out a long sigh, and Morgan felt bad for her. The woman had her whole life turned around in a matter of hours and things weren't improving any or likely to anytime soon. They weren't far from William's house, so she drove straight to Fenton Street.

Stopping the car, she turned to Bronte. 'I won't be long.'

'I don't bloody think so. I'm not staying on my own in this car. I know this is Lexie's street, I can see her house down there.'

Morgan glanced at the house then back at Bronte. 'I'll get in trouble if I take you inside.'

'You'll get in more trouble if you come out and I'm dead.'

She had a point. 'Okay, don't speak or say who you are. We'll bluff it. I only need to get a name and address off his wife; it won't take long.'

They crossed the road and didn't even have to knock on the door before the front door opened and a red-faced Will was standing there, smiling at them. 'Nice car, is that yours, Detective Brookes?'

'I wish, it's my boss's. Thanks for ringing, this won't take long.'

They walked inside. The house was in darkness, and he quickly turned on the lights. 'Sorry, I just beat you home and I thought Elizabeth would be here by now. She rang to say she'd be home before me.'

'That's okay, we can hang on.'

He pointed to the sofa and smiled at them. Morgan noticed how his eyes kept flicking towards Bronte.

'Do I know you? You look so familiar to me, but I can't place you.'

She shook her head. 'Don't think so.'

'Oh, sorry, my mistake. Look, I found some paperwork in the kitchen drawer if you'd like to take a look at it and see if it's any use. It's on the table in the dining room.'

For a moment Morgan got a bad feeling, but he smiled again at her, throwing her off guard. 'Yeah, we can do that.'

They both stood up, and he led them to the dining room where it looked as if he'd tipped out the entire contents of the kitchen drawer all over it.

'Thanks, we'll take a look.'

Bronte, who still hadn't said very much, followed her in.

'Sorry, it's a mess I'm not very organised. Look, I'll just go see if Elizabeth is coming; it's not like her to take so long.' He left them to it, and Morgan felt the tension in her shoulder slide a little.

'Come on, we're looking for a green slip from the DVLA.' She began to route through the pages of letters, pens and notes.

'Is this it?'

Bronte was waving a green slip in the air.

'Yes, it is. Well done, come on, let's get out of here.' She took the slip of paper from her.

A cool breeze ran through the house. Will was standing at the front door looking up and down the street.

'Thank you, we found it. As soon as I've finished with it, I'll pop it back.'

'No worries, we don't need it anyway, I don't think. I'm rubbish at that sort of thing, Elizabeth does it all.'

'Well, thank you for your help.'

'My pleasure, ladies, good luck with finding this guy.'

He closed the door; Morgan hadn't realised just how nervous she'd been until he was out of sight.

'He seems nice, helpful too.'

'Yes, he does.'

'You were worried in there, weren't you? Why?'

Morgan shrugged. 'I call it instinct and it's not usually wrong, but he turned out okay, so I guess it is sometimes. Let's get you back to the station. I have so much to do.'

As they got into the car, Bronte squealed. 'Crap, I left my bag on the sofa.'

Morgan rolled her eyes at her. 'Get in, I'll go get it.'

She sauntered back to the house and knocked on the door.

Will opened it with Bronte's bag in his hand. 'I was just about to chase after you.'

'That was lucky then, saved you a job.'

She took it and threw the bag into the back seat, not sure why Bronte had felt the need to take it with her in the first place.

FORTY-EIGHT

Morgan didn't feel right taking Bronte back to the station. She phoned Marc.

'Boss, where should I take Bronte?'

'We're kind of short staffed here and could do with you. Where are you?'

'Just left the Fenton Street area.'

There was a slight pause. 'Does she want to go home?'

Bronte was shaking her head.

'No.'

'You could take her to the safe house, but there are no staff to keep observations outside at this moment. Ask her what she wants to do. As soon as we can, we'll get her transferred out of the county.'

'Thanks. Where are you all?'

'Pelter Bridge car park at a crime scene, will fill you in when you get here. See you soon.'

He hung up, and she noticed a beeping sound coming from the car and let out a groan.

'Oh God, what do you think that is?'

Morgan glanced down at the dashboard, to see if there were

any engine lights on, and realised the fuel tank was almost empty. There was only nine miles left in the tank. The safe house was three miles away roughly, and the car park was another two in the other direction. The nearest petrol station was four miles away, so she should just make it.

'You're out of petrol.'

'I know, but you'd think a fancy car like this would have a better warning system than that stupid beeping noise, that's enough to drive anyone mad.'

Bronte leaned across to grab her bag, which she clutched on her knee. As Morgan left Rydal Falls, they left behind the well-lit roads and were now on the pitch-black, unforgiving country roads. She made the turn to go down the narrow lane to the small row of cottages. Bronte unzipped her bag and began to root around in it.

'I think it's my bag that's beeping.'

Morgan glanced at her. 'Is it?'

A stag jumped the hedge at the side of the road, and she slammed the brakes on as it landed with a thud right in front of Marc's Porsche, literally centimetres away. The headlights picked out the blackness of its eyes as it stared right into hers.

'Jesus, that was close.'

Bronte's head had jerked forward, and she'd let go of the bag. It tumbled to the floor, the contents spilling out into the footwell of the car. The huge animal seemed to nod to Morgan as if apologising, and then with another jump it had cleared the low drystone wall on the other side and was gone into the woods. Morgan's heart was pounding inside of her chest at the thought of almost writing Marc's car off, even though it wasn't her fault. She glanced down at the footwell of the car and felt time stand still. There, in a clear glass jar, staring up at her was a pair of eyeballs.

Bronte was also staring at the jar, and Morgan turned to her. 'Why have you got those?'

Bronte was shaking her head. 'They're not mine, I didn't put them in.'

Morgan didn't know whether to believe her or not, and she scrambled to get out of the car, away from Bronte just in case. She didn't care that she'd left Marc's car abandoned in the middle of a winding country lane; she needed to put some distance between herself and the woman who was carrying a jar containing Evelyn Reynolds's missing eyeballs, until they could clear it up. She ran to the side of the road, scrambling across the drystone wall the same way the stag had gone, and took out her phone. It only had one bar of signal. Keeping one eye on the car to see what Bronte was doing, she rang Ben. But he didn't answer. Her radio was tucked into the side pocket of the driver's door, along with her CS gas and handcuffs. She had nothing to protect herself with should she need to, except a rock she picked up off the floor that the stag must have knocked off the wall. It was sharp but not heavy enough for her liking.

Bronte got out of the car in slow motion and stood by the open door.

'Morgan, where are you? Those are not mine. I've never seen them before in my life.'

No shit they're not, thought Morgan. *Why did Bronte have Evelyn's eyes? Had Harrison known she was a killer?*

'Please don't leave me, I'm scared; I swear they're nothing to do with me. Somebody at the prison could have put them in, and so could that guy whose house you've just been to.'

She sounded terrified, and for a moment Morgan believed her, but she knew better than to trust her. As much as she didn't want the killer to be Bronte, she couldn't take the risk, so didn't answer her.

She rang Cain and began to whisper, 'Help, I think Bronte might be the killer or involved with him.'

'What? Where is she now?'

'Standing next to Marc's car. She has a jar with a pair of

eyeballs in her bag that fell out when I braked hard.'

'*Don't go near her, I'll get patrols travelling. Stay on the line.*'

'The signal is crap.'

Morgan heard the sound of a car in the distance and knew it was driving far too fast down the lane where she'd abandoned the car. She swore to herself and stood up. Bronte's outline was lit up by the interior dash lights as she stood there, one hand holding on to the door, the other clutching the jar. That car was coming their way too fast. It was a narrow, twisty road.

She screamed, 'Bronte, get off the road and close the door.'

Bronte looked around for Morgan's voice, to see what direction it had come from.

'Morgan, these are nothing to do with me.'

'I believe you, get off the bloody road.'

Headlights from behind lit her up like she was under the spotlight, and Morgan knew what was going to happen. She jumped the wall as time slowed down and everything moved in slow motion. There was a squeal of tyres on the old road as the driver slammed on the brakes too hard, losing their grip on the steering wheel, and the car that was driving towards Bronte began to spin out of control.

Morgan ran to push her out of the way, but it was too late. She was too far away from her. The car ploughed into Bronte, sending the passenger door, Bronte and the glass jar flying into the air with an almighty screech of metal and breaking glass. Morgan watched, helpless, as her body flew through the air like one of those crash test dummies. The jar went even higher as Bronte hit the tarmac with a sickening thud, followed by the splinter of broken glass as the jar shattered around her, sending Evelyn's eyeballs rolling. The car was an old-fashioned sturdy Volvo. It finally stopped spinning as it hit the drystone wall with a loud crunch.

Cain's voice was yelling her name down the phone as

Morgan was screaming Bronte's name over and over.

She ran to the lifeless figure on the road, shock and tears rolling down her cheeks. She didn't know if the woman who was bleeding and broken was a killer, but if she was, she was a product of her environment and Morgan still cared for her. Bronte's eyes were open, staring up into the night sky, and she knew then that it was too late. She couldn't help her even though she wanted to.

There was a loud groan from the Volvo, and despite the shock and horror that filled her body she kicked into police mode. She had to help the injured driver, even if they had been driving way too fast down a country lane.

She called to Cain, 'She's dead, there's no way she survived that impact, but the driver is alive and injured. How long before patrols arrive? It's so dark down here if anyone else comes they'll crash into us too.'

'I'm in a van.' She heard the sirens as he pressed the button. 'Patrols are en route, Morgan, ETA five minutes. You need to get off the road, do you hear me?'

She did hear him, but she couldn't ignore an injured person. She ran to the car and pulled open the door. The driver lifted his head from the steering wheel, there was a stream of blood running down his face, but he still managed to smile at her. His hand reaching out, he clamped hold of her wrist with an iron grip.

Morgan opened her mouth to scream. She knew him, and the fear that rushed through her veins turned everything to ice as she pulled to get free. 'William.' With her other fist she punched him in the side of the head where he was bleeding, causing him to loosen the grip on her arm, and she took off running back towards the thick undergrowth, where she'd only just emerged from, and knew she was running for her life as she heard the groaning creak of the door opening and heavy, pounding footsteps as he came running after her.

FORTY-NINE

Wendy passed Ben the final bag on which he'd written the exhibit number along with his initials and the number six next to it. He was putting it into the big brown paper evidence bag when Marc shouted, 'Holy shit, what the hell is going on?'

Ben knew, without a shadow of a doubt, that whatever it was, it involved Morgan. The brown bag slipped from his grasp onto the floor as he heard the shouts and sirens over the radio. Cain's voice was on loudspeaker.

'RTC one fatality on Grasmere Bank Lane, it's not, I repeat, not Morgan.'

Ben stumbled forwards a little bit, his legs about to give way, but he managed to catch himself. He turned to Marc as Cain's voice continued.

'Boss, your car is missing a door but otherwise good. There's a Volvo with blood on the driver's side interior and no driver.' There was a slight pause as he bellowed, 'Morgan.'

Marc was staring at Ben, his mouth open. Ben ran towards Amber. 'Stay here, I need the van.'

She passed him the keys. Not even bothering to strip off the protective clothing he had on, he climbed into the van. Marc rushed to get into the passenger seat before he sped away.

They were minutes away from Grasmere Bank Lane. How come they hadn't heard anything? Cain's voice was filling the radio.

'Control PNC check on this Volvo please.' He passed the registration over and they waited for the answer. *'Comes back to a William Dent of 101 Fenton Street.'* Cain swore over the radio for everyone to hear. *'I need a dog; I need every available patrol to make their way here. We have a missing officer most likely being chased by a murder suspect.'*

Ben was driving too fast, and Marc slammed into him as he took the sharp bend at speed, but neither of them spoke. He saw the lights from the van Cain had parked across the road and slammed the brakes on, narrowly missing driving straight into it. As he jumped out, he tore the white paper suit and gloves off and rang Morgan's phone, which went straight to voicemail.

'Crap signal around here,' panted Cain, who was out of breath as he jogged towards them. 'I suggest you and Marc take that side of the road; I'll take this one?'

Unable to speak, he nodded. Ben ran towards the gate a little further along that Morgan could have climbed over, while Cain headed towards the wall and jolted himself over with a grunt at the sharp pain in his left side where he'd been stabbed. Ben had the Find My iPhone app open and was trying to ping it, but it wouldn't connect, and he wanted to throw the stupid thing into the nearest tree.

He called out, 'Morgan.' And waited to see if she answered him.

FIFTY

Morgan heard Cain's voice in the distance, but was afraid to call out to him because she could hear William Dent thundering through the trees to find her. She looked around for a weapon, furious she'd left everything in the car, and found a thick branch. It wasn't very big, but it was heavy. Déjà vu was running through her mind on another chase through the trees, hitting Taylor over the head with a branch, and then it went too quiet, and she knew he was standing behind her. She could hear his laboured breathing. He was out of breath, which gave her a slight advantage.

Turning slowly, she stared at him. It was so dense and dark all she could make out was his shadowy form standing there, watching her, just like some horror movie killer. He raised an arm, and she saw the shape of the huge machete he was holding up. The branch she'd picked up was no match for that, but she gripped it harder. He was breathing heavy, and she wouldn't have been surprised to see him wearing a Michael Myers or Jason Voorhees mask while he watched her.

'Why?'

He didn't answer, didn't move and, for a second, she

wondered if he actually was standing there or if her mind was playing tricks on her. She opened her mouth to scream for Cain and stopped as he took a step closer. They wouldn't know he was armed with a huge blade that could chop their head off if he swung it at them. She wouldn't put her friends in that kind of danger.

'It's over, whether you kill me or not. They have the car, you killed Bronte, they have your prints, you can't escape. They'll come looking for you, and if you kill me then you're going to piss them off even more.'

She could hear footsteps heading their way as the crunching of branches got closer.

'Drop the machete and give yourself in, there is nowhere for you to go, William. What about your wife, what about Elizabeth?'

'She's dead, she was the first and you are going to be my last. All those other killers were tame, they couldn't even finish what they started, and I just proved to you that I'm far better than they are.'

Morgan thought she would feel fear, but instead she felt rage and injustice at what he'd done to Lexie, Evelyn, Bronte. She would not let him hurt Cain or Ben either. She shook her head.

'Enough, you've done whatever you thought you must.'

'I didn't though, I didn't get you.'

He ran at her, and Morgan saw a flash of black jump out of the trees and heard a vicious snarling as the huge black dog clamped its mouth around the arm holding up the machete.

William screamed in shock. Morgan thought it was Cain rushing through the trees, but she was wrong: it was Caesar, and for a second she felt nothing but pure joy at watching him take William to the ground. Even though he was trying to punch the dog in the head, it wasn't having much effect. Caesar threw his whole body weight at William, who fell to the floor with the dog growling and pressing his muzzle against his throat. Morgan saw his fingers reaching out, searching for the machete, and kicked into action. Running towards him she kicked his hand with her Dr. Martens as hard as she could, and the snap was so loud it echoed around the trees. William let out a blood-curdling scream of pain and seconds later there was a red dot on his chest as Cassie pointed her taser at him.

Cain, Ben and Marc all rushed towards the scream along with two patrol officers. Morgan took in the sight and wished she could snap a photo to pin on the board. When the two officers bent down to cuff William, Cassie called Caesar off and he backed away from the whimpering man on the floor.

Morgan couldn't stop herself, and she threw herself at Caesar, falling to her knees. She wrapped her arms around his massive, chunky neck and kissed his nose. 'I owe you, big fella, thank you.'

Cassie patted his head and tossed him a chunk of cheese, which he caught and swallowed whole. She shrugged. 'He's anyone's for a bit of mature cheddar.'

Morgan laughed despite the shock and horror. She was relieved that she was alive and no one else had got hurt, and it was all thanks to the big dog who she could swear was staring into the depths of her soul, wanting more cheese.

'I'll buy you a huge block of cheese, I promise, you've earned it.'

FIFTY-ONE

The briefing room felt lighter, the sense of relief that filled it hung in the air and it was a good feeling. Morgan, who looked a little worse for wear after her chase through the woods, knew it wasn't her finest moment. The whole team had assembled for this one, and there was so much to do enquiry wise that it would take months, but they were all in a joyous mood because the killer was in custody. Ben walked in with Marc, who looked around and smiled at everyone. Morgan couldn't hide the pain she felt at losing Bronte. The way she had doubted her innocence would stay with her forever, and the horror that she'd had to suffer the way she did made her feel a sadness so deep inside she didn't know if she could ever make it heal.

'Good job, everyone, what a bloody fantastic team you all are. Despite the gravity of the situation, you all worked your backsides off and what a result. William Dent is under armed guard while his wrist is being set at A&E. Morgan, remind me not to upset you, you managed to break it with one kick.'

Cain reached over and patted her head. 'That's my girl.'

Ben was grinning at her.

Marc continued. 'I've just had confirmation that the body

found in the boot of the silver Picasso is that of Elizabeth Dent, according to the ID in her pocket. Her place of work say that she didn't turn up six days ago, which isn't like her, and they've been unable to contact her. Ben, do you want to continue?'

He took over. 'I've had several messages from the governors of the prisons where some of our previous killers are held. They all received letters from an anonymous source telling them he was going to finish what they'd started, and asking if they had anything they could share with him. This is all brilliant evidence. Once we can prove William Dent sent them, of course, which might take some time but it's doable. I want a search team to go in and tear his house to pieces. I think we're going to find lots of evidence to help secure his guilty conviction. It's a big job, but I know we can do it.'

Morgan nodded. 'Motive, he said he was finishing what the others started because he was better than they all were. He's an egotistical, warped guy who thought he was on a mission to show the world who was the best killer.'

Cain smiled at her. 'You saved the day though and stopped him, even if it was unintentional.'

She shook her head. 'Cassie and Caesar saved the day not me.'

They all laughed, and someone asked, 'How's your car, sir?'

Which soon stopped the laughter as Marc frowned. 'It's got a new air conditioning unit that I'm trialling now the passenger door is missing.'

He stared at Morgan, who blushed and muttered, 'Sorry.'

Then he laughed. 'It's a door, it can be replaced. I'm just glad it wasn't you. Right, let's get started clearing up this mess.'

Everyone filed out of the blue room, leaving Morgan and Cain behind. She stood up, and he smiled at her. 'You did do good, and I have one last question for you.'

'What's that?'

'Would you like a hug?'

She nodded, and he pulled her into his arms for one of his huge bear hugs that she loved so much. When he finally let her go, she whispered, 'I needed that.'

He linked an arm through hers and they walked out of the blue room down to their office, where she was going to work the case and make sure they had all the evidence they needed to send William Dent to prison for the rest of his life.

A LETTER FROM HELEN

I want to say a huge thank you for choosing to read *Save Her Twice*. If you did enjoy it, and want to keep up-to-date with all my latest releases, just sign up at the following link. Your email address will never be shared, and you can unsubscribe at any time.

www.bookouture.com/helen-phifer

I've been obsessed with Final Girls since I watched the first *Halloween* movie when I was around ten, starring the brilliant Jamie Lee Curtis, who survived and fought her bogeyman, Michael Myers, many times over. So, when this idea came to me, I thought it would be great to see the past survivors having to battle against a killer again. I have to be honest I did feel bad about putting them through this after everything they've previously suffered, which is why Macy was sent to Benidorm with her mum. I just couldn't do it to her: that kid has a great future. I'm kind of sad that Lexie, Evelyn and Bronte didn't make it too, but there is a famous quote that has been used by both William Faulkner and Stephen King, even though it originally came from an English writer, Sir Arthur Quiller-Couch, but its basic meaning is: 'Kill your darlings.' Sometimes you have to write stuff that you don't really want to, but that's okay because it's all part of the creative writing process. Hopefully in time you can forgive me for doing just that in a spectacular fashion.

I hope you loved *Save Her Twice* and if you did I would be

very grateful if you could write a review. I'd love to hear what you think, and it makes such a difference helping new readers to discover one of my books for the first time.

I love hearing from my readers – you can get in touch through social media or my website.

Thanks,

Helen

www.helenphifer.com

facebook.com/Helenphifer1
x.com/helenphifer1

ACKNOWLEDGEMENTS

As always it takes a whole team to turn a rough draft into the finished story you have read on your phone, Kindle or in paperback. Maybe you listened to it on audio, which is my favourite way to read at the moment. So, here we go, my huge debt of gratitude goes to...

My wonderful, brilliant editor Jennifer Hunt for her insight and patience in making this story so much better than the one I sent to her and for the wonderful cakes she sent me on the publication of *Stolen Darlings*; they were so good I looked at the box and thought they were too good to eat. It didn't stop me though; I did eat a fair few of them.

The wonderful team at Bookouture, Lizzie Brien for all her help with everything. The wonderful Janette Currie for her copy edits and also the lovely Shirley Khan for her proofreading skills.

A massive thank you goes to the boss, Jenny Geras, for her support and sense of humour.

A huge, huge thank you to the utterly fabulous Noelle Holten for everything she does publicity wise and the rest of the amazing team, Kim Nash, Sarah Hardy and Jess Readett.

The very talented Alison Campbell brought Morgan, Ben and co. to life from book one and did a fantastic job, thank you Alison and the whole Audio Factory Team.

I couldn't do this without the support of my fabulous readers who just blow my mind with their kind words, support and love they show to me and my stories. I thank each and every one of you from the bottom of my heart.

The wonderful book bloggers are just amazing, they are the unsung heroes of an author's life, and I can never thank you all for the support you give. I love you all.

I also couldn't do this without the final read through from my dear friend Paul O'Neill, who is the fastest reader I know. Your support, Paul, means everything to me, thank you so much.

A huge thank you goes to Jessica Silvester Yeo for everything she does with my social media feeds, you are a lifesaver and my Instagram rock star. Thank you, Jess, I love working with you.

Another massive thank you goes to the wonderful staff at Mill Lane Day Care Centre who take care of my son, Jaimea, Monday to Friday so I can spend time writing. You're all amazing and Jaimea loves being with you all.

A very special thank you goes to Selena Smith, her fiancé Dan and her mum Jenny for letting Jaimea into your lives and making him a part of your family. To know that he can go and spend time with you while giving us a break from caring for him is such a huge relief. He loves you all so much and I'm pretty sure he'd move in if he could.

As always, a big shout out to my coffee gals, Samantha Thomas and Tina Sykes; you both keep me laughing and sane, I love you both.

Thank you to the amazing book club members who come each month and chat about books, some of the time – hahaha, I love our meet ups; they are always such good fun.

Krog Crosthwaite, you get a special mention because you make a decent coffee and also provide me with some much-needed therapy while drinking it.

If you're still reading, we're almost at the end of these acknowledgments.

Last but not least, a huge thank you to my husband Steve for his support, my amazing children Jessica, Joshua, Jerusha, Jaimea and Jeorgia. Their wonderful partners Tom, Danielle and Deji. My gorgeous grandkids who bring me so much joy and light up my life: Gracie, Donny, Lolly, Tilda, Sonny, Sienna and Bonnie, I love you all so much, Nanna hugs are truly the best.

Made in United States
Orlando, FL
03 February 2024

PUBLISHING TEAM

Turning a manuscript into a book requires the efforts of many people. The publishing team at Bookouture would like to acknowledge everyone who contributed to this publication.

Audio
Alba Proko
Sinead O'Connor
Melissa Tran

Commercial
Lauren Morrissette
Jil Thielen
Imogen Allport

Cover design
The Brewster Project

Data and analysis
Mark Alder
Mohamed Bussuri

Editorial
Jennifer Hunt
Sinead O'Connor

Copyeditor
Janette Currie

Proofreader
Shirley Khan

Marketing
Alex Crow
Melanie Price
Occy Carr
Ciara Rosney

Operations and distribution
Marina Valles
Stephanie Straub

Production
Hannah Snetsinger
Mandy Kullar
Jen Shannon

Publicity
Kim Nash
Noelle Holten
Myrto Kalavrezou
Jess Readett
Sarah Hardy

Rights and contracts
Peta Nightingale
Richard King
Saidah Graham

PUBLISHING TEAM

Turning a manuscript into a book requires the efforts of many people. The publishing team at Bookouture would like to acknowledge everyone who contributed to this publication.

Audio
Alba Proko
Sinead O'Connor
Melissa Tran

Commercial
Lauren Morrissette
Jil Thielen
Imogen Allport

Cover design
The Brewster Project

Data and analysis
Mark Alder
Mohamed Bussuri

Editorial
Jennifer Hunt
Sinead O'Connor

Made in United States
Orlando, FL
03 February 2024

43226140R00169